Born in Wellington 1957, Gerard Hindmarsh trained first as a cartographer before shifting to journalism in 1990. His award-winning work has featured in many publications both in New Zealand and internationally, for many years and also serving as Asian correspondent for New Zealand's National Radio. His previous books include Angelina, Swamp Fever, Kahurangi Calling, Kahurangi Stores, Outsiders, Kahawai—The People's Dish, and Kahurangi Out West. He has five children and lives on his small farm at Tukurua in Golden Bay, New Zealand with his wife Melanie.

To my wife, Melanie Walker, whose help,
and advice was invaluable.

Gerard Hindmarsh

THE TIN CRY

AUSTIN MACAULEY PUBLISHERS™
LONDON * CAMBRIDGE * NEW YORK * SHARJAH

A CIP catalogue record for this title is available from the British Library.

ISBN 9781035802647 (Paperback)
ISBN 9781035802654 (ePub e-book)

www.austinmacauley.co.uk

First Published 2024
Austin Macauley Publishers Ltd®
1 Canada Square
Canary Wharf
London
E14 5AA

Disclaimer

This work of historical fiction is based around the Great Tin Rush of 1889-91, which unfolded along the Tin Range and Port Pegasus of Stewart Island, in southern New Zealand. I have tried to keep true to all the real historical characters which I researched, but I apologise to any of their living descendants who may feel there has been any misrepresentation.

Tin cry

That characteristic crackling sound heard when a bar of tin is bent, caused by crystals deforming and sheering against each other. Bent repeatedly, the tin will cry over and over until it breaks.

Prologue

Foveaux Strait, late summer, 1946

At last, the island looms through the sea mist. Mollymawks, gulls, and terns have escorted us all the way, their cries whipped and flung about by the wind as if announcing my return. All the other dozen or so passengers have retreated to the main cabin, but I prefer to be out on deck here by myself, to smell the spray whipped up by the sea, feel the slight sting of it on my cheeks, taste its saltiness on my lips. To be honest, I am not sure if it is the salt spray I can taste on my tongue; it may well be just my tears.

If I had the ability of those wheeling albatrosses, I would get this journey over and done with, not bother with a few pathetic scraps thrown out from the galley. I'd fly straight towards those hills on the southern horizon, first soar and circle over Paterson Inlet before wheeling south over those Remarkables. I will never stop calling that range its old name, the one before they changed it to the Tin Range, because in my mind, they still deserve it, so much more magnificent than those mountains rising from Lake Wakatipu, I saw them once. What a joke that was, a few swank businessmen thinking their mountains deserved the name more. Yes, if I was those birds, I'd get caught up in the cross draughts over those giant domes of granite before swooping down over the tin workings; then I'd plummet into Port Pegasus and come to rest on the roof of the old hotel. If it was still there, that is. Pioneer Hotel belonged to Louis Rodgers, he built it, the southern-most hotel in the whole world. I still regard it as 'my hotel,' only because of that little post office out the side. Running that place gave me so much solace. Looking back, what a laugh it all was, and what heartache I went through there, how could I ever forget?

But these sea birds are determined to stay with us. Our sturdy ferry-boat is finally chugging in past the Muttonbird Islands. I can still remember their names- North Island, Women's Island, Edwards, Jackey Lee. I know they had Maori names; Tane used them all the time, but I never got to know them. Maybe I should have, those Maori fellas sure knew a few things us Europeans didn't.

This has been a slow crossing, given me time to anticipate and savour my history here. To me, those Muttonbird Islands have always looked like people, crouching and lying down, just guarding the entrance to the bay. Today, they look grey and featureless through the sea mist, although I can just make out a white necklace of breakers that crash onto their rocks, send sea foam soaring skywards before it all dissolves into the rain. There could likely be a few birders out there. You'd never know though, maybe just a few wisps of smoke from their hut in better weather. Right this very minute, they could be yanking those poor little fluffy chicks out of their warm burrows and wringing their necks. How brutal muttonbirding is, killing them before they even had a chance to fly. Their taste though is something that cannot be described, so salty for a start, no wonder they went to so much effort harvesting them.

To the last I have wanted to hold tight to the deck railing, braced by my sturdy sea legs. Twice during this crossing, the captain sent his mate out to talk the old lady in. Too late now, they've well given up on me. A woman far younger and less experienced at sea than me might want to scream each time the deck bucked and rolled and slammed into the open strait, but I've had my life, done my time on the water. Sudden shocks no longer make me cry out that I might break.

Gold may have lured the first prospectors to Pegasus, but stream tin is what they found. A few mined in the ground for tin stone too, that mad Professor Black was one of them. He was the crazy over-educated one who caused the whole rush in the first place. The men who came into my post office would bring lumps of that tinstone to show me, and I used to wonder what all the fuss was about. It was dull, hard and dark, not beautiful and shiny like gold or silver. After they dug it from the ground, they told me it had to be crushed to get the tin out by washing it clean. Using crucibles and blow pipes, they could even smelter small amounts in their camps.

We chug on, Halfmoon Bay ahead. Out to port is the little lighthouse perched on the rock of Ackers Point. Next, the sandy cove with the stone cottage. Someone told me once that Lewis Acker used to be a harpooner on a whaler before he settled here with his high-born Maori wife, Mary Pi. They built the hut; nine kids they had, stacked them up in two lots of bunks, one five high the other four. It was a hard life for a woman, him away trading most of the time, but there's something about this island that makes you up for it.

Leask Bay coming into view now, where that family never stops building their wooden boats; then Lonnikers where we always used to see those bush parrots chattering in the blue gums. Those trees had long strips of sea-grey bark which worked loose by gales, cracking and flapping in the wind like so many masts and sails.

I still have the tin brooch Syd made me. I wore it for years, every time I went out. He always played that gift down, easy to make he said, but I know it was something special from him. The tin was easy to bend and work. Some of the men would make rough trinkets, send to their sweethearts, mothers, sisters far away. They used to show them to me in the post office before they wrapped them up in brown paper to send away. I could tell they wanted my reaction as a woman, gauge how their gift would be received. It made me wonder what they all daydreamed about as they worked. Sure, all the wealth and riches they would hopefully make as a tin miner, but surely too they must have daydreamed about all the romance and love they hoped to find one day. Make their lives comfortable at last, fulfil a desire or two. How could they not hope for that? Working up at Pegasus was so hard, and no one can survive hard work forever.

Almost at the wharf in Oban now, named after that place in Argyle, Scotland. The Little Bay it means in Gaelic, I learnt that from my Scottish mother when I was a child, well before I even came out here. So similar to the coast of Scotland to here. I can already smell the big washup of seaweed sweetly rotting along the beach, even the kelp as it writhes around the tidal rocks. I can hear the land birds singing now, tui, bellbird, those raucous bush parrots. And I can't believe how many houses I can see sprinkled through the bushy hills, so many more than when I first came through. Back then, most of the Europeans, a few Maori too, lived out at The Neck. What a horrible place to end up that would have been, so open and exposed to Foveaux weather. No wonder they moved in here.

High up on the hill above the wharf I see what is clearly a newish red-roofed church with a fine-built steeple. Again, I am reminded of Scotland. I used to wonder why there weren't any graves around the churches in New Zealand, not like back at home. Here, they seem to find some paddock or out-of-the-way bit of ground, call it a cemetery. That's where they would have put old Peggy. I heard she never left the island. I tried to find Syd's grave once, asked all around Southland, but that was before I found out he got blown to pieces at the Battle of the Somme. He would have a chuckle now another big war is over, the same atrocities coming to light. "How could they have let it happen!" everyone is saying. Anything can happen anytime, even a crazy deluded tin rush on Stewart Island. Sheer insanity it was. People can do anything when they see a course, like back in Pegasus. Everyone except Peggy, of course. She knew her own mind and could tell it straight. She didn't go along with anyone except herself. Good for her too!

In the end, that Tin Rush was just a mad stampede of ill-prepared men into the miserable weather and dense impassable scrub of God-forsaken terrain at South Stewart Island. Despite all the high hopes, hardly any stream tin was ever recovered, less than one ton in total I got told once. After I left, I heard Pegasus became a fishing village with its own fish factory and freezer even. In the end, that business petered out too. I read in a newspaper not so long ago that the last miner up there let his two draught horses loose after he left them to wander the windswept moors while the burnt scrub grew back all around them. When one of those horses died, I guess the survivor became the loneliest creature in the whole wide world. When people walked up there, that mare would rush out to meet them, so keen for company was she in her lonely mountain kingdom, sheltering under a rock overhang in bad weather.

A ship's captain told me once that Port Pegasus was named after a Yankee sealing vessel which got its name from the winged horse of Greek myth. I hadn't heard of that before. Maybe that old last horse will become Pegasus history, better than any of the people who all ended up deserting the place.

Syd showed me how to make a strip of tin cry, held a piece of smelted tin metal firmly in his two hands as he slowly bent it back and forth. To my amazement, it really did begin to creak and groan, crackling almost as though it was shouting out, 'don't bend me too far, I will break!' Eventually, it did break into two. Syd said all you had to do was melt it back together again. Tin was invincible, not like Humpty Dumpty, *where all the kings' horses and all the kings' men couldn't put him together again*. Tin is a bit like the human spirit. It can keep on bending, enduring on and on until you break. But then you pick yourself up, and off you go again. On and on until we die.

You know what really fascinated me about the cry of tin? The noise the metal made each time before it broke. It's more of a crackling than a cry I thought. Made me wonder what noises our heart and soul makes just before it breaks.

Chapter 1

Invercargill Railway Station, 3 February 1889
62 years earlier

The locomotive seethed at its stationary seams, hissing steam into an air already acrid with coal smoke. Elizabeth stepped onto the platform. On both sides, a score or so passengers were bustling about with great intent as they arranged for their trunks and luggage to be heaved out and put on waiting carts, their horses all snorting with the excitement. Then almost as quickly, it was all over. One of the guards blew his whistle and held up his hand to call out in an all too familiar Scottish brogue; "All aboard for Thornberry, Longford, Tuatapere!" The train's whistle split the air in half, and the engine began creaking and gasping again like a wheezing old man slowly easing away from the station. Elizabeth watched as the faces behind the carriage windows slowly sped up until the back railing of the guard's van flew past until finally all Elizabeth could see was a plume of black boiler smoke in the distance.

Apart from one arrival talking to another in the distance, the platform was now completely deserted and silent, all sign of human activity gone. Even the last cart to be seen just about disappearing around a far corner. She looked around for the station building and it was a moment before she realised the little wooden structure that which looked like an oversized garden shed just beyond the sign which read INVERCARGILL must be it. Her trunk had already been dumped under the canvas awning, and she just stood there, dulled to her feelings of abandonment and aloneness, looking at the glistening ribbons of the railway iron stretching into the distance.

For a second or two she had to remind herself why she felt so queasy. Then it all came back; today was the last day of her life in Southland. Her old life she would never know again. For 23 years, her entire life, she had lived in the family home in Glasgow. Now, she was entirely alone in the antipodes, an island on the very opposite side of the world, as far away from home as she could possibly get.

The message had been waiting for her when she disembarked in Port Chalmers, handed to her by the kindly purser waiting at the bottom of the gangway. She thanked him and found her fingers shaking as she turned around from the hustle and bustle to get some privacy to open it. After fifteen gruelling weeks of sea passage from the docks of Greenock, she had been expecting George to meet her at Port Chalmers. But instead, it was just a letter that greeted her, and she felt dread as she pulled it out again to read. She'd realised immediately from the opening tone of the letter that it had been penned by someone other than George, as not his handwriting for a start, she had seen his distinctive cursive script in a letter he had sent to her uncle. The roughly scrawled message started by addressing her only by her Christian name Elizabeth, informing her that the arrangement had changed, and George could no longer meet her, and that she would now have to make her own way from the port of her embarkation to Dunedin Railway Station and from there catch the first train to Invercargill where she should connect with the next locomotive on the branch line to the port of Bluff. From that railway station, she would make her way with her luggage to the Town Wharf where, if she could get there by noon Tuesday, she would find the *SS Invercargill* tied up, soon to depart directly for Port Pegasus. The unsigned note ended with 'George Braithwaite will be waiting there for you at Rodger's Hotel in Port Pegasus. He conveys his sincerest apologies for this change of arrangement, due to urgent circumstances beyond anyone's control, all of which will be fully explained in due course upon your arrival.'

In a less public place, Elizabeth may at that point have broken down and burst into tears, as she had when she first read it, but she retained her countenance as her head and heart continued through the raft of emotions; disappointment, abandonment, exasperation and rising anger, all not helped by the realisation that she was weighed down by a heavy trunk with all her worldly possessions inside, and not another single person to call on for help. Several times, she felt a tear coming and reached for her cotton handkerchief tucked up her sleeve, but each time she forced the upwelling to stop, roughly wiping her eyes dry with her sleeve instead. "I must be strong," she kept telling herself. By the time her trunk was slung in a cargo net with a load of other luggage and dumped on the dock at Port Chalmers, her underlying emotions had progressed to a kind of reluctant acceptance of her unfortunate situation. Thank goodness that the weather had held. The rain clouds that had been gathering as they sailed into Port Chalmers had retreated back beyond the line of low hills which rose above the port. She had thought the scene was pretty as a picture as they'd come in, but now everything took on a new look, a decidedly grey one. At least she had plenty of time—three days before the steamer set sail from Bluff. Sitting on her trunk to take stock of her situation, she twice pulled the letter out again, the first to re-read it word by word to find anything she had missed; the second, to explore its rather bossy impersonal tone. What she noticed upon closer scrutiny was the carelessness of the handwriting, indicating to her that it had been written in a hurry, last minute perhaps. It also made her feel more than a little foolish that she was now finding herself in this situation. Strangely, she knew little about this man George Ashcroft, especially that they were betrothed to be married for the rest of their lives. One of her church-going acquaintances back home, Emily, had warned her about getting into an arranged marriage, advising her. "They may have worked once! But no more, nothin' but ol' fashioned they are! Times they were changing, far better marry for love. Then you won't feel trapped after a few years. Hysteria some doctors were calling the way women go after being with a man they didn't love anymore. They get put in an asylum you know. Don't want to end up like them now, do ya?"

But Elizabeth's father Edward was a traditional man, devoutly protestant at that, and he kept up the pressure on his eldest daughter right up to his very dying day, advising her that an arranged marriage to a hardworking and financially stable man of good faith was the most sensible, indeed, only way ahead. The man, her future husband, had already been decided, and after Edward died, his two surviving older brothers kept the pressure up on their niece as well, somehow elevating George's eligibility higher once he immigrated to the colony of New Zealand three years earlier. Dunedin was the new Edinburgh, it had even taken its ancient Gaelic name, founded by no less than the Lay Association of the Free Church of Scotland. One of the founding fathers was Reverend Thomas Burns, a nephew of the great Scottish poet Robert Burns. They had all heard how the city fathers had even erected a great bronze statue of the poet in the central plaza of Dunedin just a year or two before, which was near identical to the ones already erected in New York, London and Dundee. That endorsement spoke like no other, a city which spoke of being founded on solid Scottish values.

Obvious to the family back in Scotland now, George was a go-getter, typical of the 'leavers' who went to make new lives in the New World. "Aye, Lizzie, your best chance is this man, leave the domineering English behind and forge a new life. You'll be rich in no time, and coming from Scotland will make you feel proud."

Everything she knew about George had come from her father; a knowledge duly added to by her uncles. That he was ten years older than her, thirty-three now, was neither here nor there, somehow even more so since he'd left to reside in the town of Invercargill in the very south of the New Zealand colony. Here, they told her, he intended to open a sizeable drapery store in the main street. That he was a close relative of one of uncle's close business associates and came from a good family didn't make him reliable though, as Elizabeth was now finding out.

The idea of becoming the wife of a drapery store owner had grown on her during the long passage from home. She wouldn't have to get her hands too dirty, and she imagined the elegant gowns she could wear to social afternoons in the colony. They were all making a new Scotland in the south of New Zealand, and it sounded a far better one.

But now she knew nothing at all about this new destination, Port Pegasus. She had heard of Bluff, Invercargill's busy port, but that was the end of her known world. All her enquiries to date had all been about Invercargill, which now seemed largely irrelevant. She had heard Invercargill was a town of big wide-open skies, streets wide enough for three and even four carts to pass, streets lined with cottages and some with shops which sell all manner of things, even a genteel woman's salon where it was possible to have a cup of tea served in bone China, high tea even, cakes a price too. A place where one could attend an amateur opera or hear an expert give a social lecture to stimulate the mind, go for a picnic and promenade in their Queens Gardens on a Sunday. She felt she knew the place intimately from all she had heard, but Pegasus? She certainly didn't recall seeing that name in any New Zealand map in the Atlas of the Southern Seas. After a restless, anguished night on the train from Dunedin, she had resolved it was pointless to worry; she had to show some Scottish resilience, make her life in the colony of New Zealand a success, and there was no alternative, nothing for it but to take a deep breath and plunge on with this whole adventure. George will change everything she well appreciated, even if he hadn't turned up yet. As much as he had let her down, she felt she had to give him the benefit of the doubt.

It was still early; she had six hours to wait for the day's only train down to Bluff. Opposite the railway station was a wide, dusty, empty street, and beyond, glinting through trees in the sunlight, she was sure she could see the sparkle of water, perhaps a wide estuary or river. Looking around, down a wide, empty street, she could make out a few two-storey buildings. Guessing this was the middle of the town, she found it comforting that several of the taller buildings appeared to be made of stone, not wood. Surely a sign of well-to-do people who were building a stable future. A dense concentration of elaborate scaffolding dominated the skyline off to one side—Elizabeth had been told by a kindly gentleman on the train that it was to be the town's grand new water tower.

She shooed off a fly that was annoying her with its persistent buzzing, noticing at the same time a lone man on a bicycle pedalling up the street. Coming from the direction of the two-storey buildings, he cycled along and past her, before turning down a side road. Careful to avoid letting him notice that she was watching him, but once past her eyes followed him with a stare until he disappeared down a side street.

The day wore on. She smoothed her hair and wiped back her fringe, wishing she could change her clothes, pleased at least she could take a drink and wash her face from a faucet off the side of the platform, same thing she'd done in Gore one stop earlier when she got off for a break un-lady-like for sure, but she sure had been discreet. Still in the navy serge dress she had worn for the cool wind on the approach to land, she now longed to change her attire, at least get out of her bulky petticoat. The sun was rising higher in the sky and the day was becoming warm.

It had been a long time since she had been alone, cramped as it had been on the boat, but she had made the most of it. She had spent much time on the trip out contemplating what it would be like to be a wife, and how to be a good, devoted one at that. Her mother had died of pneumonia when she was 12, and her father passed away three years before. His dying wish, that she go to New Zealand and marry George, had affected her indelibly, and made it her only future course of action. She had no real memories of her mother managing a household, so to that end had packed in her trunk not only her Holy Bible and book of Sing Psalms, but had also included her mother's handsome volume of Mrs Beeton's Book of Household Management. At the start of the very first chapter entitled 'The Mistress' was a passage from Proverbs: 'Strength and honour are her clothing…She looketh well to the ways of her household; and eateth not the bread of idleness.'

Elizabeth moved to a wooden bench in the shade of the awning where she could keep an eye on her trunk. Inside was the trousseau she had lovingly prepared during the long and quiet Glasgow winters after uncle and Meg retired for the night: embroidered table linens; hand worked lace pillow cases and her wedding dress—cream silk, hand-stitched all over with tiny pearls that she had carefully removed from her mother's moth-eaten dress which she had found in a cupboard in the attic. All the clothes she had brought were wrapped carefully with camphor balls and stored in calico bags waiting to be opened on her wedding day, whenever that would be. No date had been discussed, but sometimes she had let her mind imagine just what a glorious occasion it was sure to be.

During the 103-day sea voyage from the docks at Greenock to Port Chalmers, Elizabeth had plenty of time to contemplate her new life in the colonies. She was still unclear about how to conduct herself as a mother. She watched the other passengers for clues: Mr and Mrs Frost had four children and Mr and Mrs Allen nine, the eldest two of whom were already in New Zealand waiting for them. The youngest seven ranged in age from 22 down to three years of age. Elizabeth had become friendly with Annie, the oldest daughter on board, and they spent long days helping with the younger children, but still Elizabeth felt she was little wiser to the task. How orderly the passengers had been on her ship, no rough miners or even the mobs of single young women that she had expected. She had read in the newspaper back in Glasgow that over 1,200 of these single women had already been shipped out to Otago from England under the province's Special Female Immigration Programme, launched in response to the massive influx of single men to the Otago Goldfields. No other province in the country had such a gender disparity, and it had to be addressed. How rowdy they would have been, pondered Elizabeth, but perhaps how much fun too. Back in Glasgow, she had spotted far smaller groups of these so-called single younger women living it up outside some of the ale halls and dram shops. A part of her was tempted to join in, but she knew it would only lead to trouble. Elizabeth had been fascinated though to read one account, in the *Glasgow Heral,* about the ship, *Savilla*, which had carried the first load of 126 single women out to Otago. Jesse Crawford had been appointed matron in-charge of all the single woman aboard, her job was described as 'onerous and unpleasant with many unfamiliar duties.' The scheme had been hastily organised, and by the sound of it, little had been arranged to receive them on their arrival in Port Chalmers. At first, the young ladies were housed in the Dunedin Barracks until such time as they could go 'into service.' Here, Jesse Crawford was kept on to find her true vocation in life, her duties listed thus: 'to look after the girls; to make them keep the place clean; see they attend to the hours; to see they get their meals at proper hours; get situations proper for them in so far as when people come wanting servants.' As more and more young women came out, the matron's primary job was to meet the parties of new arrivals at the dockside and escort them with all their bags and boxes to the depot in Princes Street. Here, they were allowed two or three days to wash all their clothes and get ready to be sent out to work.

But it was the last part of the newspaper report which intrigued Elizabeth the most, describing how the first days in the new colony of New Zealand had proved a mixture of confusion and excitement for the new female arrivals. Released from the confinement of steerage class aboard the ship, it seems they were all heartily eager to find out about life in their new country. Whatever tensions existed onboard ship often exploded once the voyage ended. Some women celebrated by participating in drunken reveries, staying out all night or refusing to take up 'situations' as they were directed to do. Mrs Crawford had to deal with their rebelliousness, intervening when men, sometimes in groups, would try to sneak into the barracks. No wonder, she got paid the fantastic sum of £90 a year, the highest matron salary in all New Zealand. Matrons were everywhere it seemed, not only in immigration barracks, but in hospitals, asylums, boarding houses. Without a doubt, you had to be a special woman to be a matron, and New Zealand it seemed had plenty.

By now, Invercargill had well and truly woken up. There were men on horseback on the streets, and two young boys ambled slowly past, involved in a serious conversation. A hansom cab and driver trotted by, which reminded her of uncle, a man who had discharged his duties to the very end, at Princess Pier at Greenock, watching her ship being towed by a valiant steam tug out into the stream of the channel. In return, she had watched his stern, black clad figure diminish. When she thought he appeared no bigger than her outstretched smallest fingernail, some of the passengers began to sing verses from the 100th Psalm. When they finished, an older woman from the Religious Tract Society stepped forward to intone a long prayer warning about separating from the almighty

Father in heaven, which Elizabeth somehow felt significant as severing her last links to home. Both uncle and Meg, his second wife who acted like her governess to her, had been kind despite their stern and uncompromising attitudes, but both were over it all, and she knew they were quietly relieved to get rid of her at last.

Elizabeth blinked, looking around to distract herself from any distressing thoughts. There was no room for tears now. The lump in her throat subsided to an ache that she tried to dispel by taking slow, deep breaths into her lungs.

The sun rose higher, the day grew warmer, and Elizabeth was glad of the shade of the awning. It had been a moment of real grief for her when her special parasol, so beautifully printed with the picture of Walking Dress in the Woods, had blown overboard somewhere in the tropics, as she was leaning over the rail to watch a pod of porpoises play in the bow wave of the ship, how they looked like shiny, slick pigs as they leapt and danced in the water. She hoped she could buy another parasol in Bluff, maybe even Pegasus which she imagined to be at least a small village on the coast.

Elizabeth wasn't surprised to feel her pangs of hunger, having last eaten since late yesterday afternoon at the Temperance Hotel opposite the railway station in Dunedin. If it hadn't been a temperance hotel, she doubted that she could have plucked up the courage to enter. Pacing the pavement for nearly an hour, she watched patrons entering and leaving, and saw they were nearly all men—indeed the only women coming and going were in the company of men, namely fathers or husbands. But eventually, hunger got the better of her. Remembering Meg's last whispered words, "Elizabeth, you're going to have to be very, very brave, and I know you can do it," she had entered the establishment, expecting the place to fall silent at her effrontery, but to her immediate relief, no one seemed to notice her. The murmured conversations of the diners didn't falter, the clink of cutlery on plates continued on as before and she was greeted by Mrs Silk, the proprietress who seated her in a discrete partially screened-off corner. Soon a barmaid delivered her out a generous plate of roast beef with potatoes and Yorkshire pudding, followed by a jam steamed pudding. After eating as much as she could, Elizabeth wrapped what remained into a brown paper bag for the next day, swigging the last of the Schweppes carbonated water she'd bought from a vendor when the train stopped in Gore. With hunger and thirst sated, and checking first to see that no one was watching her, she leaned back against the wooden bench and closed her eyes. Oh, my Great God, whatever have I got myself into? That was her last thought before drifting off.

Chapter 2

Pegasus Tin Field, 8 February 1889

"So much for this southern summer," Syd found himself muttering under his breath as he called it a day. The screaming south-westerly winds had picked up both velocity and moisture as they travelled unhindered across the thousands of miles of Southern Ocean, and now they were fair slamming into the granite crags and hillocks above him. Not that he could see any of them, all enveloped by low scudding rainclouds looking angrier by the moment. This had the potential for a serious rainstorm and he knew it as the first big drops began pinging off his tin cup and plate. Finishing his week's work on a Friday was not something hardworking Syd normally entertained, even a decent rainstorm wouldn't put him off. His basic instinct was to work all week, maybe take a few hours off on Sunday to fix his gear and put things in order around his camp, gather in some branches of dryish branches to chop up ready for the coming week. Even the most drenching rainstorms hardly put him off his claim, there was always something to get on with. There was no such thing as bad weather, just the wrong clothes, his father used to tell him. Since coming to Pegasus, he had become used to the inclement weather that routinely ranged through the extremes of four seasons in one day. Sunny and hot one minute—enough to make him strip off his shirt—then hail and icy blizzard sweeping through the next. He had thought working conditions on the Heemskirk Tin Field in Tasmania had been bad enough, made Bodmin Moor in Cornwall look tame and temperate by comparison. But then he came to Pegasus, and now appreciated what extreme weather was. This was not a place to come ill prepared, because it could mean the difference not only between making a living and ending up broke, but the difference between being alive or dead.

But Syd had an even better reason than the weather to pack up and head down to the shelter of Port Pegasus. He needed to go to the little post office there to send off his draft 'Prospectus,' to go with the Memorandum, for his solicitor in

Invercargill to type up. Only then, finally, could he begin the process of floating shares. Not a big company float, of course, more a syndicate of interested investors, and he had five interested parties lined up. There was no time to waste. It was all about getting sorted, presenting a solid case for his endeavour in the shortest possible time, and get the financial backing. Fervour for the mineral was high, but investors weren't fools; they wanted solid evidence their money was going to make them a good return. And who could blame them? For four years, Syd had worked for wages at the Mt Bischoff Tin Mine in Tasmania, the hardest work he had ever done in his life. But that was until he came to Pegasus and pegged out his own claim. Now he was working harder, and so far for far less. But he didn't care—at least he had a claim—two of them in fact—each 60 acres adjoining each other up in the head of the south branch of McArthurs Creek. Arguably, his was the best positioned combined claim in the whole Pegasus Tin Field, and it was going to make him a lot of money. He had no doubt about that.

In two years' time, Syd was going to turn 30, and he suspected it was going to be a watershed year for him. Fourteen years of hard labour was soon going to be over, and after that he was determined to do it differently. Not be like the directors of the Mt Bischoff Tin Mine for a start. They creamed off all the profits of the operation and paid a pittance to the scores of their workers toiling away with picks and shovels, year after year. That had caused so much bitterness. Everyone hated those directors for how they conducted their operation. But Syd had plans for his Pegasus Tin Mining Company, and it was going to be full of enthusiastic workers who benefited from their employment, at the same time returning him, as company director, a fair return. They might even hit the motherlode which surely lay just under the ground. After five years or so of running a profitable mining company, he might have enough to buy a sheep farm, maybe in Southland or Canterbury. Then, he would finally not only be one of the gentry but also be notable as one who had truly earned it. Marriage was not showing in his cards yet, but it would surely come to fruition as he started to prosper. A son or two to inherit his holdings, a daughter to be a success in her own right; he had so much to look forward to. The last week of sluicing had produced little stream tin, just like the week before, but Syd remained supremely optimistic. The mineral ran in his blood after all. Syd's father, Alwyn Braithwaite, had been a tin miner all his life in Cornwell. Tin doesn't occur in many places in the world, he had told his son, who had been impressed by the fact that the Romans only invaded England after tin ore was discovered in the south of the country. “Go for tin, everybody needs it,” he told his son. And his son had listened, taken it in, and gone forth to do his father’s work in the world.

It was bucketing down by the time Syd got back to his canvas tent on the little terrace above the creek which was fast becoming a raging torrent. Just upstream, a steady cascade was appearing, sending up spray high into the air. Syd was suddenly thoroughly drenched, but if he stopped moving for even a second, he knew the cold would bite into him like piercing needles. His mind kept going back to his sluicing gear in the gully—temporary fluming, riffle box, shovel, pick, crowbar, tin cup, plate—had he pulled and collected them all up so they were well out of the creek? If this rain persisted more than another hour, there would be flooding for sure and he could barely afford to lose any of his precious gear, all of which he’d carted all up on his own back.

As he set off, his rucksack slung over one shoulder, Syd made sure to adjust his hat evenly to keep both the rain off his face and stop the water dribbling off down his neck. Not that his oilskin could be relied on to keep him dry in this rain. He couldn’t help but take in the musty smell of wet vegetation mingling with odour of burnt off scrub. Strange how the rain brings out all the smells, he thought.

It would take him at least four hours to get down the hill. The track down to McFadyens was especially difficult, awash as it was with a slurry of water, silt and burnt branches all cascading off the miners claims further up the valley. The 200 or so men who now called this God-forsaken part of Stewart Island their home, a veritable ‘Lands End,’ had all done what they had considered to be the decent thing when they turned up here and burnt off the vegetation. How else could they have got around? The windblown scrub was the tightest, most impenetrable that Syd had ever encountered. Worst of all were the patches of leatherwoods, they could make a grown man cry trying to get through them. The branches were stiff and hard, even the jagged-edged leaves could lacerate you. The wholesale burning had come at a price though, for a start, this morning the slurry of stale wet ash clinging to the bottom of his trousers like treacle. Syd had forgotten what his canvas trousers had looked like when he first arrived here, near to black and encrusted as they were now. It didn’t matter anymore, as long as he had the ability to stay surefooted. A miner could not afford to break a bone or even sprain an ankle. Mobility was an essential part of the game. Coming out, Syd had been informed by the ship’s surgeon that the main cause of death in the colony wasn’t through accident or mishaps, but diseases like consumption and diarrhoea, whooping cough, convulsions, cephalitis, dysentery and remittent fever. "If you reach 50, you'll be considered old," the medical man had told him bluntly after finding out he was a miner. "Don't go adding to your risk by risking infection from unclean wounds, or drowning crossing a swollen river." The 'New Zealand death' the doctor referred to the latter as, so much it was reported happening.

Syd made the journey down the hill tolerable by letting his mind wander as he negotiated his way. He was sure the *SS Invercargill* would be in Port Pegasus by noon. It usually came in most Sundays, bringing miners, mail and provisions, not to mention nosey parkers, and there'd been a few of them lately. Captain Sundstrom usually stayed until Monday morning, unless he had some Muttonbirders to drop off on those islands around the Cape. Last month, Syd had ordered a finer grate for his sluice, to trap more of the stream tin, knowing from his washups that he was losing some of the good stuff. With any luck, that grating just might be on today's ship. All the more reason to head down early. Syd relished finding multiple justifications for everything he did, just made him feel efficient.

His route down passed through numerous claims, some he could get no view into without serious diversion. He knew them all, of course, barely an evening passed without at least a couple of miners from different claims congregating to share their toiling tales. Syd's tin mining father had earlier taught him the distinction between toiling and moiling, not exactly explaining it outright, rather using it in context. Syd just grew up knowing what they meant by how his father used them. Toiling meant you worked hard all day in a never-ending fashion. But moiling, that was another thing altogether, from old Gaelic, meaning working hard as well, but more in confusion and agitation as to what you were about. Syd knew that a lot of small claim gold miners moiled away, as some of the tin streamers were doing on this very field too. He could tell straight away what they were up to from the way they sluiced, the way they stacked their tailings, even dug their prospect pits. The toilers quickly identified the patches of paydirt and went about it step by step in a consistent fashion, working down to bedrock and following the colour and grits into richer patches, leaving nothing unturned as they went. Moilers by contrast were all over the place, never quite getting anywhere. Toilers turned their hard work into solid results; moilers they just usually ended up broke, anything they did earn just traded for stores, and that was if they were lucky. Couldn't blame them I suppose, Syd reckoned, they hadn't been brought up on Bodmin Moor like he had. Those tin miners from Cornwall knew their stuff, and why wouldn't they after two thousand years of streaming and digging for tin. Tinstone just ran in their blood. A real tin miner could smell it, damn near see it running under the ground even. "Where it is, there it is," the old Cornish tin miners saying went. Enquiring, bold, decisive—how could you lose.

The first claim workings Sid crossed which he could plainly see into was Walsh's, but he couldn't help satisfying his curiosity to divert slightly towards the edge of the terrace to see what progress the two brothers had made in the gully over the past week. A deep tailrace drained their workings, fair raging from the rain. Last time he called in, he'd admired how they had cut out an out entire loop of the stream to sluice their sizeable ground paddock. With the gully now, their workings ran for at least five chains, and he could swear the sluice faces had grown a good foot or so since he'd last looked in. There was no sign of activity today, no doubt, the two brothers were sheltering now in their little hut which was located just above the head race that fed their claim. He admired the Walsh brothers, real toiling battlers they were. They deserved to come out of this godforsaken place rich men, like I should, thought Syd. Ten minutes further on, Syd passed through the claim originally owned by Jack Edwards, but more lately by Thomas Tucker. The new owner's perfect herringbone tailings reminded him of the Old Country again, just the way a good tin miner left their 'leats' on Bodmin Moor. Syd admired Tucker's hut too whenever he had called in there. A canvas roof was stretched over on sapling poles, but all the walls were gnarly stacked rocks. Cut into the natural bank at one end was a cosy fireplace. Syd knew his hut would come in due course, when he had time to build it. But in the meantime, he was content to live under canvas. Of course, he hadn't experienced a winter at Pegasus yet. Three times already this summer, his tent had failed to hold. The worst one happened at night, and took a day of stitching before he could put it up again.

If it was a more pleasant day, he would have diverted to see how Tucker was getting on, but today, he pushed on. Through the claims of George Baker, Robert Stevens and Alex Glennie he saw not a soul, and it was only when he got to the claim of Robert Scollay that he finally stopped for a break. The tin streamer had seen him coming and wandered out to meet him, holding his oilskin over his head and firmly clenching the clay pipe in his mouth that no one ever seen him without.

"So, tell me Bob, how you going down there?" Syd enquired.

Scollay could be dour, "Huh, I pay my provisions, a few pennies left over. To be honest, nothing but hard labour when we all should be making ten bob a day. Be lucky to clear sixpence at the rate we going."

A great fraternity existed between all the streamers, but it didn't mean they could exactly trust each other when it came to their returns. They all knew the game and kept it close to their chest. For all Syd knew, Scollay was doing far better than he was making out, the man had a canny almost instinctive nature when it came to his work, and he'd been one of the first on the field. On his previous visit to the claim, Syd had been intrigued by Scollay's tailrace which was divided down the middle by cut timbers which plainly showed axe marks, this arrangement positioned by larger rocks to make two channels. Clever, thought Syd, he could have two flows going out at once, one back out to the creek and the other down to his lower paddock. It wasn't worth asking him about it though, Scollay wasn't one to give much away unless there was something in it for him.

Only when the track from McFaydens hit the Surveyors Track did Syd finally begin to relax. This last stretch down to Pegasus Hotel had only been cut the year before, a marathon job that had consumed three surveyors led by Thomas Miller, equipped with axes and slashers, for a full nine months. Their work had facilitated the surveying off of all the claims, Syd's included. In its short existence, the track had been used by hundreds of diggers trudging back and forth to their claims with more and more gear, leaving it in exceedingly bad condition. Apart from one steep section, the track kept a remarkably even gradient and fairly straight course for its entire last two miles, but Syd knew it would take him at least two hours to negotiate it in the wet conditions. In the worst parts, he would find surer footing up alongside the track, just as all the other miners did, causing the track to be up to a chain wide in some places. Going back uphill with a 50lb bag of flour on your back could double that time, sinking in at every step. Whatever way you went, no man could do this track and avoid ending up covered in mud at least up to his waist. One of Syd's prospecting mates had worked out that over the track's distance to their claims, a miner would lift up, on his boots alone, around one ton of mud to a height of one foot, an unintended accomplishment indeed. Tough enough, thought Syd, and how bad it would have been for the very first prospectors, with no trails or burnt bush to negotiate. The hillsides of stiffly branched leatherwoods were the worst, and there were plenty of them. They grew in thick swathes, vegetation that was too short to crawl beneath and too tall to step over. The only way was to bush-bash straight through, a method that afforded the stiff branches ample opportunity to rip clothing and draw blood. Even retriever dogs were known to baulk at going through, just give up and whimper off. Any progress through the blasted leatherwoods was excruciatingly slow, leaving the traveller bruised, scratched, and thoroughly exhausted.

Thank God for tracks, a small mercy, thought Syd. The hotel was barely a furlong off now. He knew every part of the route; he had been up and down it so many times.

Stopping under the shelter of a branching tree gave him the opportunity to take a short break and compose himself before arriving at the respectable establishment. Barely respectable he well appreciated, but the only guaranteed dry structure for 30 miles gave it some standing. Syd didn't need a mirror to appreciate just how filthy he was, even the lower half of his rucksack was coated in mud. The rain was no longer torrential, and Syd had even spotted a small piece of blue sky in the distance. His claim was high above and behind him now and he had left it behind in his mind. Instead, he began to think of what he might encounter in the hotel. Come to think of it, he might even meet George's new wife-to-be who he'd heard was coming all the way out from Scotland. All the miners had heard about George's arranged bride, and more than a few jokes were in circulation.

Syd shook his head, a smile playing around his mouth. It'll take a special type of woman to take on Pegasus, let alone George, he mused to himself. All this mud for a start. Peggy the barwoman and housemaid was always complaining about it, she had even taken to wearing all her skirts hitched half way up to her knees when trudging around the hotel. That was her story anyway, but Syd suspected she wasn't averse to showing a bit of ankle and the effect it had on the men. The miners were mostly a decent bunch even if a bit rough round the edges. He hoped George's new wife could give as good as she got, because living down here was not going to be easy for her.

George, now he's a strange one, thought Syd. He couldn't understand why now, of all times, George had decided to get married—from all accounts he'd been happily muddling along as a bachelor in Invercargill, planning to set up a drapery shop and all, but a month earlier he had turned up at Pegasus out of the blue to manage the hotel while Rodgers attended to his liquor license. Rodgers had been operating without one and when the authorities in Invercargill found out, they fined him a substantial amount. Made him go over to the mainland too and apply for one in person, no way were they going to grant it to him by letter, not when he'd broken the law. The rules of law were toughly applied. That's when his old mate George turned up to run the show. Syd had often wondered—he had never said this out loud, nor ever would—if George was a bit of a pansy deep down. Didn't like getting his hands too dirty, just a feeling Syd had, the way he spoke even.

Anyway, none of that was any of his business and he knew it. He had more important things to think about in his life, like making his fortune and settling down himself. He knew without a doubt he wasn't a pansy, so a wife was absolutely in order. Sometimes, he felt he was still fending off Peggy—she was a bit old for him—but it was hard at times when a bloke got a bit lonesome up on the fields and you knew there was a warm welcome down on that little promontory out in the harbour. Syd had sensed old Peggy would be more trouble than she was worth. Make life easier for him for sure, but at what price?

The last of the big leatherwoods were giving way to the crown ferns, big cutty grasses and shiny-leaved muttonbird scrub of the coast; he was nearly there, and just in time too. The light was fading, and he could tell by the loud voices below that the steamer had arrived. Why hadn't he heard the whistle as it came through the narrows? Must have been the rain, he put it down to. Finally, through the trees, he could make it out, the tender from the *Invercargill* pulling up to the shoreline. And hitching up her skirt to take a step out towards it was Peggy, a strange thing to do thought Syd, until he spied the pale, dark clothed woman who Peggy was now helping from the boat. Syd squinted his eyes to focus on her, looking lost and bedraggled, and ignored by all the men as they manhandled cargo all around her, lifting it out of the longboat to stack on shore. Surely, this new woman couldn't be the new wife. "Where the blazes was George?" Syd muttered to himself. As he drew close, he could vaguely see by her demeanour that the new arrival was young, maybe early to mid-twenties. Looking so out of place here. Peggy, yes, she belonged, but not this new arrival, surely this new girl had breeding. Her feet were now on dry land, and she turned back around to face Peggy directly, causing her full face to be exposed to Syd now standing back in the fringe of tall manuka above them.

"Most welcome to Port Pegasus, ma'am, I'm Peggy," he could plainly hear the barmaid greet her. "George sent me down to meet you, he got caught up with getting the postal bag ready for the boat, but he'll be down shortly. Don't you worry about him now, lassie. You've come a long way. Let me take you up to the hotel and settle you in."

Syd was sure now that the new arrival was out of sorts, he could see it on her face. Where was George anyway? Her future husband for God sakes! Why hadn't he come down to meet her? Bad enough he hadn't met off the immigrant boat in Port Chalmers. Another miner had found out about it and told him.

Just at that moment, the new arrival looked up, maybe sensing something, to look directly at his face. At that exact moment, the sun came out, and Syd was sure it illuminated a single glinting tear running down one of her cheeks. But it was his own cheeks which he felt flush with sudden warmth, the embarrassment of being caught out spying through the trees.

Chapter 3

For the son of an English crofter, Professor James Gow Black could rightfully feel proud of the position he now found himself. He turned over the palm-sized piece of cassiterite, the latest sample of tinstone to be sent to him from the wild, remarkable mountains of Stewart Island. Despite a considerable unintended leave of absence, he still had his position at the university. But even more importantly, he was feeling quietly confident that he had cleverly positioned himself to be the New Zealand colony's main claimholder of tinstone, the mother lode. Slipping out his magnifying glass, he examined the quartz and mica glittering out the tin dioxide rock darkened by intrusion of iron. But it was only the glint of thin translucent crystals of tin oxide that made his heart beat faster. Even without assaying it, he could tell that this latest sample was almost certainly the richest he had handled so far. For several minutes, he examined the rock from every angle before the strain of looking so intensely through the glass caused him to put it down and remove his spectacles. Leaning back in his chair, he rubbed his eyes with both hands, taking the opportunity to reflect on the immensity of his discovery. Everyone was looking for stream tin, but he knew now exactly where the mother lode was now, deep within the granite mountain. And his hilltop claim was the only place that mother lode came anywhere near the surface. The two Cornish miners now under his employ, recruited from the Tuapeka Goldfield, had come at a price, but they were going to repay his financial outlay most handsomely. He imagined them at that very moment digging with picks and chisels into the granite mountain, getting closer and closer to the motherlode with every passing day. And that thought made him immensely satisfied.

His spacious office at the university could look shambolic at times, but it was as comfortable as the salon he shared with his wife and family in their impressive Calton Hill home in South Dunedin. And it would be fair to say he had earned his standing well. The Foundation Council of the University of Otago had been convened 20 years earlier in 1867, only two years later appointing the newly arrived Black as its first professor of Natural Science to teach chemistry and minerology. He held this position with distinction until 1877 when he relinquished his geology portfolio to specialise in industrial chemistry, allowing Otago Provincial Geologist Captain FW Hutton to replace him as the university's new geology professor. It was a tactical expansion for the budding institution, and Black used it to his advantage, for he was now able to concentrate his full attention on his favourite interest—industrial chemistry, in particular, developing processes to leverage the worth of the raw mineral treasures which lay unexploited beneath the earth's surface. The growing colony not only urgently needed new mineral discoveries, but develop the ability to process them economically as possible. For over two decades, everyone had only looked for gold, went absolutely mad with the frenzy of it, nowhere more than on the Otago Goldfields. But the professor well appreciated more than anyone else that the alluvial gold was finite, he could clearly see that in the monthly returns filed from the gold buyers which were routinely passed onto him from the provincial government. Without a doubt, the precious metal was running out for the alluvial miner, and he knew that by the turn of the century, the hard rock gold miners would have ascended to supremacy. Far greater efforts would soon be required to extract the precious metal from the deeper, tight gravels and dense quartz reefs. Risks and costs would rise accordingly. More than anyone else, the professor appreciated that the post-rush story of the goldfield belonged to the 'Companies' as they struggled to harness enough water for their hillside-busting sluicing cannons. It was destruction on a grand scale, whole hillsides reduced to slurry to profit the venturesome shareholders. Anything was possible, the latest government purchases of huge tracts of Maori land meant his new country comprising three islands was now fully available for exploitation.

Iron, magnesite, serpentine, talc, dolomite, bituminous coal, he had advised on them all. But there was one mineral that the professor had over the last 18 months become utterly obsessed with, and that was tinstone. To make the metal Tin, element symbol *Sn,* derived from the Latin for the metal the Romans called *stannum.* He could still hear the laboured voice of his old emeritus professor pontificating about it at the University of Edinburgh. And rightly so, Black now fully appreciated, just what a splendid mineral it was. He had come to look down and almost despise the way people derided the use of the metal, calling items made of it as tinpot, tingod, tinhorn and the like, to imply cheapness and inferiority, because nothing could have been further from the truth. Probably no one else at this point of time in the whole colony appreciated just how noble a resource of tin metal could be. For thousands of years, copper had been the sole working metal used by ancient peoples. Then sometime at least around 3,500 years before the birth of Jesus Christ, an unknown metalsmith in Persia discovered that adding a little tin ore to copper in the smelting process resulted in a much harder and near indestructible alloy-bronze. An age was born, one that would last more than two thousand years until the advent of smelting iron and subsequent steel transformed metal-making production. Of course, the professor had read every historical tome on the subject he could get his hands on, endeavouring to decipher what part the metal had played in the advancement of the civilised world. And his findings had illuminated him, indeed, filled him with an entire life purpose. Tin deposits he knew were scarce, occurring in only a few places in the world. The very discovery of stream tin in Cornwell facilitated the Roman Invasion of England around half a century before Christ was born. If it wasn't for tin, they wouldn't have bothered crossing the English Channel to subdue a few primitive lawless tribes. Apart from there, tin ore was known to exist in France, Germany, Spain, Portugal and Italy, the professor had seen the field notes for all of those, but lately, he had heard an exciting rumour that extraordinary deposits had been found in the far reaches of China. No one ever expected it to be found it in the New Zealand colony, not until 18 months ago when a plain wrapped sample of dark sand had arrived addressed to him at the University of Otago's front desk.

The receptionist recorded it was dropped off by Stewart Island settler and prospector Charles Robertson, the attached letter sealed with wax and simply addressed James Gow Black, underneath it marked urgent. The parcel was promptly delivered to Professor Black's office.

From the weight of the parcel addressed to him, the professor had immediately assumed it was a sample of crushed gold-bearing quartz, but the curt note from within the sealed envelope soon heightened his interest.

"I will call in again tomorrow late afternoon to discuss mineral sample attached, sluice pannings from Pagasus Creek. Mention to no one in meantime. Charles Robertson."

Black cleared his work desk to lay out the parcel, unwrapping away its inner and outer wrappings of heavy brown paper to find several pounds of dark, almost black sand. It was not iron sand; the professor could tell that immediately from its lack of lustre. Tin did come to mind, but surely not, he mulled, his mind taken up by the meeting he was about to attend in five minutes. Taking care not to spill a grain, he re-wrapped the delivery to examine later.

"You look somewhat distracted today, Professor Black!" his chancellor said to him at the end of the heads of faculty meeting, routine for a Thursday afternoon.

"Aye, perhaps, I am." Black replied curtly, before adding, "A pressing industrial inquiry which I must attend to in the laboratory before I go home. Excuse me, gentlemen."

"Could you possibly be stream tin?" The professor found himself asking this as he unwrapped the little brown paper parcel for the second time. Putting a few grains under his microscope, he focused on the crystalline structure. Sure enough, coming into focus were the distinctive spikey crystals that he was looking for. Suddenly, the sample could be nothing else.

"By jingo, it is tin!" Black found himself declaring out loud, but he knew a definitive judgement about its purity could not be made until he assayed it. He hesitated for a few seconds as he ran the old tried and proven Cornish tin miners' procedure by himself. He had only ever done it a few times, and that was back in Scotland.

On the balance scales, he went about weighing out exactly twenty troy ounces of the black sand from the sample, about half of it, mixed it with four troy ounces of powdered culm on a flat copper pan, careful to choose the one with a long-shaped lip to ensure he could more easily brush the mix into the black lead crucible held in the stout tripod at the edge of the furnace attached to the laboratory. The professor felt thankful that one of his research students had only used it previously that afternoon to assay a promising sample of magnesite from the Cobb Valley in Nelson. It was still hot, meaning he could get straight underway with a little pumping of the bellows and judicious use of a blow pipe to get it to the 450 degrees heat Fahrenheit temperature he would need. For an hour he worked, blowing the pipe and pumping the bellows alternately with his feet, until the mix became frothing white hot, a state of flux he kept for the required twelve minutes. Only when he judged that every ebullition had died down, did he select a number three sized scraper and set about carefully drawing aside the culm-ash which had risen to the top, after which he proceeded to pour what was left into a 30-troy ounce iron ingot mould. This he placed on the copper pan to make sure it collected the culm slag, not to mention any adherent metals oozing out of it. After carefully scraping out what remained in the crucible, he mixed these scrapings with the contents of the mould and pan, which he then transferred to a mortar. Only now could the 'lump' be freed from its slag and taken to the scales. This lump he then pounded to the consistency of powder, passing it all through a sieve so that nothing but the tiniest flattened particles of tin metal remained, adding these as well to the scales for the final reckoning. The professor was well aware that some assayers used a little flour-spar to assist the fusion of refractory slag, even a dash of borax for when the silica level was high. But this professor was putting his money on old Cornish wisdom—they'd been doing it far longer than anyone else after all. Still perspiring from the furnace, the professor stopped to take a long drink of water. Ready now for the calculations, he sat down at his desk to divide the final weight of pure tin against the stream sample he started with. It all came down to defining how many pounds of tin metal you could get out of a hundred weight of stream tin. Often these samples came from a prospect pit, typically four feet by two, just long and wide enough for a man to shovel down four feet or so. The assay of the sample taken out told you whether it was worth streaming the area. But the professor rightly guessed from its purity this sample had come straight from the riffle box, and had conservatively allowed for it. The professor did his calculations, pencil scuffing on pad, double checking to make sure he hadn't made any errors. His first result came out at 14/20, enough for him to go through the calculations again. Same result, 14/20. That meant 78 pounds for every hundredweight of sluiced stream tin alluvium. The realisation of the certainty of the result made the professor drop his pencil and rub his eyes. The last thing he did before leaving the room was tear off the page with his numbers, ripping it into tiny pieces before throwing them all into the red embers of his furnace. No record should exist, he had given his word by accepting the parcel.

By the following morning, the professor could think of nothing else. Seven times, he had gone to his library shelves of geological and chemistry books in his study after he'd got home late, checking up on anything else he may have missed about the mineral which had so suddenly and without warning entered his life. In the insightful journals from James Cook's voyages, Black was absolutely astounded to read how in March 1770, the urgent cry of 'Land Ahoy!' had come from the crow's nest of the *HMS Endeavour* off southern Stewart Island from the crow's nest of Cook's *HMS Endeavour.* So startling were the granite monoliths which greeted them out of the dawn, that several officers felt compelled to put pen to paper to describe them in their logs. The ship's draughtsman, Sydney Parkinson, wrote how they reminded him of 'Sugar Loaf.' Skimming through the lines, the professor knew that real insight would come from the most venerable scientist aboard, Joseph Banks, who spent his hours passing the great outcrops under scudding sails by observing them with his telescope. Only when they were all out of sight did the scientist sat down at the narrow desk in his cabin to pen his impressions.

The phrases jumped out to the professor. "…amazingly full of Large Veins and patches of some mineral that shone as if it was polished or rather looked like it had been pavd *[sic]* in glass; what it was I could not at all guess but it certainly was some mineral and seemed to argue by its immediate abundance a countrey *[sic]* abounding in minerals, where one may judge by the corresponding latitudes of South America in all human probability something very valuable may be found."

The professor now realised how prophetic Bank's words were turning out to be. Just over one hundred years later, in 1882, gold was discovered in 'Strong Creek' on southern Stewart Island by Louis Longuet and Harry Allen. This watercourse which fed the magnificent waterfall that flowed into the head of North Arm would shortly after be officially named Pegasus Creek. The two pioneering prospectors worked inland to the rugged heart of the range, then dubbed the Remarkables, and completed the first known traverse along the backbone range of the island, returning overland to Paterson Inlet. Their discovery had brought about a minor rush of activity, but complaints soon started to be heard from prospecting explorers about how their yields were low, thanks mainly to a contamination, a curious 'black plague' of sand which always seemed to fill their wash-ups. It was near impossible to separate off too, because it was heavy, almost exactly the same as the gold. The miners had no choice but to put up with it, and but only the hardy ended up staying, so trying the situation became. Lucky for indefatigable Longuet too, who went on to Preservation Inlet where he picked up his famous 16oz nugget just sitting upon the beach near Moonlight Point.

Professor put it down to Dame Fortune, who seemingly visited the Pegasus field again in December 1888, when George Swain and James Thompson of Halfmoon Bay finally managed to isolate off a quantity of a strange mineral amongst the 'beastly' black sand which plagued their claim in Pegasus Creek. Filling a chamois bag with their precious findings, they gave their sample to another island prospecting colleague, Charles Robertson, who was on his way to Dunedin, with strict instructions to deliver it without delay to James Gow Black, Otago University's esteemed professor of chemistry and expert on all things geologic.

After delivering his parcel, Robertson returned the following day to the University in Leith Street. His meeting with the professor had proved near explosive. The two men were like powder kegs ready to go off together. Robertson already suspected what the professor had now proved, and they instantly became secret comrades.

"We must leave for Pegasus immediately," said Robertson in a hushed voice. "If word gets out of what we have found, every man and his retriever will surely beat us there."

Although not a mining man in the practical sense, the professor well appreciated exactly what the experienced prospector was saying. Whoever pegged out a claim on the ground was in, and whoever didn't was clear out of the race. The gold seekers were there already, frustrated by that confounded black sand. If more got wind of what real riches lay in that alluvium, there would be a stampede.

"Mr Robertson," the professor addressed him in his gravest tone. "What we have discussed is now between just you and myself, absolutely no one else should find out what we now know in Dunedin. We must travel with haste down to Port Pegasus. When can you make yourself available to leave?"

"Give me an hour to collect my belongings," said the miner without hesitation. "There is a mail train to Invercargill later tonight, we could make Bluff by nine o'clock tomorrow morning. I know Scollay's cutter *Bob* is tied up there, loading supplies and mining gear. With luck and fair weather, we could even be in Halfmoon Bay by tomorrow evening. Now, if you would excuse me, good sir, I had better get going, I have a couple of urgent legal matters to attend to before we leave."

It wasn't until Robertson left that the reality of the situation began to dawn on the professor. Thank the generous Lord, the university student holidays were about to start, otherwise he would still be delivering Chemistry lectures that day, let alone more classes tomorrow, the next day and every week thereafter. But there was still the question of his wife, Carolyn, to whom he had mentioned nothing about the sample delivered to him the previous day. Missing the festive season with his three children was relatively easy, at heart, he was from stoical crofter stock after all. But his mind faltered over the slurry of appointments stretching out into the new year which he now realised he all would have to cancel, at least postpone. But before he had even one chance to go dizzy over the sudden turn of fate, he sat down, pulled a sheet of clean white watermarked paper from his draw and began penning a letter to his boss. “Dear Chancellor, it is with extreme regret that I must take unexpected and urgent leave until early February at the earliest, maybe into March. A matter of the utmost and serious importance has bestowed itself upon me without the slightest warning…”

He would explain the situation to his wife, Carolyn, when he went home to collect his rucksack, clothes, blanket and miscellaneous gear, a few food items, ready for imminent departure on the afternoon train. She was used to his disappearances, though this would surely be his most sudden yet, but he knew she would get over it, especially if he returned a victorious man. True riches were surely within his grasp, and all would be forgiven in due course.

****

The two men did make to Bluff the following morning, where they hurriedly went about purchasing last minute equipment and supplies. For the professor, this included a sharp tomahawk from the hardware merchant in Gore Street, something he would surely need from what he had been warned of the dastardly leatherwoods. It was a flurry, and one that was observed by more than a few around the port. Gold fever was rife, and their hasty preparations had not gone unnoticed. Scollay had made no bones about departing his cutter on the turn of the tide, eleven thirty at the latest. Everyone was known, or at least known of, and the professor was displaying a flamboyantly excitable and urgent demeanour.

Even before the little cutter, *Bob* hit the choppy Foveaux Strait, they spied over their shoulders, a pursuing cutter. Robertson knew the race was on, with whom no one was quite sure, so the professor spent the next hour convincing Scollay that he must abandon Halfmoon Bay as their first port of call; it was now essential to head directly for Pegasus. Scollay was initially reluctant because the sea conditions had become exceedingly rough, but eventually after some ardent badgering by the pushy professor, he altered course. The wind calmed down a tad as the dusk settled, and all night they sailed under the waxing moon, barely discerning the coastline as they followed it south, past Port Adventure where they sailed out to give Weka Rock a wide berth, then sneaking back in towards Abraham's Bosom which they knew would at least offer them some protection from a wicked easterly if it should suddenly spring up. That refuge was not required, and early the following morning, they made Pegasus, sailing with great relief into that magnificent harbour, no pursuer in sight. Without delay. Robertson found George Swain up at his gold claim, instructing him not only to gather the half the dozen other miners around, but tell them to bring a sample of their latest washes with them for the professor to assay without obligation. The urgency of request saw them all soon congregate, the professor now revealing to them all what he suspected, still shrewdly playing it down. It was just like a lecture, grab their attentions and knead them along in your palm awhile.

"Please do not get excited, gentlemen, my assay was preliminary only, I must now, if you can all be so kind as to avail me to take your samples away with me. You will be the first to know the results."

Some muffled talk ensued amongst the miners, but eventually they all relinquished their various sized chamois bags after they marked them as to ownership.

On the cutter back to Halfmoon Bay that afternoon, the professor opened the small sacksful of bagged samples, careful not to mix any of them up. Even under his glass he could attest to the quality of the stream tin, the promising peppering of tiny garnets too which he could plainly identify, always a good indicator that tin was present in greater concentration. At Halfmoon Bay, they wasted no time crudely smelting the small sackfuls into tin at Scollay's smithy; this time, the combined rough results coming out even better than his Dunedin calculations. On the professor's advice, Scollay departed immediately again for Pegasus, this time to peg out 120 acres of the most promising lower ground. For three whole days Scollay slept barely a wink, so excited was he after pegging out his claim in the lower reaches of Pegasus Creek, returning then to Invercargill with two comrades to apply for the permission to work it. With nervous excitement, he lodged his claim in the Land Office in Invercargill, knowing that his act would now make it open slather. There was no way the news of a tin strike would not spread like wildfire, across all the goldfields, even across the Tasman Sea where hordes of disgruntled miners waited to hear even the slightest rumour of any new mineral discovery in any of Her Majesty's far-flung Dominions. Even before Scollay prepared to depart yet again for Pegasus, this time to defend his claim, he got urgent word that a whole shipload of miners had already departed from

Melbourne, one report claiming they had made excellent time and had made Port Adventure, where they were now weatherbound. Agitation gripped Scollay's party, making the professor mad keen to charter the *SS Despatch* to get them to Pegasus first and so beat the wretched Australians. They set off, but the weather was against them too, the captain refusing to battle the boisterous south-easterlies they were soon encountering.

Back in Halfmoon Bay, the professor pulled the miners together for an urgent meeting, there was no alternative now but to tackle the overland track to Port Pegasus, down the near impenetrable backbone of the island from Paterson Inlet. So began their epic bush-bash, through the untracked country of the island's interior, the domain of the dreaded leatherwoods. Thank goodness, I bought a tomahawk, the professor thought to himself as he set out.

Bruised and utterly exhausted, the band of six arrived on the Pegasus field on the morning of the fifth day. All were immensely relieved to see the field still unoccupied apart from the few incumbent goldminers. Feverishly, they newcomers went about pegging claims on fresh ground up and down the creeks. That night, they enjoyed their first slumber under canvas, only to be awoken in the still dawn by the shrill whistle of an approaching steamer.

"The Australians have arrived!" went out the cry from their camp. Four men were immediately despatched to peg out the remnants of fresh ground further on which lay still unclaimed. It proved a false alarm; it was nothing but the *Awarua* on a 'friendly visit.' But their relief was short lived, two hours in fact, when Scollay's cutter sailed back in to join them. Immediately behind followed a flotilla of boats big and small, all full of rival prospectors, all infected with feverish intent. The first to land after Scollay was a pinnace with four men in it, a big-bearded man in the bow jumping into the water as soon as it became knee deep. As he dragged the boat in, his mate immediately behind handed him a bundle of square cut pointed wooden pegs tied together with twine. Without hesitation, this lead man ran up the beach, hesitating only briefly to make out the track entrance, then disappeared up it running as fast as he could. Two days later, the ship full of Tasmanians arrived.

The Tin Rush was on.

Chapter 4

If there was one thing the commotion of the tin rush had done for Captain Sundstrom, it had made him extremely proficient at negotiating his 1245-ton steel ship through The Narrows into Port Pegasus. On the bridge of the *SS Invercargill,* he instructed his new helmsman to take the middle course between Black Rock and White Rock. Now that the tide had turned, the current would be running more slowly.

Sundstrom had brought his ship in through these narrows at least a dozen times in the last year alone since the rush had taken off, but he still always made sure he had on hand William Stewart's 1809 chart of Port Pegasus. Like every mariner in these southern latitudes, Sundstrom appreciated how great the sealing captain of the brig *Pegasus* had been, using the time while his men wiped out all the fur seals in the area to chart the great port deemed by the British Admiralty as big enough to moor every ship in the entire Dominion. But Sundstrom was under no illusions, the commander of the sealing ship paled in comparison to the skill of Cook, the Explorer. After all, Captain Cook had produced his chart of far bigger Dusky Sound in far less time and with virtually no errors, while Stewart's chart, eventually published in 1816 in *Purdies-The Oriental Navigator*, contained some significant errors. Ones that could cause a ship to wreck.

"Helm steady ahead," said Sundstrom, at the same time reaching to swing the lever on the ship's telegraph to Slow Ahead. Once past The Sisters, he pointed out to his helmsman Orphans Rock, along with the wee rock just to the south of it.

Followed by wheeling mollymawks, the voyage from Bluff across Foveaux Strait had taken them across steely grey seas which had become noticeably rougher once they passed Port Adventure. Sundstrom was pleased to be finally entering The Narrows along Whale Passage, leaving the rough water behind, even if the roll coming in was still giving the boat a good sway. In smoother weather, he would have taken his ship through the deep channel on the north side of Orphans, but there would be no tempting fate today. Sundstrom always listened to his seaman's instincts.

As they emerged out of the tight passage, he gave a long hoot of his whistle to let everyone around know they would soon be pulling up off the hotel. The ship steamed quietly into North Arm, past Burnt Island. Rodger's hotel soon came into view, gleaming white-washed against the dark green hues of bush.

"Slight left rudder…now straighten up," ordered the captain, his telegraph already to Standby. The throbbing from the bowels of the vessel became little more than a pulsating murmur as the huge steam piston in its bowels wound down. The captain let his ship's gentle momentum take it another couple of ship-lengths further on, before ordering the anchor dropped. "Sixteen shackle-lengths of chain, no more," he called out to the bosun from the side of the bridge. He knew there was a good sand bottom here, not too shelly, and he'd never had a problem with the anchor holding in here before. Although he was an experienced seaman, he had never lost that feeling of relief at the end of every voyage. At first light tomorrow, they would head back out around South Cape and up to the big Muttonbird Island, Taukihepa, where they would drop off another party of birders. Exposed to the full fury of the Southern Ocean, that would be an even bigger challenge, but today, they were all safe, and his ship was still floating without a single scrape on it.

Sundstrom now could not help but turn his mind to one of the passengers. On his manifest as Miss EW MacDonald, he had noticed her from the moment she'd come onboard at the Town Pier in Bluff, definitely the odd one out amongst his mixed bag of passengers, otherwise all made up of roughneck miners and a few Maori birders.

Soon after leaving Bluff Harbour, the captain had called up to his second mate; "Keep an eye out for the lass, will ya? Make sure she stays in the cabin. Never know what might happen to her out on deck."

After writing a brief entry in his log, the captain stopped to keep an eye on his longboat which was about to take the young lass ashore with the first load of miners, noticing the crew almost dropped her bulky trunk into the drink as they were transferring it to the boat. That would have given her a fright, he thought. The trunk looked like a coffin sitting centre midships on the longboat, like some crazy Viking funeral pyre ready to push off. Well, that was until the bottoms of four hefty miners sat firmly on it. He was glad the lass was seated safe up front with the bosun. The curiosity of the whole situation even made the captain pause for a few seconds to ponder what her story might be—asking himself why ever would a fine young lass like her want to come out to this God-forsaken place, a day's steaming from anywhere? It was only when he saw the young lass helped ashore by another woman, hitching up her dress in the tide, that he suddenly lost interest, calling down to his first mate, "Make sure none of those birders get off, would you please, Mr Bishop! You'll never get them back on board in time to leave tomorrow. Wouldn't know a schedule if they could read one, those Maori fellas."

Coming into North Arm after The Narrows of Whale Passage, Elizabeth's suspicion that a very small village lay ahead was fast realising. As they edged ever closer, it began to dawn on her that it wasn't even a village, just three or maybe four smallish white, wooden buildings huddled together on a low promontory beside a tiny scrap of beach. As they got closer, she could see it wasn't even a beach, more a sloping rock shelf, the only access up to the buildings looking like a wooden ladder leaning against the rocks, all of it surrounded by scrubby trees and patches of dark burnt off vegetation. It was wild country in all directions, with no sign of any other huts, houses or even tents anywhere. Two small cutters lay with their stern anchors out, their bows just tied out to trunks of spindly trees. By the time she was being rowed to shore in the longboat, Elizabeth found her asking herself the very same question which the sea captain had wondered. How had she found herself in such a godforsaken place?

"Dear Lord," she prayed under her breath, "please help me now at my darkest hour."

When Elizabeth finally stood on that little beach, greeted by Peggy, she felt the world start to spin. The last few weeks began to collapse in upon her. She recalled the small figure of her vanishing uncle on Princess Pier back in Greenock; the weeks-long journey across a massive ocean; her dashed hopes of living in Invercargill; the sleepless, overnight train trip; the wretched and rough nineteen-hour crossing she had just endured. But now, finally in Port Pegasus, being greeted by this rough, unkempt woman and still no sign of her so-called husband, ignored by all those men throwing supplies around, even being spied on by one man hiding up the bank, it was a situation straight out of a nightmare. Worse still, she now realised she would soon have to climb that flimsy wooden ladder. It was the final straw; she had just reached the limits of her endurance.

A tall rough man in a floppy hat and wearing the dirtiest clothes she had ever seen was approaching them. Surely, this couldn't be George? He didn't look that old. She was acutely aware of her own dishevelled appearance and a musty animal smell rising from her clothes after days of travelling without a proper wash, the perfume she had liberally applied earlier making little difference.

"Excuse us now, Syd," Peggy blurted out before he could say anything. "Ma'am, may I introduce you to Mr Braithwaite, one of the tin streamers out here. We must get you up to the hotel."

Only then did Elizabeth realise that this was the man who she had caught watching her. Thank goodness it wasn't George, this man was surely a vile creature beyond words, a man of the peat. She averted her gaze and looked around at the ladder again.

"Sorry, ma'am, about over there," Syd blurted out, refusing to back off. "I wasn't staring or anything, just wondering if you needed some assistance."

Elizabeth felt a rage rising inside that made her heart pound in her ears, so she could barely hear what the man was trying to say. After all she had endured, there wasn't even a George here to meet her. Whether he had forgotten or didn't even exist, it hardly mattered now.

"Call me, Syd, please, welcome to Port Pegasus. May I help you two ladies up with that trunk?"

"Yes, that would be dandy indeed, Syd," said Peggy curtly, "And after that, would you kindly excuse us…"

"I'm not going up that ladder," Elizabeth butted in.

"Say again now, ma'am, what was that?" Peggy asked.

"I said, I am not going up that ladder! I'll catch the boat back to Bluff, that's exactly what I am going to do." And with that, she turned away and sat down on her trunk, folding her arms tight and keeping her gaze firmly on the water now starting to ripple in the rising breeze.

"Miss," Syd couldn't restrain himself. "The boat is going on with the birders and it won't be back this way until next week. You can't sit on the beach for three days. The tide'll come in for a start…"

"Aww, shut up, will ya now, Syd," said Peggy, joining Elizabeth on the trunk. "Can't ya see she's a woman with feelings, she ain't got a tinpot heart like you blasted miners! Get this trunk up the ladder, then shove off or I might have to give you a bash around the ear!"

Elizabeth did not trust herself to speak. Besides, she hadn't heard another woman quite speak like Peggy before. A woman threatening to bash a man! And this woman beside her looked tough enough to mean it. All Elizabeth could manage was yet another upwelling in her eyes. Certainly, this was the very worst day in her life. And she was about to meet her future husband, if he actually existed that was. Damn father, damn uncle, she thought, pushing me into this.

The two women stood off while Syd did the proper thing, hefting the trunk up the ladder with the help of a newly arrived hopeful he had called over. As they carried it towards the front steps of the hotel, Syd couldn't help but notice the young man also had that half-dazed look of a new arrival about him. The whole situation seemed ridiculous to Syd now, but he was used to Peggy's heavy-handed tactics every time he came down to the hotel, it was just the way she dealt with all the miners.

"Listen, Lassie," Peggy said in a low voice when they were alone. She leaned her head towards Elizabeth until it was almost touching hers. "I know you come a long, long way now, but soon, I'm gonna take you up to meet George. He's been talking about you all week. You're only going to have to stay here another month or two, then you can go back to Invercargill and get married proper. Your time here will be a fine time to get to know him. If you ask me, and to be truthful, I dunno why he got you down here so soon, but that's your business to sort out. It's just my job now to help you settle in, make you feel welcome, teach you a few of the ropes. We're run off our feet here with all this rush. George needs your help, and I do too. I'm gonna call you Lizzie now, is that alright? You're one of us from now on! Come on, let's go up. I thought that George might be down by now, but he must be still busy up there with getting the mail out, always is when the boat comes in, mind you."

Elizabeth knew there was no point arguing. Peggy steadied the ladder for her as she gingerly worked her way up, pulling up one side of her dress after another as her feet found each new rung. She didn't want to admit to Peggy that she'd never climbed a proper outside ladder before, no wonder she felt terrified, not like Peggy who immediately romped up after her.

"He must be in the post office. Follow me now, hope you're ready for him!" Peggy finished with a raucous laugh.

"As ready as I could be, considering the circumstances," Elizabeth found herself muttering back.

“Here he is, we found him!” cried Peggy. Before Elizabeth had time to indulge in any more thoughts, a man appeared, walking busily down the track with great concentration. This must be George, real now, bowing his head slightly and extending his hand out in welcome. “Elizabeth, it is my pleasure to finally meet you, welcome to Port Pegasus.”

Elizabeth was momentarily silent as she took in the man before her. He had a short-cropped beard, a demure stature, certainly no taller than her, maybe even shorter. “Welcome to Port Pegasus, Elizabeth,” he said again in a voice that she couldn’t help effeminate voice, bowing his head slightly.

“A pleasure to meet you at last, George,” she extended her hand and he took it, leaning forward to bend down and brush his beard across the back of it, effecting a kiss of sorts. At least, he was a gentleman. His hand felt soft, not like the calloused claws of the ships’ crew who had grabbed her arm to help her aboard. It could be worse I suppose, she thought.

“Elizabeth, if I may, this is indeed my pleasure to finally have you here. You look as fair and beautiful as your uncle wrote. I must apologise for all the trouble I have put you through, but please let me explain as soon as we have you settled in. May we…” He flourished his hand out to indicate the entrance to the hotel.

“Thank you, George, of course you can call me Elizabeth. It is a pleasure to finally meet you too. Uncle had told me much about you. Yes, please show me the way, I would like to see this establishment. It is, to be honest, the last place on earth I thought I would find myself. You have much to tell me, and I too you with news of home. The last few days have not been easy for me. I was beginning to wonder if I had found a living hell. I need to wash and unpack my things, then perhaps I will feel a little better.”

George turned briskly to Peggy. “The mailbags are ready, take them down to boat,” he barked. “Syd left a packet to post; can you make sure it makes one of the bags I left unpadlocked and put the postage on his ledger? There are three new arrivals to register, tell the two brothers they can share a bunk room, give the big man the north room, but make sure, he pays in advance, don’t know nothing about him. Throw those empty bottles from last night down the bank, and can you check the stores were all brought up and packed away. I will attend to Miss MacDonald.” His attention went back onto Elizabeth, who noticed his voice becoming gracious again as he addressed her.

“The kettle is hanging on the fire; we’ll make a cup of tea and fetch you something to eat. I hope you like cod, we eat a lot of that out here…and parrot…”

Peggy cut him short, "George, a woman surely knows how to look after another woman. I have jobs to do, so will leave you two to get acquainted. I'll fetch some tea and something to eat later. We'll be darn busy in the bar tonight for sure, so let's spend some more time together then. Don't you worry now, this will all work out, Lizzie, I'm sure of it."

Elizabeth wondered if Peggy could sense the panic rising within her. In just a few minutes, Elizabeth felt she had at least made an ally, and now that ally was going to disappear, leaving her with this man, still a stranger. The idea that she was going to end up married to him was too much to bear thinking about. One step at a time, she kept reminding herself.

Elizabeth certainly did feel a little better, earlier queasiness now subsiding, now she was on solid ground. George showed her around the hotel, what there was of it. The front door of the main building led straight into the barroom with rough-hewn wooden chairs around three tables. A fire smouldered in the brick fireplace at one end. Off to one side, a door appeared to lead to three bunkrooms, while on the other were four single rooms. "No married couples around here," George said by way of explanation. Following him, she inspected them all except one that was occupied. "A hard-drinking miner, if he ain't up by this evening, I will have check to see he ain't dead. We get all sorts, but no real ruffians," he assured her. She took it all in, including the rudimentary cookhouse out the back. There was no finesse about the place, not like the buildings back in the old country. This one had been thrown together quickly, Everywhere, inside and out, was rough-sawn, the only difference between inside and outside being the interior that looked more freshly cut, neither oiled by a brush nor varnished, while the exterior had been roughly whitewashed. Some of the bedrooms had scrim tacked up on the wall to stop the drafts, others didn't. There was a pervading smell, not only of woodsmoke, but a staleness that comes from too much human occupation and not enough scrubbing. As he was showing her the bar, a ginger cat softly padded up, pausing quietly for a second before leaning its sleek body against the bottom of her dress, purring gently.

"Millie certainly approves of you," said George. "Best mouse catcher around, best bird catcher too. She brings in all sorts during the day. Leaves feathers everywhere. If you see any around, sweep them outside will you."

There was one thing Elizabeth was beginning to appreciate though, and that was George's frankness, almost bluntness.

"Now, Elizabeth. I would not expect you to lay with me yet of course, we do not even know each other, let alone be engaged to be married yet, so I reserved the front single room for you. Peggy gave it a good mop out yesterday, even put some clean sheets on the bed. We don't do that for everyone, you know."

"Why, thank you, I will indeed take up your offer," replied Elizabeth, suddenly finding herself blushing. "But I am keen to know, George, why ever did you get me down here? Surely, you could have waited, at least asked me to find cheap lodgings in Dunedin or Invercargill to await your return."

"It's not that simple. You see my employment here for Mr Rodgers may not be temporary after all. If this Tin Rush takes off, which everybody seems to think is almost certain, the hotel will need a shareholder to expand. If it gets any busier, there is no way Rodgers will cope by himself. He had many interests in Invercargill, and I want to be able to be take over from him. He isn't exactly…what is the best way to say this…financially secure, stretched is a better way to put it. I suspect getting fined for not having a liquor license has been a huge setback for him. He may even need to sell the hotel, and I will get first option."

"But what about your drapery in Invercargill? Uncle kept telling me you…"

"Listen, Elizabeth," George butted in. "This colony is a land of opportunity. You must be versatile, ready for new opportunities, quick off the mark, be able to change. The drapery was a good idea, but now that tin has been discovered here, it has changed everything. Imagine a huge smelter right here, with big mines in the hills, tramways bringing down the ore night and day for the furnaces. Hundreds of workers always coming and going. How wonderful it would be for all of Southland, entire New Zealand even. This could be our greatest opportunity. Besides, I needed extra help, and you were coming anyway."

Peggy came in, preventing Elizabeth blurting out something she might regret.

"Good evening, you two. I need to set up the bar. George, fetch me a crate of whisky will you, and a couple of bottles of that bourbon? We're short on both. Someone asked me about our license this afternoon, heard a rumour we didn't have one. I told 'em we had a temporary one while the owner sorts it out. I hope that's true now, George."

Elizabeth noticed George didn't answer. As soon as he went out, Peggy sidled up to her, "So, Lizzie, what do you think of your new husband?"

“He’s not my husband yet, I’ll let you know. He seems a decent enough man, I suppose. Obviously, I need more time to make his acquaintance. Let’s say that it may take some time. I’m not one to rush into things now, Peggy.”

“Plenty of that time down here now, Lizzie,” the barmaid laughed. “Now, if you could pass me some of those glasses there, and help me set the table here. We have five in for dinner that I know of tonight. A special treat too, leg of mutton just in off the boat, it’s in the big camp oven already. Make a change from cod or parrot now, well, for us who been here awhile, won’t it?”

Elizabeth put on her apron, relieved she had survived her arrival at Pegasus, and slightly surprised that her Scottish resilience had come to the fore. She would help Peggy in the kitchen and perhaps help take out the meals. After laying out the tables, she went to set herself up in the little room allocated her on the eastern side of the building. She had had a rough week, but as the afternoon drew to a close, her spirits began to pick up. She felt almost plucky again, and she felt an overwhelming determination that no one, absolutely no one, was going to boss her around.

Chapter 5

For the first time since arriving at Port Pegasus, Syd felt slightly worried. His fifth prospect pit had proved a flop, the sample he panned off revealing barely any stream tin, certainly none at all under one foot of depth. He thought his third and fourth had been bad enough, but this one had not even been worth digging. Still, he knew from his experience in both Cornwell and Tasmania that tin fields could be like that. But what really concerned him the most was the gossip he'd heard from another miner at the hotel, that the best prospects were coming out of the bed of Smiths Creek, a branch of the Robertson River over in the eastern part of the field. The stream tin they were finding sounded far cleaner and coarser than what he was getting in his creek in the valley of the Pegasus. He'd even taken a whole day off to go and investigate, the claimholders working there happy enough to let him to have a poke about. After all, no one could take their claims away now they had them pegged out and registered at the Land Office in Invercargill. They were sounding hopeful alright, but he could tell fairly quickly that they were working in not much more than a foot of wash, and that their prospects, once washed, never exceeded a half ounce of tin to a dishful of the stuff. Coarser for sure, but nevertheless not much of it.

Syd thought back to the surveyor, Thomas Miller, who had come up to map the claims, 111 of them in total. The job had taken him a full nine months, had to cut his way through leatherwoods everywhere he went, tight as a hedge in most places. No matter how much you burnt, there was still so much of it left. Syd had been left curious as to why the surveyor had put in such a big dam reserve at the very head of McArthur Creek, not to mention peg out a tramway up into the field tops from Diprose, that bay just east of the hotel named after a highly respected Tasmanian tin miner whom Syd had personally met when he was working over there. Syd suspected nothing would become of either the dam or tramway, it just wasn't that sort of field. It was just no use to anyone unless they were prepared to undergo the hardship of the digger's life and settle gown to steady hard slog. There was no escaping it, otherwise the riches would surely evade you.

On his way back, Syd had diverted up a small creek to seek out another Tasmanian miner who everyone knew as just Conliffe. He had turned up soon after the survey, an amicable chap, but hard-nosed when it came to assessing a payable claim. Rightly so, he had been contracted to prospect seven claims in this field for their absentee owners.

"Come on in, laddie," he called out to Syd when the man's black retriever had started barking at the new arrival. "Now quiet on, Billie," the prospector called out to his dog, who soon started wagging its tail to escort Syd into camp. Over a billy of tea, Conliffe had unrolled Miller's survey map showing all the claims, almost all of them concentrated around the southern end of the Remarkables, from McArthur's on the western side to Smith's and Scollay's in the east.

"Look at 'em all, will ya?" Conliffe was blunt when he got going, a no-nonsense man, certainly not one to exhibit fevered optimism when it wasn't due.

"How many of these claims do you reckon seen a pick or even a shovel would you say now?"

"Maybe half, maybe more, I see activity wherever I walk," replied Syd.

"Nah, you wrong there, laddie. I went through them all and I say 40 at most. Why do ya think that is?" He paused to glance at Syd, but did not wait for his reply. "Because most are not worth spending money on now, that's why."

"Why ever do people bother keeping them then?" Syd countered. "The license fees are not cheap; I pay for two and that's too much."

"I'll tell ya why they keep them, laddie, it's the rumours of riches just waiting to be dug up like some treasure chest, that's what gets everyone going, makes them lose their minds like. They can't even think straight. Let's face it, considering how big this field is, very little is being done. Most of the ground is being held for shepherding. I know, because that's what I get paid to do, reportin' to the absentee owners who hope other discoveries are made. Surely, you've noticed the dark wolfram in your dish, not tin ore at all, but ore of this new metal everyone is going on about, what's it called…tungsten. You can hardly spot the difference, can ya now, laddie? Damn near same weight as stream tin too, makes it hard to separate, it's part of the problem here, but who knows, it might prove in the end to be the answer to all our problems, make us richer than tin ever would in the long run. Have to admit though, it's not worth a flippin' penny right now, but wouldn't surprise me if that tungsten could be like the new gold. If you mix it with knife steel, it never goes blunt, can you imagine such a thing now."

Syd didn't want to admit he had hardly heard of this tungsten. The rain outside was pelting down again now and rivulets of water were seeping in under the sides of the Conliffe's calico tent.

"You might not be going home tonight, laddie. God forsaken this country is, made for the devil himself, makes you wonder what makes a man come here. Majestic, I know, the way those peaks can shine. Have you been up at sunset and seen the colours on those two peaks, Gog and Magog? Whoever named them got it dead right, straight out of the bible, Ezekiel 38. I'm not a religious man by no means, but I know a good story when I hear one. Don't they just look like ancient gods rising out of the land? You have a lot of time to think when you're a prospector. How many of us triumph, not that many, don't ya think?"

Syd had to agree, but he didn't say anything, He only knew his spirit hadn't quite got to the low point Conliffe's had.

The gritty old prospector reached over to the edge of the smouldering fire in the rough stone hearth of his fireplace built unattached at one end of his tent. Using two sticks in the deep faintly glowing embers; the gritty old miner deftly excavated extracted a steaming, black charred bundle of sacking. "You can share this with me," he said. "Yet another owl parrot, wouldn't know what we'd eat up here if there weren't a few of these around."

Syd had never seen one cooked in charcoal like this before, wrapped up in wet sacking.

"Got to make sure you smear the outside of the sack all in damp mud, otherwise it'll catch fire and the bird will burn. Mostly bury it in the coals from late morning, on the edge of the fire, just let it simmer away all day. Come back in mid-afternoon to turn it. Wet it again when you do. Bush pigeon you can do the same too, shoot it in the morning and wrap it up like this with coals around it, take in the saddlebag of your pack horse even, ready for when you stop at lunchtime, eat it still hot while the billy boils. I always say a pigeon makes the best lunch, but there's nothing like an owl parrot for supper. Don't like those kiwis that much, kind of musty taste the ones I had anyway."

The smell of the sack-roasted bird was now filling the tent, and Syd suddenly found himself voraciously hungry.

"Don't know what I'd do without my dog," said Conliffe. "An old Maori told me once you didn't need a dog to get those owl parrots, kakapo he called 'em.

He said just find their scratching bowls, then go there at night, couple hours before dawn is best, before they go back into their hidey holes in the forest. They hang around in packs, feeding up on fern roots. Be real quiet and still, watch them awhile from way back, look for the sentry bird. It'll be sitting up in a tree, looking around, this old Maori told me. Creep up behind it and with a good stout stick and whack it across the head. If you get that lookout bird, the rest are easy picking, knock them all off with your stick easy, one by one they go down, all confused like. Makes ya laugh how stupid those owl parrots can be."

"I've heard, a flaming torch blinds them," offered Syd.

"Yeah, I tried that once, but they all scattered. Best to creep up, that's the only way. Unless you got a dog." Conliffe extended his hand over to give his faithful dog's neck an affectionate scratch. Don't know how young miners exist up here without a retriever."

The dog was salivating now, licking its lips and pawing forward in anticipation. Conliffe carefully unwrapped the sacking, revealing the plump steaming bird carcase.

"Only got me own tin plate," said Conliffe, you'll have to tear it off with your fingers, I'm afraid.

"I'm certainly used to that, Mr Conliffe," commented Syd as he tore off some of the fatty breast meat. "Oh, my Lord, this is tasty, good as the most tender lamb."

"Aye, it is. You can always pick the tastiest ones as soon as you kill them, while they're still warm. Grab a tuft of feathers from its neck and give them a good yank. If they come away easily, that's a young one good to roast. If you can't pull the feathers out, then you're stuck with boiling it up for four or five hours."

"I get more kiwis up my way," said Syd. "Lately, I been finding them drowned in my prospect pits, at least one a week. As long as they look fairly fresh, I just eat 'em. Not as delicate as a parrot though, I have to admit, more gamey, like a pheasant."

The two men sat without talking now, only their chewing rising above the rain heavy on calico, the soft crackle of leatherwood burning on the fire, and the dog shuffling around on its tummy in restlessness as it anticipated the scraps.

It didn't take long for the conversation to turn back to mining. "I'll tell ya what, laddie. Rumour has it James McKay is coming down for a field inspection, maybe next month or three, gonna turn up here to have a look for himself. Now, there's a man who knows his business, not born yesterday that man. He's the government geologist for the whole country, what he says, people listen to, not like that mad professor Black in Dunedin. He started this whole thing, but you know, laddie, he's no better than you young prospectors all taken with fever. The only trouble with him, he thinks he more knows more about the business, which he don't know, never so much as held a pick or shovel in his life I bet ya. Men like him, they're downright dangerous. Get men to go where they shouldn't know…"

"Guess you've heard the professor staked his claim of course," piped in Syd. "Right at the top of the mountain, 120 acres just under the wooden trig. There must be something up there."

"Aye, laddie, he's going underground. Two Cornish miners he's hired who'd been working up Tuapeka, I heard. They might be up there now, pick 'n' chiselling 'n' hammering into the hard granite. I know what he was thinking, follow the stream tin up to the motherlode. Ha! We'll see how he gets on. One thing I do know already. It will cost him a fortune. It's a bet what he's doing, a gamble, and you shouldn't gamble what you can't walk away from, that's why the rest of us go for the stream tin, ain't that true now, laddie."

They talked on, throwing the odd bit of leatherwood trunk onto the fire which smouldered on into the night. Syd got under his borrowed blanket, the dry piled-up fern underneath giving him some comfort against the cold coming up from the ground. In the morning, he would be damp for sure, but it didn't matter tonight, at least he would go to sleep comfortable. He couldn't help going over everything the old miner had told him, but as he began drifting off to sleep, his mind wandered back down to the hotel, and in particular, the newly arrived Elizabeth who he had not seen since the day of her arrival. He needed to go back down next week, to collect his mail, hopefully an encouraging letter or two from his prospective shareholders awaited him. But he also found himself thinking more now about the woman, a strange stirring within him that he struggled to understand. Even when streaming, shovelling hour after hour into his sluice, he had caught himself thinking about her. Maybe it was the embarrassment of their first meeting, caught out watching her and all, or just the roughness of how Peggy had handled their introduction, nothing unusual for the callous barmaid of course. Syd understood her well enough, even wondered if she fancied him, just the way she always went out of her way to abuse him whenever he turned up.

"Attraction can take many forms, Mr Braithwaite," an elderly matron had informed him once while staying in a boarding house in Invercargill. "Sometimes, a woman who appears to fend off a man can also feel secretly within herself a simmering passion for him that she does not even realise. It is up to the man to woo her until she realises and turns. When it comes to men and women, the human condition can be most curious."

Syd had never forgotten her words. Six months at Port Pegasus and Peggy was the only woman he had seen until this new one turned up. Even though he suspected Peggy had feelings for him, he didn't feel them back. She was too rough for him; he liked a bit of tender sometimes. This new woman though, well, something was different about her. Every time he thought of her, he had to remind himself that she was betrothed to George. But no matter how hard he tried, he couldn't imagine them together. He knew George a bit, Elizabeth not at all, but his inner instinct told him they could never be together. The rain had remained incessant all night. The last thing Syd heard before drifting off to sleep was the dog, crunching away on the owl parrot carcase just outside the tent.

Chapter 6

News of the Tin Rush had made headlines throughout the New Zealand colony and more than a few newspapers in the Dominions of the British Empire featured blow by blow accounts of how it was unfolding. And no one more than Professor Black was being painted as the hero of the campaign. The picture was clear; with his superior intellect, insight and endurance, this remarkable man had led an advance guard of trusted miners into the very heart of the Remarkables Range in the deepest south of the Third Island of New Zealand. The triumph was all his, and at his encampment high in the Tin Range, he felt most pleased with himself.

Everyone was wanting to be his accomplice now, visiting him at every opportunity for any advice he would part with. But Black was being cautious, and in no hurry to get back to Dunedin either. Both his family and the university would have to wait their patience, and he knew that the newspaper reports would be supplying them with all the information they needed to know that he was taking the right course of action. He would return to Dunedin the hero of the campaign in due course, but for now, they could all wait. He had to admit, he was amazed how fast the published reports were arriving. Some had been delivered to his camp just two days after appearing in the newspaper. It didn't surprise him though; the rush had created a huge flurry of activity, and no more feverish than on the Bluff wharf. Three ships were now servicing the island. Along with the *Invercargill*, there was the 100-ton paddle steamer *Awarua* which, when it got its paddles, chunking could hit eight-and-a-half-knots. It only took three-and-a-half hours to get across Foveaux Strait now. Then there was the slightly smaller SS Despatch which had started up in direct daily competition, as well as all the little local cutters which criss-crossed the strait, each commandeered by yet another group of hopeful miners. Some barely stayed a few days, the reality of the field hitting them as though they'd suddenly fallen through the ice into a frozen pond. Hopefuls in one direction, the skepticals in the other, mused the professor to himself each time he read another newspaper report. There was no better coverage than in the *Southland Times* who had appointed their top reporter, James Barkley, as 'Our Correspondent' to write blow by blow accounts of the rush, all of which were heartily devoured by fixated readers.

But it wasn't only miners that came flocking, entrepreneurs and businessmen with an eye for the main chance were also descending on the island, the biggest party of 40 organised by indefatigable William Todd, one of Invercargill's most prominent businessmen. Quick off the mark as soon as the first whiff of news of the rush broke, he chartered the *Invercargill* to sail directly down to Pegasus, bringing with him forty southern gentlemen, each paying 40 shillings for the privilege of the three-day trip.

Dressed in his finest threads, including a splendid new silk Belltopper hat, Todd was in his element as the ship steamed up Whale Passage and into the Northern Arm of Port Pegasus. He had shrewdly spent the whole passage down from Bluff interrogating every one of 'his' passengers as to their interests and intentions. Some were forthcoming, others not. Only four or five he deduced were genuine prospectors, the rest budding industrialists, shipping contractors, a couple of government officials, and an Invercargill merchant named Louis Rodgers, a shrewd Dutchman who had the idea of setting up a store and accommodation house upon the shores of the fine harbour. 'Hell's End,' this man described the place without a hotel to Todd. "How could a miner not resist a good bed when faced with a godforsaken place like this?" Of all his assorted passengers, Todd had a hunch that this man's prospects might actually succeed.

All were rowed ashore in four longboat loads to a small flat of cutty grasses near the head of the arm, not far from where Pegasus Creek flowed out over a magnificent waterfall. Todd waited for them all to assemble before putting on his fine Belltopper hat to address them. "Ha hmmmm!" he started, clearing his throat loudly to get the group's attention.

"Our itinerary today, gentlemen, will first take in these magnificent falls which so far remain unnamed. From here, we will make our way up Pegasus Creek to inspect some alluvial claims, and from there, ascend to the lode deposits. Gentlemen, we are indeed privileged that our most experienced guide today will be Robert Scollay, there being no one more experienced in this field than him." Todd turned his attention to Scollay, asking him in a loud voice so everyone could hear, "Mr Scollay, please tell us, what are the chances of meeting the professor today?" Todd was pleased to discern a small tremor of excitement ripple through thc crowd.

"Every chance, sir," replied Scollay loudly to the assembled. "It is not an easy walk I will warn you all, but the professor is expecting us later this afternoon." A few of the men attempted to break out an applause, but Scollay cut them off with an upraised hand. "No time must be wasted. Please follow me, it's only a short walk to the falls."

Reporting on the excursion, 'Our Correspondent," from the *Southland Times*, had taken the time while waiting for the party to assemble to write in his notebook the hope 'that it would not be long before Stewart Island Oysters in Stewart Island tins may be familiar to the world as Bass Beer.' The insightful reporter was pleased; he also had some humour to impart when Todd promptly lost his Belltopper hat when it got caught in an overhanging branch while admiring the magnificent falls. The group let out a collective laugh as the fine silk hat bobbed down the rapids and disappeared irretrievably over the falls. "Those that come in unsuitable attire are reminded," Scollay found himself saying, after first making sure he was out of Todd's earshot. "When we arrived, these falls had no name, now they will forever be known as Belltopper Falls." The reporter pulled out his notepad to record the incident, noting Todd not only looked a little less formally attired, but decidedly crestfallen at the loss of his new hat.

Immediately up from the falls, the going was relatively easy, thanks to the near continuous sluicing operations which had transformed the bed of Pegasus Creek. It was here that Scollay came into his own, stopping at periodic intervals to impart his knowledge of the alluvial workings, starting with the basics.

"No other form of mining is more efficient than ground sluicing," he informed them through the wash pit of the first claim. At its headrace, he paused again. "With just digging implements, and untold stamina, the miner diverts the water above his claim by way of a head race, such as this into the area of alluvium he wishes to work. This area becomes his paddock. That water goes back to the stream by way of a tail race. It sounds easy but let me assure you that much labour must be expended before any mining can begin."

They moved to the next claim, the two claimholders standing back, leaning on their shovel handles, to allow Scollay to give his next lesson.

"Once the water supply is laid on, mining can proceed by directing the water over a scarp, just like you see here. Assisted by picks and shovels, thc water flow breaks up the ground, which gets washed down the tail race over the tin-saving riffles. This is where the heavy stream tin settles out, while the lighter sediments and gravels are washed away."

Scollay swivelled around and extended his arm out to the big pile of tailings. "The miner's work is cut out for them here, stacking all these heavy cobbles and rocks that get worked out into orderly stacks, usually on the ground that's just been worked. You will see these tailings throughout the field as we go along. Let us go on, gentleman."

As the men progressed through another three claims, Scollay made the point that there was a considerable number of factors determining exactly how the ground was worked.

"The depth of the payable ore, how it's distributed, the lay of the land, even the preferences of individual miners. These all influence how a claim is worked. An experienced miner can tell just by looking how the claim should be worked. He must take in the location of the head and tail races, the final shape of the worked ground and the pattern of tailings exactly. See here," he pointed up the ravine, "We have a long thin sluice gully created by working back into a steep face, notice will you the tailings stacked up inside the workings in no discernible pattern. Completely different from the next we will come upon. Let us go on."

Large ridges of tailings characterised the next claim which were swarming with half a dozen toiling men. "See the tailings here, all stacked as this broad area was worked into the face. Six men work here, that's a sizeable workforce for up here, meaning that as one area is worked out, another adjacent area can be started. It all works like clockwork, the tailings piled back not only into the worked-out area, but along the length of its tailrace. This main tailrace is kept open, but the point at which it was fed would change as the area migrated."

Scollay pointed out more variations as they passed them, culminating by leading them into a large broad expanse of ground being worked right alongside the stream. Here there was no need for a single large tailrace, but rather short discrete races that fed directly back into the stream.

After spending all morning, touring the alluvial workings in Pegasus Creek, Scollay escorted the sightseers to the lode claims high up in the southern end of the Remarkables. The reality of the excursion into this now largely rocky, burnt off wilderness began to take its toll. The fine clothes that some of the men had arrived with were now well and truly discoloured, ripped, tattered, and in some cases, discarded. The burnt skeletons of leatherwood trees were the worst offenders, scratching and even ripping their skin. One poor man was stabbed in the white of his eye by an extended branch which had been burnt off to a sharp point. Two men suffered bad falls after tripping on hidden rocks, one badly banging his head causing profuse bleeding which required one man to give his white shirt up as a bandage to tie wrap around the injured head. It was a case of the walking wounded, and Barkley, the ever-observant reporter who missed nothing, later recorded:

'By the map, the lode claim is distant from the anchorage by only three miles, measured from the way we travelled through the alluvial claims, six miles; measured by the exertion required—well, fifty miles is a moderate estimate. It would take you longer to go fifty miles, but you would not be so tired.'

It took them a full five hours to finally make the professor's encampment. How strange it seemed, to some of them at least, that in this vast untamed country they would find an esteemed professor, living like a hermit near the top of the windswept mountain. A few had met him before and were amazed now to find him looking so uncouth in ripped clothes, sporting an untrimmed beard and hair. If they had not known who he was, they might well have considered him a vagabond and given him a wide berth.

"He has turned into a true mad professor," one of the sightseers commented quietly to his companions.

The professor got straight into it. "I know the day is fast running out, so welcome one and all, honourable gentlemen, welcome to Pegasus and my humble encampment." He paused as they gathered around him. "Like the winged horse of Greek myth, these mountains will soon take off and fly, mark my words."

It had not escaped him that some of the new arrivals were at the end of their physical endurance, several were sprawled across the ground. Others were now sitting down attentively, waiting for the professor to carry on. He shuffled around a few minutes until they were all ready, had all caught their breath, then positioned himself again to address the small throng.

"Gentlemen, I know you are all curious as to why I am still here in a place derived of all comforts. Please, let me explain."

He paused for effect, knowing full well he was starting to spin a story, much like a spider sets off to spin a web, strand by strand.

"During the initial flurry of pegging out alluvial claims on both sides of the range, I took a day out for some scientific rumination. I thought of all the world and its creation, thinking my way down to the ice period when immense glaciers ground down the sides of these Remarkables, crunching off even the very noses off Gog and Magog, those magnificent peaks, you will soon spy in that direction, even gouging out this most fine port of Pegasus. The boulders I know, the gravels I understand, but what of the tin? I concentrated all my thought, and it was at that point I had a revelation, one that bordered on being divinely inspired. By the living jingo, the ice has ground the tin out of the mountain. Look up, look up to the source. The rest of it is still there yet. I'll peg it off!"

An appreciative murmur excitedly rippled through the small outdoor assembly. The professor was creating the same atmosphere that he could conjure up in the lecture hall back at the university. He paused a split second for effect again, picking up his tomahawk which he had handily positioned to brandish aloft, well aware how every presentation could be enhanced by a suitable prop.

"By the earliest dawn, still dark, I set out to tomahawk my way up through the leatherwoods to this highest summit where I attacked the outcrop with hammer and pick." The tenor of his voice changed at this point, became more urgent as he pretended to be hacking his way through the leatherwoods.

"There was no time to be sluggish. As with all my party, notably Messer's Swain and Robertson, we were plainly aware we only had two days at most to peg out all the promising lodes before rival parties made their way up there. And by jingo, they did! On the third morning of our arrival, we spied the first rival party emerging from the bush line." He stopped, using the pause to build suspense before continuing. "Rushing down to encounter them, it was with considerable difficulty that we beguiled them into proceeding towards a likely looking flat about four miles to eastward that still lay unclaimed."

A ripple of laughter spread through the listeners. The professor reached down for a mug of water, sipping it before going on.

"It may be said, and I think fairly correctly, that it was by some such deception that Messers Swain, Robertson and myself became the only prospectors to take possession of claims where tin was clearly visible in veins in the granite. That was why the bush telegraph, emanating from this field, ended up telling you all in Invercargill that the 'professor's party was on the metal,' which resulted in this mad nocturnal scramble we have seen here over the last week, the very reason you are here today. Imagine this scene if you can, gentlemen. All through the night, we spied the flaming torches of men in the hills as they climbed to position themselves ready to peg at first light. It was a spectacle that I'll never forget as long as I breathe."

The professor put his head down, appearing to go into deep concentration before coming back to conclude in a more measured tone.

"So, that is my story. Two months ago, I was a chemistry professor at Otago University, much of my time taken up by lecturing to senior students and conducting experiments. Now, I find myself camped on a huge knob of rock exposed to all the fury that the Southern Ocean can throw at me. It has not been easy, nor comfortable, but I feel full of confidence that this lode which lies beneath us may well be the motherlode, all the stream tin spread out over the valleys below nothing but a scratching off its back."

The men broke out in a rapturous applause, which he heartily received, bowing gently before holding up his hands in a gesture of mock humility. The last thing he wanted was for any of them to think he was grandstanding. He waited for silence before saying his farewell. "Thank you for making the effort to come to my claim today. Remember, true riches await those that strive, not only with hard work, but with concise knowledge and the benefit of science to hasten their goal. When you return here one day, there may well be a hard rock mine tunnelling into the mountain, the one which I believe contains the motherlode. Now, gentlemen, I understand from Mr Scollay that you will be making your way down to the former surveyor's camp where you will be spending the night. If any of you need to talk to me in private before you go, please avail yourselves forthwith. Thank you." His show was over.

While Scollay rallied his weary party, half a dozen of the men one by one took the professor aside, asking advice, offering advice, suggesting partnership deals, even the loan of money at a reasonable rate.

It wasn't only the professor who was solicited that day. 'Our Correspondent' Barkley and his brother were later enthusiastically offered a share in one of the claims, 'just a portion of an immense fortune,' only because the claimholder had no ready money. This never before-known shareholder used Professor Black's name most freely which he used as the authority for his statements, before waltzing them around over great outcrops of lodes, all supposedly black with tin ore. For £200, a 48 per cent interest could be acquired, securing a fortune of thousands of pounds a year for unborn generations.

So taken by the words, Barkley and his brother had thoughts of how their rich English uncle could maybe be persuaded to forward them the money.

Picking up some scattered samples they enquired of the vendor, "Any tin in this?"

"That's more than half tin."

"What about this one?"

"That's at least three-quarters tin."

"And what about this?"

"That's pure tin."

They carried on, taking their samples with them. Halfway down, they ran into one of the newly arrived Tasmanian miners.

"How much tin is in these then?" They asked him.

The miner looked the samples over before replying decisively, "None."

"What, none at all?"

"None at all. I don't think there is any."

"Well, what's the black stuff then?"

"That's wolfram. A worthless mineral."

"But is there really no tin?'

"Well, put it this way," the miner replied, "If all the tin in them was gold, and you had a mountain of it, it would still not be worth working."

Despite such warning stories, all widely published, public interest in the Tin Rush continued to escalate, becoming fever pitch in Southland after Professor Black abandoned his mountain camp and returned to Invercargill on 23 January 1890. To a waiting reporter from the *Southland Times,* he announced that two rich lodes of tin-bearing granite had been discovered in the Remarkable Mountains. "Should they not be renamed the Tin Range, as many prospectors were referring to them already?" Black was quick to ask. Within hours of his quote appearing in the newspaper the following morning, the Land Office in Invercargill was deluged with a second round of applications. Eleven areas of 60 acres each, plus ten new licenses were issued on that day alone.

A month later, a public meeting was called in Invercargill to hear Mr James Ashcroft's account of his tour of the field had to be shifted at the last minute to William Todd's expansive salerooms due to the exceedingly high turnout. Ashcroft was a true business strategist, addressing the crowd to call for an amalgamation of all the claims into one giant syndicate, and the formation of a company with capital of £100,000 to properly develop the diggings. This man openly admitted he knew little about the business, but he sincerely offered his conviction that the tin lode was a gigantic opportunity for the entire province, its future returns to be measured in hundreds of thousands of pounds per annum.

"A second Mt Bischoff!" he exclaimed with hands aloft. Everyone in the throng knew exactly what he meant, the famed tin mining area in Tasmania around then held up as the ultimate success story.

Among the near-frenzied crowd, Louis Rodgers had listened quietly. One of the original members of the Todd excursion that had taken place one month before, the Dutchman with aristocratic blood in him was also an experienced merchant, and he had quietly left the meeting utterly convinced that the best opportunity which everyone seemed to be missing was not going to be obtained from chipping away at the granites or working in the streams, but rather supplying the field with essential stores, liquor included. And there was no time to waste. Within just two weeks, Rodgers had contracted two builders to start constructing his Pioneer Hotel at Port Pegasus, which made it the southernmost boarding house in New Zealand. Even before all the sawn timber could be shipped down from a sawmill in Paterson Inlet, Rodgers went about amassing ten tons of general supplies in a warehouse in Bluff, to be shipped down as soon as the storeroom at the hotel could be completed. Few buildings in the entire country would ever be built so fast, especially one in such an isolated place. As soon as the storeroom was weatherproof, and lockable, Rodgers shifted down with all his stores to begin trading with the prospectors, proving himself to be one of the most colourful men in the fields. His advertisements, in both the *Southland Times* and *Otago Daily Times,* promoted the area as 'the future Broken Hills of New Zealand.' Just one month after moving down, the government approved his plan for a post office, appointing him the postmaster and paying him an annual salary for maintaining it. The contract for delivering the mail went to the 100-ton screw steamer *Despatch*, which henceforth was required to undertake the mail delivery run from Bluff every two weeks. What with the *Invercargill and Awarua* ploughing back and forth as well, Port Pegasus became well-serviced indeed. Everything seemed to be falling into place for Rodgers, but his haste in getting up and running also proved his undoing. The news that he was selling hard liquor to the miners without a license made its way to the Temperance Society in Invercargill. Before long, he was formally summoned by the licensing authority of the Provincial Government to attend a hearing where he was charged with the offence of supplying alcohol in the absence of a legal license, slapped with a considerable fine, then told to apply for a new liquor license. There was no way he could do that by mail, he had to turn up and do it all in person at an interview. That was when George had gone to look after the Pioneer Hotel.

Chapter 7

Elizabeth enjoyed being made postmistress of the tiny Port Pegasus Post Office. For the whole month after her arrival, she made herself useful helping both George and Peggy run the hotel. She helped in the kitchen, getting the meals ready for the lodgers, and sweeping and scrubbing when Peggy needed a hand including boiling the water in the copper when it was washday. There were hundreds of things to do running a hotel, no wonder, George had been so eager for her to come, she cynically observed. From what she could make out, he spent most of his time talking to the lodgers as they turned up or departed. Of course, he was running the place, but exactly what chores he did, she was never quite sure. He disappeared for most of the day, until another party turned up, and suddenly, he was there, talking to them like they were long lost friends.

"That's my job, talking to our guests," he had replied in his usual blunt way when she asked him what he did all day. He then wasted no time explaining how important it was for a publican to spend time with his customers; it encouraged them to come back. But there was something that didn't quite seem right to her. Elizabeth had even brought it up with Peggy, unimpressed as she was.

"What do you expect, Lizzie? The man thinks he owns the place, stands around acting like it too. I've watched him too, hardly does anything. Throws a few bottles and a bit of rubbish over the bank when he can't find me to do it, otherwise he wouldn't even do that. Wouldn't it be great to be like that? Not for us, I'm afraid, a woman's work is never done. That's why men need us."

"Sometimes, I feel like a maid servant here," admitted Elizabeth.

"Ahh, lassie, don't worry, you're going to marry George one day, then you can start being his boss." Peggy giggled. "That's the way it works, you know. One day, I'm going to find a fine man, look after him best I can, then he'll look after me."

"Have you ever met a fine man, Peggy?"

"Of course, I have, more than one, but none I'd ever wanted to marry and settle down with. There's one up on the field I quite like the look of, but far too early to let him know yet, or you for that matter." She let out a little laugh before adding, "Now, come on, the ship'll be in soon, we have much to get ready."

The arrival of the *SS Invercargill* every second week was always the busiest day on the hotel's calendar; lodgers to check in, stores to unpack and put in the storehouse, wooden crates of bottles to stash away, and of course the mail to sort. Running the little post office had quickly become Elizabeth's favourite job. The size of the building, just 10 feet by 8 feet, made her feel secure, like being in her own little world. It was manageable, not like the hotel which fast became overwhelming. That place always reeked of sweat, spilt alcohol, cold fat and pipe smoke. Not like her little post office, which smelt sweet, of sawn timber, ink and gum. She could keep it perfectly clean and tidy, file everything away in the three drawers and two shelves. The New Zealand Post Office had even supplied a Rule Book of instructions about how to complete every postal procedure step by step. Luckily for Elizabeth, only the month before her arrival at Port Pegasus, the onerous double-docket postal system in use around the country had been replaced by the Collection Postage system, copied from the far more progressive United States Postal Service. Under the older system, two dockets had to filled out for every mail item—the Docket proper and the Advice. The Office of Despatch and the Postal Charge had to be entered on both dockets which were then affixed to the mail article and sent to the General Post Office Accountant in Wellington. After being verified as having the correct postage, the docket proper was re-affixed to the letter which was then forwarded to the Receiving Office who would reverify the postage, attach the stamps to the back of the docket, which then had to be cancelled by the postmaster or postmistress by writing their initials across the stamps. The final step was despatching the docket back to Wellington for filing. Only then could the letter be delivered; not only was this system deemed onerous, but it caused long delays in getting a simple letter to its destination. Now, all Elizabeth had to do when someone came in with an item to mail was calculate the postage, attach the required stamp or stamps, and then cancel it with her Port Pegasus Post Office letter stamp, so that it was ready to send off on the next boat.

No wonder that little post office quickly became Elizabeth's domain. She approved of the proper procedures that were required of her, even felt appreciated there. George had quickly recognised this, handing over his postal duties entirely to her by making her the new postmistress of Port Pegasus Post Office. He even wrote a letter to the post office in Invercargill, informing them of his new appointee. Everyone knew of course it was really Louis Rodgers who held the postal license, but Elizabeth didn't care. It was her job now.

Elizabeth had also made it her business, when no one was looking of course, to read every message written on the leaves of muttonbird scrub before she postmarked them. The leathery leaves, easily obtainable around the coast of Stewart Island and Southland, had in recent years become nothing short of a craze in Victorian society, both throughout New Zealand and England, indeed all throughout the Dominions of the British Empire to which the Royal Mail was delivered to. The pale underside of the large-veined leaves lent themselves perfectly to pen and ink, strong enough to take the pressure of a pen without being gouged, yet soft enough for the ink not to run. They would never curl up after being picked, nor go black or rotted when thrown into a mail bag. They could survive months at sea, to be pulled out undamaged at their final destination. What's more, the agar gum on the reverse side of the stamps easily affixed themselves to the outer glossy side of the leaves. Most muttonbird scrub 'postcards' had in recent years emanated from Paterson Inlet Post Office, but since the little post office opened at Port Pegasus, more than half of its outward mail was now being written on these leaves. No wonder though, thought Elizabeth, miners kept little or no paper in their camps. It was far too damp to keep anything dry, let alone have an ink pen to write with. All they had to do when they wanted to post a letter was pick their paper as they came down to the coast, then borrow the pen at the post office to write their messages. If they were illiterate, they would dictate it to Elizabeth who wrote directly onto the leaf.

What impressed Elizabeth the most was, being postcards, how curt and to the point the messages read. The first one she had postmarked on this day read:

"Dearest Sarah, I cherish you in my heart, please wait for me. Yours, Richard."

The next, addressed to an Invercargill solicitor, revealed an urgent business matter:

'It is important that claim number App Nvii/21 be added to my Land Office application by 27th following latest. Yours faithfully, Thomas Morecombe Jnr."

The third postcard brought tears to her eyes.

"My dearest Bridgit, no words can describe my heavy heart upon hearing the news about the sad loss of our unborn daughter. Please, take care of yourself, thank goodness you have your mother around to help. I shall return when I can and pray for you every day. Forever yours in love, Samuel."

Peggy had told her about the leaf of the rangiora too. "You can write on them as well, bit small though, but mostly they just good for wiping your bottom if you don't have anything softer around. The bushman's friend, they're called."

Elizabeth had to admit that in her five weeks at Pegasus, she had learnt a lot from Peggy, things she didn't know about before, certainly stuff she'd never heard in Sunday School. Like about laying with a man. Peggy had made her squirm when she first brought it up one day, Elizabeth sure her face had flushed so red Peggy would surely have noticed.

It had just started to rain when Peggy suddenly reappeared at the door of the post office.

"I can always tell when you're working in here, I hear the thump, thump, thump of your stamper from the far end of the hotel. Sometimes, you stop awhile, then start up again. I bet you read all those leaf postcards."

Damn her, thought Elizabeth gritting her teeth. Nothing escapes the woman. "Most certainly, I do not," replied Elizabeth defensively, averting her gaze to put away her stamper and inkpad.

"Well, I would if I were you, always used to do that myself. Rodgers even used to say to tell me if there was anything he should know about, like hearing a rumour that someone was planning to leave who hadn't paid their ledger. I always told him everything. Once I even opened a letter to read that hadn't been sealed properly. All I had to do gum it up again. Was interesting too, about some money owed that was overdue. Told Rodgers about all that too."

"I just follow the rule book here." Elizabeth found herself saying, pulling it out to slap down. "Says all the business here is confidential…"

Peggy roared with laughter. "Like Flaming Hell, it is! I like to know everything going on around here, even if it does mean reading their mail. One thing I can't make out though, it's about you and George. Pray tell me, Lizzie, so why ain't you laying with him yet? Never seen even an ounce of affection between yas yet. What's all that about then?"

Elizabeth also realised she was fidgeting with her fingers as she tried to fend the question off, but Peggy persisted with her inquiry.

"I mean, it just ain't natural. You been here five weeks now and I hardly see you together, not so much as see you holding hands. I have to ask you now, Lizzie, woman to woman, do you even have any affection for him?"

"Of course, I do. He's always polite to me, never so much even raised his voice or been annoyed about anything. A bit bossy sometimes. Let's just say, we're taking a bit of time to warm to each other. It's all been a bit of a shock for me to come out here from Glasgow."

"Well, I have to admit, I think he could be wooing you a bit harder I reckon," offered Peggy. "A man has to show interest in a good woman like you. To tell you the truth, I feel like having a good talk to him, tell him he doesn't know a good opportunity if it bit him on the bottom. Sometimes, I think he only thinks of himself, makes me mad, so far, I've kept it all to myself, but watching you two, I might not be able to help myself for much longer."

Just at that moment, George called out from the hotel, "Peggy, where are you?" She ignored it and kept her gaze on Elizabeth who took in a deep breath before responding.

"Oh, Peggy, don't worry about us. It's between him and me. All in good time. Something as sacred as marriage should not be hurried. It wasn't my idea, you know; it was all arranged by my family."

"Hah, for what's that worth. I have seen lots of those arranged marriages, some work good, others end up a living hell and nothing either party can do about it. There needs to be a spark to start a fire you know."

George's voice piped up from somewhere over by the hotel again. "Peggy! Peggy! Are you around?"

Peggy lowered her voice now. "If I was you, I'd be looking around for a new fella. Keep your options open. Not much opportunity around here though, must admit, but when you get back to the mainland, they'll be jumping for you. There's far more men than women down south, and a lot of them are single. You're a well-bred, pretty lass, you'll find someone in no time. They'll find you more like it, you just gotta make yourself available. And enjoy yourself, if you know what I mean?"

Elizabeth felt a rising uncomfortableness, her hands had taken on a clammy sweat, and she wanted out of the conversation. "Peggy, the ship will be in soon and I have much to do before it does. George sounds like he needs your assistance also. You must excuse me now."

Elizabeth disengaged from the conversation by swivelling slightly to focus her attention on adjusting the padlock around the neck of the mailbag. Peggy went to go, but instead turned around by the door.

"Well, don't forget what I said, it's important! I don't like to see someone I like not getting the tenderness they deserve. I know a bit about this sort of thing. I've had a few men that gave me nothing. Not one thing, it was all me giving out. See you for a cuppa later if you get some time. I meant to tell ya too, a whole bunch of miners are on their way down, got business here to attend too, three of them are going back to Invercargill on the boat too. Bound to get busy. I might need a hand tonight in the kitchen. Bound to be more than a few new diggers on board too. Now a good day to ya, Lizzie, let you get on with your business here."

As Peggy turned around, they could hear George hollering out again. "Peggy, Peggy. Where the blazes are you? I need you!"

Elizabeth wasted no time grabbing the broom to sweep around her office, she prided herself in keeping it spick and span ready for the next influx. She went outside to wet a cloth from the swivel tap on the barrel of rainwater collected from the corrugated iron roof, pausing to watch a parson bird delicately feeding upside down from the flowering stalk of a flax bush. The bird almost looked drunk, she thought. Squeezing out the cloth to wipe down her desk, she made sure to take off the odd smears of ink from her stamper that had somehow managed to get on the tabletop. There was also something she needed to check up on in the Rule Book. George had told her that one of the miners had indicated that he would soon be getting a sizeable money order transfer from England, so she flicked through the pages until she came to the procedure, checking she had the available forms on hand which would need to be filled in, so the transaction could be accepted. She hoped no one else knew about the transfer, because she would have to hide the money in a better place than her cashbox under the counter if they did. She then made sure her stamp book was handy, ready to pull out, and her gum roller topped up. She felt all ready now for the mad rush hour that would come with the ship's arrival. The brief shower had stopped, and she wandered outside to stretch her legs, strolling out to the edge of the manuka to look out over North Arm. There wasn't a breath of wind, the water still as a mirror reflecting the wisps of mist tangled through the treetops. The tranquil scene reminded her of the moody lochs back home, taking her breath away with nostalgia. A fish jumped, sending out near perfect circular ripples in all directions. Maybe a seal was chasing it, she mused, casting her eyes around to see any sign of the sleek animal. Sealers from the *Pegasus* had slaughtered almost every last one around here, so the attentive mate of the *Invercargill* had told her as they were coming in. But she had since figured the *Pegasus* had come

70 years before, so the few that did survive must have bred up. She had even spotted a couple since she'd had arrived, just swimming past. Could they be the descendants of the survivors, or had others come in to replace them? She then wondered back to her voyage from Bluff, why that mate had seemed so protective of her, using every trick in the book to keep her in the main cabin. He'd been absolutely determined not to let her go out on deck; even told her she might fall overboard if she tripped up on her dress. Strange, he didn't say anything to the men, even when they were all fooling about, one even tried to climb the rigging, swinging out on one while the others watched and laughed. It was like the mate was trying to keep her into a gilded cage, to be guarded and watched at all costs.

Holding onto the trunk of a manuka tree, she leaned out to look down the arm. There was no black funnel smoke in sight, it was too early for the boat anyway. She felt the urge to take a little stroll, to get away from it all. She strode back to the post office to lock it, then set off to the little inlet only a couple of chain off to the eastern side of the hotel promontory. The tide was out, so hitching up her dress, she carefully made her way down the big rocks which defined the narrow incision of inlet. Apart from a few small boats that sneaked up here at high tide to offload a passenger or stores to the hotel when it was rough, this little backwater beside the hotel escaped all notice. It was a place no one seemed to know of or care about. This little canyon cove burrowed into the seashore lay all hidden by the branches of trees. It was all her domain, and she had started coming to find solace here when everything became overwhelming at the hotel. At first, she had been tempted to walk up the Surveyors Track but changed her mind after George warned her it was not an ideal place for a woman to take a stroll.

"More mud than you could poke a stick into," he had warned. "And who knows what strange men might come your way. And I can't guarantee I have met even half the miners who live in these hills. Best stay around the hotel, Elizabeth, then I won't have to come looking for you. We're busy enough here without you disappearing off."

His advice had left her with a strange feeling, one that she had struggled to understand. Mostly, it also annoyed her that the only reason she shouldn't go up the Surveyors Track was so he didn't have to find her if he needed something done in a hurry. It wasn't 'don't go up there because I care for you.' It was all about him wanting her around so he could do less work.

The previous night, after lying fitfully awake for several hours, she had finally fallen into deep sleep and dreamt that she was trapped inside a huge open enclosure. Pacing the perimeter, she finally found an opening along the fence which she could just squeeze through. A man suddenly appeared on the outside to help her, pulling on her arms when she got stuck, and together they had run off, high into the hills. It was dusk and the sky was on fire. Elizabeth had woken in a sweat, relieved to find herself in her own bed, but the struggle of her dream remained. The man she had dreamt of hadn't been George, it was someone else who she did not recognise. The dream had left her with the frightening feeling of being relentlessly pursued, and it had stayed with her for days after.

The little pirate cove of an inlet was perfect to her, cut down deep out of sight, it was like a fairy world. Once she'd seen a penguin sheltering in there, standing like a sentinel, fine yellow feathered crests growing out of its head like magnificent eyebrows. She found herself right in front of it before realising she was blocking its path back out to the sea. It dashed this way and that until she had finally climbed a rock to allow it to escape. She had seen a few little blue coloured penguins sneaking up the rocks at dusk around the hotel, but this was the first time she'd ever seen a penguin like that, so beautifully crested. The creature waddled down to the water like a drunken soldier, leaving her delighted as she watched it dive onto its belly, swimming out effortlessly before disappearing beneath the surface. She kept an eye out awhile, to see where it would come up, but there was no sign of it anywhere.

A trickle of a creek at the head of the inlet, less than two chain in, tumbled down the rocks before meandering down to the Arm proper. Elizabeth loved sitting on the fallen log beside the miniature cascade, its quiet gurgling soothing to her ears. Walking up towards it, she picked up a stick and made patterns in the sand as she went over Peggy's words from earlier in the morning. Ruminating about things which Peggy said always made her stomach churn. Out loud she found herself saying, "Oh, dear Lord, let my mind be still. You have sent me here for a purpose." Then she found herself laughing, adding, "Well then, Lord, it would be great if you let me in on your secret purpose, for once in my life. Come on now, I want to hear from you." Oh dear, she went quiet now, what was she saying, demanding of the good Lord? Maybe the spirit of Peggy had flown into her.

She stayed in the inlet for a good half hour before she heard the first distant sound of the ship's whistle echoing out of Whale Passage, warning everyone near and far that soon the boat would be pulling up off the hotel. Time to get back and open up her little post office again. Just as sure, she knew the tide would soon come in and fill up her little inlet again. Already in her 23 years, she appreciated her life also had an ebb and flow to it. Ever since leaving Scotland she had felt her spirit ebbing away. Now, as she climbed up the rocks, she felt for the first time a new murmur within, like the tide had turned. Something was about to happen, and she felt strangely excited.

Chapter 8

Syd was hugely relieved to have his first day off digging in over a month. Apart from visiting a couple of neighbouring miners, including Conliffe's encampment where rain had forced him to stay the night, he had barely left his claim, sluicing from near dawn to dusk to widen out his sluice faces, redirecting the entire creek sideways half a chain and extending his headrace in the process. Initially, his wash-ups had proved more and more productive, but the more he got into the bank the more the promise of a good strike eluded him as he hit bedrock and the stream tin petered out. It was all part of the journey to success he reassured himself. Anyway, he had too much invested now to pull out. And he would soon find out exactly how much his shareholders were prepared to back him. Their letters responding to his Memorandum offer would surely be waiting for him at the post office. Maybe he would even run into the new girl there, Elizabeth. Surely, she'd settled in by now. No matter how hard he tried, he just couldn't imagine the woman with George, couldn't imagine any woman with him in fact. Syd couldn't quite put his finger on the man. George could talk alright, but Syd suspected he lacked real depth and understanding. Like he wasn't quite there emotionally. Syd just couldn't put his finger on it.

Except for a few scudding showers, it had been relatively dry and windy for days, so Syd knew the mud going down would be passable. Last time he turned up at the hotel, he looked like a swamp creature, so splattered with mud and blackened from charcoal from his trek down the mountain. This time he was determined to arrive more like a gentleman. After all, one day he might be one. Syd could hardly believe how happy he felt today, like his life suddenly had the promise of coming together, and he put it down to the letters he knew would be waiting for him. Maybe by tonight, he could toast himself as a real claimholder, with real backers. There was no way he would have been this happy if he'd stayed back in the home country. There weren't the opportunities open to him that there were here. Back 'home,' he would have been a worker for a company, slogging 10 hours a day, six days a week. He knew that he was putting in the same sort of hours into his claim, even more, but at least he didn't work for 'the man;' company boss, slave driver, gaffer, call them him what you like, they all meant the same.

Syd got into his moleskins, the only good trousers he owned, noticing how loose they felt around his waist. He couldn't recall when he had worn them last, Invercargill perhaps, special occasions being the rule. He'd even washed them the day before, pinning them down with a rock in the headrace, letting the current do the rinsing before throwing them over a leatherwood to dry. Slipping the belt off his canvas work pants, and re-threading it around his waist, he scanned the horizon. A few clouds were coming over from the hill from the south east, so he picked his warmest wool shirt. No matter what the weather ended up doing, it would at least keep him warm until he got back. The moon was waxing gibbous, rising not long after nightfall he guessed knew from the previous night, so he knew would easily find his way back in the dark if he had to. Syd adjusted the red scarf he had loosely tied around his neck, going over to check his elongated reflection in the shiny steel of his big bowie knife. That knife was special to Syd, one of his old Tasmanian tin mining mates had given it to him when he left to come out to New Zealand.

By the time he hit the first mud bog just a furlong down from his camp, Syd reminded himself that few mud splashes were inevitable. The second section of string bogs were slightly worse, and by the third, he knew that just keeping the mud splatters below his knees was going to be an acceptable compromise.

Below the last rocky knob, Syd waved out to Tucker who was slashing a new access track into the lower gully of his claim, a sure sign that he was preparing to work new ground. The two met halfway and shook hands, before getting straight into it, the tin field gossip.

"Fred called in the other day, told me about Old Dad going up Ned's peak," said Tucker, referring to the one and only Christian salvationist on the field. "Must have been moved by the spirit of discovery rather than the Lord that day, going up to oblige a new group of prospectors who wanted the lay of the land. With the help of a few braces from the bottle on the way up, he got himself drunk, first time ever in his whole life he reckoned, but I doubt that. As he was coming down, he let himself go, singing all the Glory songs he knew as loud as he could. Trouble was, weather turned to freezing, and his canvas trousers kept freezing up solid on him, could hardly bend his knees. Over he'd go, time and time again.

But he kept everyone's spirits up, singing out, 'Hold the fort, I am coming!' every time he got up again.

Syd hadn't laughed so much in a long time. "I hear Old Dad's son is coming to help him soon. He's done pretty good so far on his lode by himself though, must be near 70 now. I hear he still packs 70 lb sacks of tinstone down off his mountain most weeks."

"Yes, puts us to shame alright," agreed Tucker. "You noticed that he always wears something red. Like a red jersey, a red scarf, a red knitted hat, even a piece of red ribbon pinned to his lapel. If anyone asks him about it, he always says, 'It's a fire, it's a fire'."

Tucker paused, looking Syd up and down. "You ain't turning into Old Dad yourself, are you? Red scarf and all I see. Where you going all dressed up like that anyway?"

"Just down to the hotel, nothing special, just felt like getting out of my muddy digging gear that's all. Only got two sets of clothes, work and no work ones." Syd laughed at himself. "No dance to go too after all, not around here anyway." They both laughed at that. "Better get on my way then," said Syd, tipping his hat.

"Aye, then. If you could cast an eye over my ol' row boat while you're down there, that would be much appreciated."

It was nearly one o'clock in the afternoon when Syd finally made the hotel. George was the first person he ran into, standing on the front doorstep. Typical, thought Syd, not working. Never seen him do much at all.

"Good day, Syd, haven't seen you in a few weeks. You'd be famished or thirsty, I guess, come in and have a drink. Peggy can sort you out. The boat will be in soon with the mail too, come to think of it I saw an important looking letter or two for you at the post office, came in last week on the *Despatch*..."

"My word, Syd!" Peggy just inside suddenly took over the conversation, using her shoulder to push her boss out the way so she could share the doorway. "Look at ya, now, never seen you in such fine threads, you look like you've come down to get married now." She looked down at his trousers. "At least you got some mud on ya like a true digger."

Syd felt a sudden warmth in his cheeks. He hated the way the barmaid always noticed odd things about him. She had her hands on her hips, like she meant business too. Syd didn't answer the woman who just flicked her head back to get the fallen hair out of her eyes.

"Well, come on in and sit down then," Peggy finally said. "A dram or two of whisky maybe. Get in before the rush I say, boat will be in soon and I'll be run off my feet. Won't have time to serve a humble miner like you, probably all sorts of important people coming ashore, rich types if you know what I mean. We getting all sorts of business people since that professor gone and told everyone about the treasure trove up there."

Syd looked around to make sure George was out of earshot. "So, how is the new girl getting on? How are George and her getting on?"

"Oh, you should mind your own business, that's what I should be telling ya." She lowered her voice now, checking around to make sure no one was listening. "Not exactly a romance, not exactly anything from what I can make out. She lives in that room down the passage over there, he lives in the store, she's all the day out in her post office, all a bit weird to me. She's taken over the post office, perfect for her though. By the way, I saw a letter or two for you the other day when I was there."

At that moment, the ship's whistle sounded in the distance, indicating that it would soon be arriving at its anchorage just offshore. "If I was you," said Peggy, "I'd go and pick up your letters, before it gets busy. Twenty minutes, and a whole lot of ruffians just like you will be swarming all over the place. I hear a big party is on board the boat, at least a few of 'em bound to be staying here tonight."

As he crossed from the hotel down the little path to the post office, Syd felt curious why Peggy was being so helpful, courteous even towards him, it quite didn't figure out considering how she normally acted towards him. When he came to the post office door, Syd found it shut, strange on such a warm day. Then he spotted Elizabeth approaching from the other side with the key in her hand. She was wearing a mottled beige dress, which Syd quickly realised had a light imprint of flowers. Around her neck hung a necklace with a little silver locket. But the first thing Syd had noticed the whisp of hair hanging down one side of her face, the rest of her hair tied back into an elegant chignon. So different from Peggy, he couldn't help but thinking. Peggy's hair more resembled a bundle, tidy enough, but still a bunched-up bundle.

"Good day, sir," Elizabeth said, "Bear with me, I will be with you as soon as I unlock this door…"

"I believe we have met already, Elizabeth, isn't it? I was here the day you arrived. I carried your trunk up the ladder. My name is Syd Braithwaite, Peggy did introduce us." Syd felt his heart do an unmistakeable flutter.

“Why yes, that was very kind of you,” said Elizabeth as she opened the door and stepped inside, using her foot to push over a rock to keep the door open. Only at this point did it dawn on her, this was the man who watched her from the trees.

“I have to say, you look quite different today, Mr Braithwaite…” She gave out a hint of a smile, making sure to avert his attentive gaze.

“Yes, you could be forgiven for not recognising me,” said Syd. “I recall that day being most wet. Mud everywhere. I’m sorry we met under such circumstances.”

“Worry not, sir, I was not quite myself either. Now how can I help you? There may well be a queue soon if I’m not mistaken.”

“I hear from both George and Peggy that there is a letter…”

“Two, in fact, Mr Braithwaite,” she said, turning to retrieve them from the A-D slot of her inward mail shelf. She slid them across the table, Syd took them to stash down his shirt. His desire to read them had been superseded by a sudden inclination to loiter.

“So, ma’am, may I ask how have you been finding Port Pegasus?” The way Elizabeth paused and pursed her lips made him instantly regret asking.

Finally, she did reply. “I must admit, it has taken a bit of getting used to, but I have more-or-less settled in. I haven’t left the hotel much though, except to explore around the edges of this promontory.”

“What! Surely, George has taken you at least to see the falls?” Even before he finished asking the question, he knew he’d overstepped his welcome. “Excuse me, ma’am, I didn’t mean to to…”

“No, no, no, Mr Braithwaite. It’s alright. Peggy mentioned the falls. She even suggested one day she will borrow a dinghy and row me there, when we not too busy of course.”

“Yes, they are not far by water. Try walking around to them through the bush from the hotel, you’ll find endless gullies to cross, down and up all the time, it can take you a good two hours, you reach them exhausted. By rowing, that’s the way to go, you can be there in quarter of an hour, easy.”

“Well, then, I shall certainly look forward to seeing them one day,” said Elizabeth, suddenly aware the boat had pulled in.

Just off in the Arm, the sudden splash and rattle of anchor chain was quickly followed by the commotion of men calling to each other. A boat was being pushed off the shore, they heard the swish swash of the oars in the water, and the squeaky rowlocks too.

"Ma'am, you'll be busy in a minute or so, please excuse me and thank you for the mail…I'm sure I shall see you again. Oh, and please call me Syd, if you may."

"I will, Syd, why thank you…and you can call me Elizabeth."

As Syd turned to leave, he wondered if their eyes met in a way that was different, some sort of understanding maybe. It wasn't until he was walking down the path back to the hotel that he realised his heart was surely trembling. Back inside the hotel and seated at a table, he pulled out his two letters. His heart sunk a little as he digested the contents of the first one. It was from Thomas Mapleston of Milton, a prominent landowner whom Syd had discussed his venture with on a prior occasion. While not exactly discouraging, the cautionary last sentence of the letter read, "While we acknowledge the gains obtained by your thorough prospecting, attributable of course to your hard labour and continuous attendance at your claim, we are hesitant to commit any funds to advancing a partnership until such time as government geologist James McKay has prepared his overall report on the field. If this is encouraging, we will then reconsider in a more favourable light."

Syd put his head in his hands and rubbed his eyes for a few seconds before opening the second letter, aware Peggy was watching him from behind the bar as she sprottled away transferring glasses from a wooden tray. The second letter, from Gore businessman James Hargraves, started, "Thank you for the memorandum which we received today. While we feel the results are…" Syd was skimming now, picking out pertinent phrases; "…concern about an abundance of optimism…a lack of provincial government backing…assay samples relating specifically to your claims will be required…whilst we are of the opinion the prospect is exciting…further exploration is needed…" Syd didn't bother finishing it. He would read them both properly when he got back to camp. Suddenly, there seemed no hurry to do anything. The first passenger off the boat was making his way into the hotel. Just outside, Syd could hear George waylaying the two following, thinking how ingenuine his greeting really was, it sounded more like a covert interrogation. He watched Peggy serve the newcomer a straight scotch, observing that although her demeanour was welcoming, she was in fact grilling him just like her boss.

"So fine, sir, what brings you to Pegasus?" She said sliding the glass across the counter with a beaming smile. The new arrival mumbled something about coming down to investigate a business proposition. Syd couldn't help but notice the man was evasive. Won't be getting much out of him, he thought. Peggy waited for the man to move to a table before coming out from behind the bar to sidle up to Syd.

"You, ok? You don't look happy since you read those two letters. Not too bad news I hope." She moved close, bending over to put her arm half around him.

Damn Peggy, thought Syd, makes everyone's business her own.

"Nah, not too bad. You just wonder why you're here sometimes. Slogging your guts out and getting nowhere, just how I feel right now." Clutching his drink off the table, Syd sat back in his chair to give out a pronounced sigh.

"You're not alone, Syd, that's for sure," said Peggy frowning in solidarity. "Maybe you need a break, get your mind going on something else, even for a day. You miners never stop, you should stay tonight here at the hotel, give yourself a day off tomorrow. Its Sunday, after all. The hotel will be quiet once this lot take off in the morning."

"Have you ever been to the falls?" Syd found himself suddenly asking.

"Why no, I was saying to Elizabeth just the other day, I'd row her up there sometime, but if you're offering, maybe we could all go. You can get Tucker's boat, can't you? Save me going up the hill begging for it. You keep an eye on his rowboat, don't ya? I know you do, cos he told me so. That boat, it's ten feet long he told me, it should fit the three of us easy, George too if he wants to come. Doubt he will though, he ain't interested in anything like sightseeing, more likes to just hang around. Let me talk to Lizzie…must go, I got some serving to do." She was already halfway back to the bar before she finished the sentence, and by the time she was serving again, the tone of her voice had changed back completely.

"And so, what would you two fine gentlemen like to drink, a dram or two of whisky maybe? Maybe just a Schweppes to brighten you up. I can tell you got some serious business to do out here. My word, I can always spot the successful ones! So, what brings you here?"

Chapter 9

Upon his return to Invercargill, the professor had wasted no time courting many a monied suitor to join him on his hard rock mining project. Although he had pegged out his own block, he had also shrewdly negotiated another adjoining 60 acre claim originally pegged out by William Smith, Section 13, Block VIII of the Pegasus Land District. Going in with Harold Gordon had been a shrewd move too. Not only was he a man well versed in hard rock mining operations, but he was the government's Inspector of Mines. Together, they formed the Cornish Mining Company, immediately enlisting the labour of two Cornish miners working in the Tuapeka field, Branock Curnow and Arthur Trethowan. The professor promptly met them in Bluff to accompany them down to get started, and they sailed directly to Port Pegasus on the *Despatch*. Bypassing the hotel, a waste of time the three agreed, they trudged straight up the Surveyors Track, the three of them carrying hefty packs of tools and supplies, not to mention pushing a sturdy wooden wheelbarrow laden with extra equipment. When it got muddy, the two burly miners took turns to push it. On the steeper sections, they attached a rope through the tray braces so the one going ahead could pull it. After much grunting, they finally made it out of the windswept thickets to the more open tops of the mountain where no plants grew much higher than a foot, all shorn off and bent over by the prevailing winds. The wild wind made it exceedingly difficult even to keep the barrow upright, let along themselves. On a better day, they might have stopped to admire the splendid view out over the fine harbour stretching to the horizon, its islands and myriad of indentations making for a most pleasing view. But no such thought entered their minds today, they were just on a mission to skirt around the trig as quickly as possible and get out of the wind.

"Gentlemen," the professor was forced to yell to them standing alongside, just to get them to hear, "It's just down there, in the lee of this last hillock. Follow me." They went on and down another two hundred yards before stopping in a pronounced recess of the hill.

Apart from swirling gusts, it was much calmer here, although the temperature all around was beginning to plummet. The professor rubbed his hands to warm them up, turning his back at one stage to get his face out of a gust so sudden it sucked the breath out of his mouth. Waiting for the worst to pass, he started delivering his instructions in his sternest lecturing tone.

"Gentlemen, this is where I need you to start digging," He pointed at a spot on the incline around half a chain directly ahead. "Make sure you keep to a bearing of 220 degrees, with an upward gradient of one in seventy to allow for dewatering." The two miners went forward to inspect the inclined face. The scrub had all been burnt off, revealing the ground to be littered with loose black rocks, all specked strongly with some sort of shiny mineral. Arthur picked up one of the loose rocks, examining it closely, mumbling to his mate so the professor wouldn't hear. "Tinstone for sure, but not that rich by my reckoning. Full of wolfram." He called to the professor who was holding back. "So, how far in do you estimate this motherlode?"

"No more than 100 yards, 150 yards at most, you should strike it before then. Send me samples from the face every two weeks. The broad hollow here lends itself to a couple of good mullocks, dump the spoil all out here on either side, but make sure you preserve good access and drainage, we don't need a mud pit at the entry." Arthur went back to his barrow, returning with his spalling hammer and two pegs which he drove in either side of the face where the professor had indicated.

"Dropcut marked," he called out to the professor. "Come and check we got it right, will you?"

The professor came alongside them. "The tunnel face needs to be no less than 27 square feet, that's four feet 8 inches wide and 6 feet two inches high. Taper the roof on each side to one foot six inches. If I'm not mistaken, the granite should provide an excellent finish."

As the professor turned away, the two miners exchanged knowing glances. "Easy for someone who ain't ever mined in his life to come out with something like that," Branock mumbled to his mate.

"Granite, for sure the hardest rock around, only one inch every thousand years it weathers. I'd say we might do two yards a day at the most in this sort of ground, not including bogging out."

"That's if we strike it right," added Arthur. To the professor, he turned again. "Pit props? So, what if we need a few? Bound to be ceiling crevices, we need to shore up along the way.

I'll arrange that with Scollay, contact him if you need them, you could also cut some pit posts out of the forest down the hill, there's a gully with some timber trees there. Hopefully, you won't need many. Any more last questions?"

He waited a few seconds, noting the two men exchanging glances again. "Well, gentlemen, I wish you all the best. Good luck setting up your camp. I will make sure your supplies are despatched every month from today's date." He pulled two envelopes out his pocket, handing one each to the men.

"Your contracts gentlemen. My specifications. An order to the Cornish Mining Company account in the Bank of New South Wales in Gore will honour wages every month. I shall advise you if the money is due to run out, but at this stage, that is not envisaged. Now, if you have no further queries, would you now please excuse me, I need to catch the boat which will be coming back up from South Pegasus tonight. Good day. We will keep in contact, I'm sure of that."

The two miners shook his hand in turn. Crouching down in the lee of some scrub growing all bent and twisted in the wind, they watched the professor head back around the trig, sniggering to each other as the wind buffeted him about.

"He looks like a drunk going off," joked Arthur.

"Yeah, a drunk who knows absolutely nothing about mining," Branock replied.

When he was finally out of sight, Arthur turned to his mate.

"What have we got ourselves into up here? They never mentioned this polar weather we'd be working in, did they? Makes Cornwall look like one of those South Sea islands you see in those books, Tasmania for that matter too. Got a bit of cheek calling themselves the Cornish Mining Company, don't ya think?"

The man paused, looking back up to the top of the mountain. "You know something too, Branock, something ain't quite right up here. Did you see the way the veins in the rock were running as we were coming around the top? And which way he wants us to dig in. It just don't add up if you ask me!"

"Who cares?" Branock replied. "He told us straight what he wants, and he's the boss. We just do what he wants. Not up to us to question anything. Let him say something when he gets the samples, they will speak for themselves." He turned around to survey the hillside. "I say let's set up camp over there in the lee, best spot out of a bad bunch. Beggars can't be choosers now, can we?"

Chapter 10

It was with an air of boyish excitement that Syd untied Tucker's upturned row boat from the manuka tree it was tied to. Gone entirely was his disappointment of the prospective shareholder responses. Peggy and Elizabeth both leaned in to turn the clinker dinghy over and grab its gunnels to help him drag it down the slight incline and leave half in the tide. Peggy had made sure it was her business to bring a spare bottle cork or two in case the bung needed replacing, she was brought up in a coastal village after all.

"It's been out of the water so long, the planks will surely leak," Syd warned them. "We should've sunk it a few days back, let them swell tight, but then, spur of the moment outing and all, can't always get it right. I'll do the rowing; you two lasses can do the bailing. I found a couple of tin cans down the bank on the way here, one for each of you. Don't throw them overboard by mischance now, just make sure you hang onto them as you bail."

Elizabeth hitched up her lilac dress with one hand, instinctively holding out the other for Syd to help her balance as she stepped over the bow, the feel of his hand so rough against hers so tender, big too, it encased her hand like a warm glove. She found herself holding it as long as she politely could while balancing her way down the boat, only willing releasing it when she swivelled around to sit down on the rear thwart. Syd put the oars in their rowlocks and pushed the boat out a little further, just enough to get in without the rowboat getting stuck on the bottom.

"I'm getting in," pronounced Peggy finally, pushing it out a bit more and hitching her leg over the bow at the same time. "Aye, what an adventure, I seen enough of that hotel, washing and cooking and cleaning all the time. George doesn't know what he's missing out on. Didn't even look interested. Someone's got to keep an eye on the place I suppose. Those two men from Tuatapere, ain't even up yet, dunno why they bother coming out here if they spend all day in bed." Peggy bent forward to rearrange her skirt before sitting down on the front thwart.

"Probably has something to do with how much bourbon they drank last night," offered Syd, using one oar to push off the bottom. "I had to listen to 'em going on all night. Made the mistake of laying my head on the back porch, had to listen to them go on half the night."

"And I served them half the night too, reckon they ended up guzzling a good three bottles between them. Wouldn't surprise me if at least one of them didn't wake up at all, dead drunk they were," added Peggy.

The head of the Arm was unusually calm as Syd rowed out in a wide arc that put them directly on course for the falls. It had been a few months since he'd taken Tucker's boat out and it took him more than a few strokes to get back into the rhythm of rowing. As soon as Syd had hopped in, Elizabeth had realised she would be directly face to face with Syd who was rowing backwards. When he leaned forward to lift his oars out of the water and draw them back, his face came to within a foot of hers. She made a point of not looking directly at him, but she was close enough to take in the detail of his broad nose, cheeks full of colour, his pronounced forehead. She thought him handsome in a rugged way.

"Look!" said Peggy, waving her hand at two pointed peaks that were rising into view above the bush line. "Have you ever seen anything quite like them?"

"Nothing like the outlook from the hotel, I have to agree," said Elizabeth. "So wild up behind, I had no idea how the low hills around the hotel block the view back into the interior. It certainly makes the rolling hills of bonny Scotland look tame enough."

"You know what us miners call those two matching peaks?" Syd didn't wait for them to guess, because he knew they never would. "The Nipples!"

Peggy gave a hearty laugh; "Oh, my goodness, they'd surely be teenage titties then. About a 15 or 16-year-olds, wouldn't you say now, Lizzie?"

Elizabeth couldn't help herself, bursting out in unrestrained giggling. Suddenly, not much seemed to matter, out here on the water she felt free.

"What do you expect from a bunch of rowdy miners?" Syd chimed in. "We men inhabit a different world up there in the mountains. Just can't help ourselves. All these hills we give names to. One day I can take you up the Buttocks if you like. Two humps side by side they are. Only been up 'em once. Had to go hide down the big crack when it sleeted over, nearly froze me to death in that crevice too."

"That would have served ya right, now, wouldn't it?" Peggy roared. "You wouldn't catch me up between some buttocks."

Water was already beginning to swirl around their feet, and Syd reminded them to bail. "We don't need the boat sinking under us now, I got me boots on, I'd sink like a stone."

Elizabeth couldn't believe how free she felt, and how enjoyable everything suddenly seemed, even the bailing. She was getting into it with a newfound relish. It surely must be that she was having a break from the hotel, she thought, she hadn't realised how bound she had come to feel to the place, a place not even of her choosing. But there was something else as well, and she was trying to put her finger on it. Her laughing had woken her up. She couldn't remember the last time she had laughed so out loud.

"Oh, look a seal!" shouted Peggy, pointing ahead.

Syd stopped rowing to take in the surface disturbance, the raised slick of water now heading directly for them. He lifted his oars to watch it as it got closer and closer.

"Ain't a normal seal," said Syd. "Bigger for a start. But look at its head too when it sticks it out again, different shape, more like a big snake." The animal was almost right alongside them, giving out a low almost imperceivable rumble as it edged closer. Peggy found herself instinctively pulling back as the creature stuck its head out of the water to stare at them. They could plainly see its big black shining eyes, and the yellow slits of irises as they fixed on them. The top of its head was black, its throat light grey, unlike the mottling of grey and black spots which surrounded its huge muzzle that looked out of proportion to its head. It was as if a sea monster from the deep had come to inspect them.

"Oh, my God," whispered Elizabeth, feeling real terror now rippling through her body. Her voice trembled now as she talked. "Should we be afraid of such a sea monster? I swear its longer than our boat. Maybe it wishes to tip us out and devour us one by one?"

"Nah," said Syd, reassuring her. "I'd say it's simply curious, did you see its giant flippers when it rolled over? Must admit I've never seen a beast quite like it before. Maybe it's one of those sea leopards? Aye, that's what it must be, could only be. A sailor told me once about them. Said he' d seen one attack and kill a fur seal, when they were anchored in a harbour at Campbell Island. The thing didn't stand a chance either. They go round eating penguins too, tear them apart just like that, first of all hold them in their jaws then flick them with such force it skins them just like that!"

Peggy was leaning right over on Syd now. "I don't like it, Syd, just keep rowing, I say, let's leave it behind."

"What a beautiful creature though," said Elizabeth. "So sleek and shiny. It gets through the water so effortlessly. Oh, my goodness, did you see its teeth just then? Nothing short of fangs!" Syd started rowing again, soon leaving the monster behind. They all watched it in silence as it carried on its way, back towards Whale Passage.

"Makes me never want to go down to the water again, imagine that rearing out of the water and grabbing ya?" Peggy said.

"Me too!" agreed Elizabeth. "I go down to that little inlet at the far end of the hotel all the time, imagine if it was hiding in there, waiting for me. No one would even know if I was taken. Might not even have time to scream. Did you see the size of its jaws?"

"It's gone now, don't worry, lasses," Syd assured them. "We won't see him again most likely. Look up ahead, the falls will be coming into full view soon." Within a minute, they spotted the first sliver of falling water behind the dead limbs of a fallen tree protruding out over the water. As the bay narrowed, the falls grew wider and wider until they were fully exposed. And what a sight they were, a broad vista of tumbling water coming down in two spectacular cascades before plunging into the salty sea at the head of the Arm. The noise grew and grew the closer they got, finally drowning out all their conversations.

They watched in silence as Syd got them closer, into the little waves emanating out from the falling water. The power of the water crashing continuously down into the sea silenced them anyway, and it wasn't until Elizabeth felt damp all over from the fine spray that she was finally able to offer some words.

"Oh, they are just so beautiful," she cried out. "Thank you so much for taking us here. Everything seems so different here. It has even always made me forget about that horrible sea leopard."

"Fine indeed," yelled Peggy above the din. "So much better than I ever imagined them to be. All that water coming down all the time. Wherever does it come from? Can we get ashore and climb above them?

"We surely can," said Syd, working to get the dinghy out of the current now. "Over here, by that fallen branch, we can tie up there."

Clambering ashore onto a bank of cutty grass and crown ferns, they were soon level with the wide lip of the upper cascade, watching as the water flowed ceaselessly over. A wood pigeon whooshing from behind took them by surprise, it coming so close to Elizabeth that she ducked, causing them all to laugh. Syd urged them to climb up further to where the torrent came down a chute in the rock. "See how the channel has been cut through the rock? There is nothing like the power of flowing water to dig out the earth. On the diggings, we direct it to sluice out whole faces in our claims. Do it right, and it works for you, get it wrong and it can become a cruel master."

Peggy ventured further up the creek, looking in the pools and eddies as she went, before kneeling to scoop out a cupped handful of water which she put to her mouth.

"Syd, this is so beautiful here. Thank you for taking the day to bring us here," said Elizabeth. The song of a bellbird somewhere in the trees serenaded them.

"Elizabeth, it is my pleasure. Everything I do is work, so it is a treat for me also. But particularly, that I can be in the company of such a fine woman such as yourself."

Elizabeth put out her hand for Syd to hold as she followed him down a slippery incline to the water's edge. "Why thank you, Syd, that is most kind of you to say," she replied once back on a sure footing. "To be honest, I have never met many kind men. Not here in New Zealand anyway. Well apart from you now, of course. They always expect you to do something for them. Not that I've been here that long, of course."

Syd could see Peggy getting up. He had to say it, what was stirring inside him, before they were interrupted.

"Elizabeth. Ever since the day I first spied you through the trees, something has stirred in me…"

"Oh, Syd, that's so kind," she replied, turning her face from his gaze to take in the waterfall again. "But you know I am betrothed to George. Perhaps, it is not the best to indulge in such words, do you think?"

"Maybe not, and excuse me then, but I do know one thing for certain. You are not meant to be with that George, and I suspect you think so too. He isn't the man for you. It's a queer situation if you ask me. Even Peggy has mentioned it."

"Well, luckily, then I am not asking you, or Peggy for that matter either. I'm sure, I will sort it out one way or another, but all in my own good time."

Seeing that Peggy was about to re-join them, Syd turned his gaze back to the waterfall.

"So, what you two been talking about?" Peggy asked alongside them now, eyeballing them both directly in turn.

Elizabeth jumped in before Syd could say a word. "Oh, Peggy, you missed something most interesting."

Oh no thought Syd, surely not. "Syd was telling me about the finer details of how the water is utilised on the field. Most interesting too. I'm sure he wouldn't mind repeating it if you were interested."

"Not to me, he won't," blurted Peggy. "Not interested, never will be. That's a man's business." She paused briefly as a couple of parson birds did their wild acrobatics beside them before disappearing as fast as they had come. "These falls are great, but that's enough for me, think we should be getting back soon."

Back on the water, Syd watched how excitable his two companions had become. Peggy, in particular, just couldn't sit still.

"That sea leopard better not come back," she said more than once. "Never been so scared in all my whole life. I hate that creature, and to think it swims past the hotel. Wouldn't be the first time, probably hauls out here somewhere."

"I've heard every wild animal can be tamed," replied Elizabeth. "You need to exhibit a mixture of kindness, discipline and reward, that's what the keeper at the zoological gardens in London told us when we visited there once..."

Peggy butted in. "Nah, what you talking 'bout, lass, couldn't be right. Bet that only works with land creatures, not wild sea creatures, surely."

"Well, it works on all us miners," said Syd. "You got us all tamed and trained, Peggy." Elizabeth laughed as Peggy picked up a length of rope and gave him a playful lash across his back, surprising him. "Yep, trained alright I got you, Syd. Anything I say you have to do, now keep rowing."

"And you lasses keep bailing, came back, Syd, can't you feel that water around your feet again. You'll have us sunk in no time."

"Row, row, row your boat gently down the stream..." Peggy was singing the nursery rhyme now at the top of her voice. Her voice must have carried across the still arm, because no sooner had they pulled the boat up outside the hotel than they spotted George, and he was hollering from the edge of the bank. "Peggy. Peggy, hurry on back, will ya? The two gentlemen from Tuatapere have woken up, and they want some lunch."

“Oh Lord, please excuse me if I go and give that George a right bash. That’s what I feel like doing anyway,” said Peggy as she jumped out to trudge back to the hotel. Elizabeth helped Syd pull the boat back up the bank, watching as he turned it over and secured it back to the manuka tree again. After safely stashing the oars under a bush up the bank, he turned to Elizabeth, “I’d better be going back up to my claim. Thank you for a morning I will always remember,”

Their eyes met for a few prolonged moments.

“Why thank you too, Syd. I won’t forget it either.” Before he had a chance to turn and leave, she walked over the cobbled rocks towards him, stopping to bend over slightly and kiss him gently on his left cheek. Syd couldn’t believe it. Did that just happen, he wondered?

“I shall see you soon enough, no doubt. Goodbye now,” said Elizabeth smiling, turning away to head back for the hotel. Syd watched her go, his heart fair pounding in his chest. It was then that he spotted her, Peggy standing up amongst the manuka. She hadn’t gone straight back to the hotel; she’d been watching them.

Chapter 11

The rumour went around the field like wildfire. A consortium of miners was secretly preparing a consignment of five-and-a-half tons of tin ore to ship out. The first Syd heard it was when he was walking back up the hill after his excursion to the falls. Tucker spied him coming up the track and came out specially to ask him if he knew anything about it.

"What, five tons and more, I don't believe it," said Syd, noticing one of the miner's front teeth was missing, he was absolutely sure he had it only two days before, or was it that he was only just now noticing it. He wanted to ask him, but thought better, keeping to the subject. "Who would have amassed that much without anyone noticing?"

"It was even mentioned in the paper I hear, so it must be true" Tucker said before breaking out into roaring laughter. "Can't believe anything you read. Mind you, it'll keep the investors interested while we carry on doing the hard yards."

Syd thought of his investors and wondered if they had just read about it in the paper. Funny though that no one had mentioned it when he was down at the hotel yesterday. Most Southlanders appreciated what all the miners already suspected that the successful prospects of the field were being stunted by a lack of capital. Every miner had signed the petition which was sent to the provincial government, asking for assistance in developing capital works, namely upgrading the Surveyors track and building a wharf, but despite all the pleas, the reply was always the same; they were unwilling to invest before the field was proven. Like all the miners, Syd felt trapped between a rock and a hard place.

"Wait till McKay gets here," said Tucker, referring to the impending visit of the government geologist. "What he says will dictate what happens."

After thanking Tucker for the use of his boat and informing him of the new place, he had stashed the oars, Syd farewelled the man and carried on, speculating in his mind about what the esteemed McKay might say when he visited. Surely, he will agree with the professor, they were colleagues in a way, after all. His thoughts soon drifted back to Elizabeth, the meeting in the post office, the stolen conversation at the falls, and that goodbye kiss, still warm upon his course whiskered cheek. The question he was soon asking himself was not now, 'Would he see her again?' but 'When will I see her again?' By the time he got to the turnoff to his claim, he realised he was utterly fixated with thoughts of the woman. It was as if all the tin fever in his body was suddenly replaced by another sort of energy. "I think I have feelings for her," he even found himself saying out loud. Then came the questioning, 'But does she think of me?" She gave me a kiss after all. He went back over the words they had exchanged by the waterfall when Peggy was out of earshot. At first, he thought Elizabeth's responses had been off-putting, but then he remembered what the matron in Invercargill had told him about the reaction of women being at first discouraging. *You have to woo them.*

He thought about writing her a letter, even taking it down to leave for her to find. The only trouble with that was Peggy would read it for sure. He knew what she was like, capable of opening someone else's letter before they even had a chance to open it themselves. Maybe he could take Elizabeth something when he went down to the hotel again, a gift of some sort. Something that could speak for itself. I know, thought Syd. I could make a brooch and give it to her, something she might cherish. Out of tin, a tin brooch. He thought about it for a while. Gold and silver brooches, he'd heard of, but a tin one? He thought hard, trying to remember how many tin broches he'd ever seen. His mother or grandmother certainly hadn't owned one, and they were both wives of Cornish tin miners. But what option did he have, apart from going back to Invercargill and buying her a gift in one of the fancy shops? None! He tried to picture the broach he was going to make, and how Elizabeth might wear it. He had fallen for the lass, and he knew it,

Coming up to his tent, Syd noticed the paw prints of a small animal in the mud, a wild cat for sure he thought after kneeling to inspect them. It didn't surprise him that they had reached this far, visiting ships had been leaving their cats in Port Pegasus for nearly a hundred years, and they were well established around the shore.

Back up at his claim, before getting into his working clothes, Syd went to the side of his rough bedding and pulled out a small tin, its contents were his entire output of stream tin from his sluice for the last month, little more than six pounds in weight. From his small satchel, given to him by his father in Cornwall, he pulled out his porcelain miner's crucible along with its tongs and two short lengths of blowpipe, all items handed down through his family—at least four generations of tin miners that he knew of. His father had made a ceremony of handing them over to Syd as he had begun packing to leave. Unpacking them now gave him a pang of regret that he hadn't asked his father more about his Cornish ancestors. They hadn't seemed that important to him when he was growing up.

He had one more thing to find, a safety pin. He was sure there was one somewhere. Ferreting around, he finally found it, stuck into the small bandage he kept in case he cut himself. Miners had been found dead before, bled out after cutting open their upper legs on sharp mining gear, or even falling on them. That was the last thing his father had warned him about, the danger of working alone and unassisted. He remembered his words "Work in a gang, you're far safer, there'll always be someone looking out for you and ready to help. Working alone, you're on your own, and that's it if anything happens."

Syd attended to his chores now, he had much to catch up on if he was to do a touch of smelting latter. His tailrace needed sorting if he wanted to start sluicing again in the morning. He changed into his work clothes, noticing how ragged they looked in comparison to what he had taken off. Making a good campfire was his last task before he left, knowing he would need red hot embers for later, and lots of them. He rooted through his stack of gathered firewood and picked out all the dryish pieces of leatherwood trunk to lay out in the sun, making a mental note to bring them in if it rained.

Extending his tailrace and stacking rocks took up the rest of the afternoon. The weather had held, he certainly had that to be thankful for as he returned to camp, carrying a tin of clay and a hefty flat rock around the size of a big dinner plate. The rock, with a slight inward bevel, had been easy to find, but the fine clay had proved much harder to locate. He had finally found a patch of suitable stuff to dig into near the big rock at the edge of his claim. He tested it by kneading it in the palm of his hand until he was satisfied it was fine enough for his purpose.

Coming back to his tent starving hungry, he mixed up some flour. yeast and water to make damper in his camp oven, smothering the steaming bread with lard before devouring it. Sometimes, he hated his endless diet of stodge, but he knew it kept him going.

Before setting to work, he built up the fire and set up his rock in the middle of his tent, making sure it was thoroughly wetted. Dusk was falling, and after setting up his lantern, he used his hand to scrape all the clay out of the tin, kneading it around in his hands again. When he was satisfied that he had it right, he pushed the clay into the middle of the rock and flattened it across with the blade of his bowie knife. He was ready now to make the reverse impression which would serve as his cast for the finished brooch.

For an hour, he worked solidly on his creation, using all his metal implements he could muster—spoon, bowie knife, fork, a metal pin, needle and the safety pin—to make the impression of a flowering thistle rising out of the fern. The was not random. While he was sluicing, his mind had been going over and over a suitable design for the brooch. Finally, he had settled on the contrast of a Scottish thistle growing out of two New Zealand fern fronds. We may have been born in the old country, he thought, but we have settled here in the new land of New Zealand. Surely, she would appreciate what such a design signified, the coming together in the new land of opportunity.

He used the point of his knife to scratch out the basic design in the clay, working with the teaspoon and the tine of his fork to dig out the stem and head of the thistle. Its spikey flower and the ferns he applied with the sharp-edged tip of his bowie knife, twisting his body around this way and that to get the flourishes right. Finally, when he was happy with it, he set about raking out the wood from the coals to leave a concentrated red-hot centre. Carefully, he poured the tin ore into the little crucible until it was three quarters full. Using the tongs to grip it, he placed it upright directly in the coals. Fitting his two lengths of blowpipes together, he immediately set about creating a little furnace around his crucible, the heat searing his face every time he took a deep breath and blew into the pipe. His father's advice came back to him, "Concentrate when you're blowing, always remove the pipe from your lips when you breath back in, otherwise your lungs will catch fire." Syd fetched some water in a bucket and found some relief by wetting his face every few minutes. Soon a rising steam began rising off the ore, and before long, it was bubbling. He kept it at this state, bubbling away, for what he thought must be ten minutes, before scraping off the lump of slag which had risen to the top. After much blowing, the substance turned molten. At first, it was golden, then it became red, and finally it turned bright glowing white, the glow from it filling the whole tent. Syd was happy now, and out of breath too. Carefully wrapping the tongs around the crucible, he lifted it off the fire, tilting it with one hand and using the tip of the bowie knife in the other to drag out the last of the floating slag. It wouldn't be the purest smelter he'd ever done, but it would be good enough. Wasting no time, he placed the crucible over the clay impression and gently poured the molten tin into the mould until it was level with the top. While he waited for it to stop bubbling, he used his knife to dig out another impression in the clay, this time rectangular, then poured the leftover tin into it to make a thin ingot, not much bigger than a stout pencil. He waited for the brooch to stop bubbling, then carefully inserted his knife through the safety pin before gently lowering it longways down into the molten mix. When he saw the blade of his knife gently touch the molten mix, he lifted it up a hairs-width, holding it there with both hands to keep it steady for a full five minutes before he was satisfied it had taken.

Wiping his sweating brow, Syd felt truly proud of what he had just accomplished, and all with the bare minimum of tools and equipment. He couldn't help thinking of his family home back in the old country, tinges of homesickness, and he knew it. But as he lay on his bed of fern, his thoughts kept turning back to Elizabeth. She was his hope for the future now. Who knows, maybe one day they could travel back to England together. Catching himself in his thoughts made him suddenly sit bolt upright. Did he actually think this was possible, he asked himself. It didn't matter, he ended up reassuring himself, whatever will be will be. Laying back on his bed of fern, he closed his eyes and let his mind run with the thought of her. Oh, what must she be like to hold, to passionately kiss even. He would go down to the hotel and see her next week, for sure.

His night was restless, the cat had returned and made strange crying noises outside his tent. At one stage, the noise had become too heated, making him deduce there were two of them. At one stage, he crawled over to pull aside the tent flap, but he couldn't see any sign of movement.

The sun was already up when he finally opened his eyes for the day. Going straight over to his casting, he held his hand close above it to gauge its warmth. Even though a whole night had passed, it was still ever so slightly warm to the touch. He was pleased to see the safety pin had embedded, and that its clasp still opened properly. The casting looked great, and although it was peppered with a number of pin-prick airholes, that was to be to be expected. The back didn't matter anyway, it was the front of the brooch that did, and soon it would be revealed. Without putting on his boots, he took the clay straight to a quiet part of the creek where he crouched down, submerging the mould. As the clay softened, he gently broke bits off the outer edge and through the middle until he was left with two palm-sized pieces, one with the brooch still embedded, the other with the ingot. He worked on the ingot first, rubbing off the clay to finally expose it. Using his fingers, he cleaned it until all the clay had gone and all that was left was the pale grey strip of metal. Syd turned it around several times, inspecting it for signs of imperfection. Apart from a few tiny air holes, it was a near perfect casting. Carefully putting it aside on the bank, he set to work on the embedded brooch, taking far more care this time as he gently rubbed the softening clay off in the water. A small plume of discoloured water dissipated downstream as it merged into the main current. As he got closer to the metal of the brooch, he stopped his rubbing to just let it soak between two submerged rocks. For a full five minutes he watched it, going back at one point to pick up the ingot again for another inspection. He felt immensely proud; an ingot of tin produced by his very hands. How many men in the whole world could claim they had smelted metal which they had dug out of the ground? His Cornish pride swelled.

It was time to reveal his work. He picked up the clay, satisfied it was wet enough and took it out into the main flow. Ignoring the icy cold water stabbing his feet like hundreds of needles, he cupped the clay in both hands and swished it about. He waited for the plume of dissolving clay to completely dissipate out before heading back to the bank. Finally, he was looking at the casting only, the reverse impression of what he had created in the clay. And it was near perfect! Even the detail of the fern fronds had worked out, every little frilly crevice filled in by the molten tin. Just like the ingot, it wasn't shiny, more a gun metal shade of light grey, but he couldn't help thinking it looked most royal in an unassuming way. He stared at it for several minutes, an immense pride flooding through him. Walking back to his tent, gently holding the brooch in one hand and the ingot in the other, he couldn't help himself. Raising his head to the sky, he let out a wild 'Whooaaaa hooooo…'

He couldn't wait to give the brooch it to Elizabeth now.

Chapter 12

"So, Lizzie, I saw you kiss him," said Peggy, her two arms resting on the desk and her body leaning forward on them in an interrogating way. She stared directly at Elizabeth. "Haven't seen you do anything like that to George. Fancy Syd, do ya?"

Taken aback with the bluntness of the question, Elizabeth reeled back in her chair. How dare Peggy corner her in her little post office, the only place she felt safe? Peggy had chosen the perfect spot for the confrontation, and she knew it.

It had been four days since the outing to the falls, and Elizabeth had thought of not much else but her rising feelings for Syd. It was time to admit them.

"Yes, Peggy, I do. I fancy him. Alright, now you have your answer, I would like you to excuse me."

"Not so fast now, Lizzie. I ain't finished asking you about it. We are the only two women for forty miles, I have a right to know what you're planning. It affects me."

"Absolutely nothing, I have no intentions, I swear to you," said Elizabeth. Tears welled up in her eyes, her face was flushing. "It's confusing for me. Somehow, I have got myself into this mad mess with George, a man who obviously doesn't love me, who has never shown me an ounce of affection. He treats me like his maid around here, his postmistress and extra help to holler for! He has no interest in me whatsoever. The only reason he wants to marry me is so he has a housekeeper and a cook back in Invercargill, his shop assistant to banter to his female customers I suspect as well, a worker he won't even have to pay."

Peggy's body visibly relaxed as she let out a deep breath. "Aye, Lizzie, I think you're right, but you don't wanna run off with the first man who does show you a bit of affection. That's my advice, it's why I came in to ask you these prying questions. Don't think I'm just being nosey. We're both vulnerable down here, don't ya know, stuck in a man's world. It takes a special type of woman to survive it, it does. We're not like those suffragettes out protesting in Dunedin."

Elizabeth pushed her chair back to get up. "I'm well aware of all that, Peggy, thank you for coming in, but I would appreciate some time alone now. Please if you would…" She grabbed her book of stamps and thrust them into the shelf.

"As you wish." Peggy half turned to go, adding, "But I'd appreciate a hand later in the cookhouse if you could. Tane dropped off one of those kelp sacks of muttonbirds to pay for the grog on his tab. Didn't know those Maori fellas could drink like he does. You can give me a hand to cook a few of 'em up. You'll have to boil 'em up outside 'cos they stink the place out." Peggy was pondering now. "I wonder what's his business down here. Birding I know, but I thought he'd be going back on the ship. Not even sure where he hangs out, up the track somewhere or along the coast, I guess. I asked him about it once, why he comes here so often. 'Maori business,' he told me. Reckoned I wouldn't understand. I'm off, bye now."

Elizabeth waited for Peggy to make the hotel before getting up to shut the door. Her stomach was in turmoil, not to mention her heart. Syd's words about having feelings for her had quietly resonated in a way she didn't understand, or really acknowledge. She had to admit to herself that she barely knew what was happening, this feeling rising up inside. George could not, and would not, be her husband. In her heart, she knew the time was drawing near to close the book on George completely. But a despair was creeping in. How could she possibly escape now? She was trapped at the bottom of the world, miles from anywhere. Where could she go? To Dunedin maybe, where she might, at best, get a housekeeping job. Slave the rest of her life away in some vain hope of meeting a rich gentleman who would whisk her away to live happily ever after. What a fairy tale that was. She well appreciated what chances she had in a colony dominated by an over-supply of men. There were dreams, and then there was cold hard reality; one in which she knew she would not fare well.

It was an early close that day. Elizabeth liked to keep the post office open until five o'clock; in case any last-minute miners came down from the hills with something to post, maybe a late cutter coming down from the top of the island, Bluff even. They could spend hours battling the chop, and you never knew when they could turn up. But today, she had a desire to check up on something. A cruel wind had come up, and she wrapped her shawl around herself before locking up and crossing to the hotel. Autumn had been mild, but the approach of winter had brought a never-ending damp. Rain clouds swept through most days, the blustery south easterlies bringing a biting cold. How like Scotland it could be, just more extreme.

Going straight back to her room, Elizabeth double checked she'd locked the door. More than once, Peggy had barged in, wanting to know this or that. The woman couldn't stop poking her nose where it didn't belong. It was like everyone was fair game, maybe it was the Irish in her coming out, mused Elizabeth. Her father always used to go on about the Irish. The English he loathed, but the Irish he laughed about. "Always in poddle, lookin' aft' everyone's business not thy own." Elizabeth used to get annoyed with her father for talking about the Irish the way he did. He hardly knew any Irish people for a start. But the more she got to know Peggy, the more she began finding herself thinking just like her father.

She ferreted around for the key to her trunk in her purse, thinking how out of place the little handbag was down here now. She opened her trunk, the strong smell of camphor immediately rising to fill the room. She could only stare at the first thing she saw, her folded wedding dress on the top. "Oh, my Lord, how naive I have been," she mumbled to herself, lifting it out to lay on the bed. She went back to the trunk, lifting out the various layers, four everyday dresses, two fancy ones for 'occasions.' All her lace underwear, sown by her *piuthar*, singlets, woollen stockings, fine socks. Her psalm book and bible lay in there too, the sight of them reminding her she hadn't had much use for them since coming out. Could this misfortune have befallen her because of her lack of faith? She wondered. Maybe Port Pegasus was an ungodly place. The very reason no one had ever settled down here before. That trunk represented all her dreams, the dreams of a new life, dreams that had all been tucked away under lock and key. She had to set them free, but how? And more importantly, when? It was at that moment she felt as if someone grabbed her and was flinging her about. She put her head in her hands and began to sob.

She spent two hours locked away in her room. Twice Peggy had come calling, but she ignored her. When she finally emerged, her eyes were red and swollen, so she spent the first five minutes at the mirror above the outside wash basin, bathing her face in cold water. George had come by twice on his way to the storeroom, appearing to barely notice her. Finally, moving her face this way and that in the mirror, she deemed herself passable, retying her hair back as she went to join Peggy in the cookhouse.

"Here they are, four muttonbirds to cook tonight," Peggy wasted no time instructing. "Put them in the big pot and boil 'em for two hours. Like I said before, far too smelly to do inside sorry. I lit the fire outside already. I'll come out with a few potatoes to throw in later. I'm gonna do a piece of mutton, can't expect many of those gentlemen will like muttonbird, acquired taste after all."

"Whatever do they taste like?" Elizabeth inquired.

Peggy thrust the four little carcases at her, Elizabeth almost dropping one as she tried to hold them in her outstretched arms. Already, the two on top had fallen against the bodice of her dress, and she could smell the result.

"Fishy mutton, that's what they taste like," said Peggy, not looking up as she wiped off the bench. "Tell you the truth now, some people hate 'em, absolutely revolted by 'em, reckon they're far too strong. That's why we boil the hell outta 'em, get some of that strong taste away. I don't mind a bit of muttonbird myself, but not every day like."

"Oh, they're really quite small, why do they get them so young?"

"That's the whole point, they're sitting ducks in their burrows, all fluffy still, don't even have feathers, never so much as flapped their wings out in the open. All those birders got to do is reach down and pull 'em out and wring their necks. See, how they cut them; it pays to have them splayed out before you put them in. Makes 'em cook evenly."

Elizabeth clearly was not resolved about how and why the chicks were caught. "Oh, that's so cruel, the mother birds must kick up such a fuss."

"Nah, chicks get left all day while the parents go fishing. They come back at night to throw up whatever they have eaten. That's why the birds taste so strong and salty, they eat nothing but fish vomit. Tane told me all about it, he been doing it all his life, ever since he was a boy. Now look, stop asking so many questions and go cook 'em why don't ya? Otherwise, they won't be ready for when the men come in soon."

"What men? I haven't heard of no boat coming in."

"They're coming in over the top. Scollay mentioned it to me. George knew about, but he didn't bother telling anyone. That big-wig geologist from the government, what's his name…" Peggy paused to remember… "McKay… Alexander McKay, that's right. Bringing three of three other government men with him, walking all the way over from Big Glory Bay. They stayed somewhere up the tops last night, Old Dad talked to them when he was coming down off his lode, and he told Goodall who told Scollay who told me. Dunno what their business is exactly, but one thing is for sure, all the miners fairly excited about him being around." Peggy picked up the tea towel and flicked it at Elizabeth, "For God sakes, get those birds on the boil, will ya? You already stink like one from just holding them too long."

Elizabeth couldn't help staring at the little bodies in the pot as they finally came to the boil. Imagine if some monster suddenly reached into her post office and tore her out and wrung her neck before she even had a chance of knowing what was happening. Would it be like that frightful sea leopard coming into her little inlet and grabbing her with its huge fangs? If the good Lord had the power to work miracles, why didn't he stop all the suffering?

An excited commotion from the front of the hotel interrupted her thoughts. She could hear George, with some other men talking excitedly. "Peggy, fetch these good men a drink will you," George called out. Elizabeth strained to hear what they were saying. Louis Rodgers, she caught his name being mentioned, they were saying something about the owner of the hotel. Moving over to the door of the cookhouse, Elizabeth could see Peggy serving drinks from behind the bar, the men's backs to her. They looked bedraggled, not surprising considering how far they'd come through inhospitable country. One of the men stood out, not only in height, but his big mop of unkempt grey hair matched only by his overgrown beard protruding out both sides of his head. As he turned, Elizabeth noticed his wild untrimmed moustache drooping down to obscure his mouth. At first glance, she thought he was an old tramp, but the more she studied him, the more venerable and statelier he began to look. Elizabeth noticed the imposing man commanding the conversation, the other men all grouped around him, attentive to his every word.

"Please don't call it a track if you'd please..." she heard the big man say to George. "Far better from Big Glory to head straight for the tops. Besides, I wanted to appreciate the continuity of the landscape, the jumbled, broken country east of Anglem and the Deceit Peaks. Traversing the land is the key to understanding what is beneath, in a way one cannot realise by sailing here."

"Aye, the weather though, a man can be blown clean off the mountains," George replied. "I'm sure you all experienced the fury of the wind these last few days." The men all laughed and raised their glasses. "To survival!" roared McKay.

After a few sips more, the big-bearded man put down his glass and got up. Elizabeth could hear every word; no doubt Peggy was listening in too.

"Now, George, before I forget I have a letter for you from Louis Rodgers, he gave it to me in Invercargill, and said I must give it to you straight away. Please forgive me for not doing it earlier when we arrived. Overtaken by weary exhaustion my only excuse." Elizabeth moved closer, pretending to tidy up the bench closer to the door now. She watched the man go out and return a minute later with a white envelope.

"Why, thank you, sir," said George. "Personal delivery I see. And how is Mr Rodgers, did you speak with him much?"

"Yes, I did, at the provincial offices where he was finalising his liquor license. He looked in good spirits, rather pleased I gather that he seems to have satisfied the authorities of his fitness to hold his license. I think he should be granted it next week from what he told me. He has been biding his time wisely in Invercargill by all reports, just last week he filed a patent for a 'The Pegasus Tin Opener'." The bearded man became theatrical now, flourishing out his arms and putting on an exaggerated aristocratic voice. "For more rapidly opening all sorts of tinned meats, condiments, spices, or anything else used when tinned."

The men all erupted in laughter. Piped up one, "You have to give it to Rodgers, scheme a minute that man. He should have been a showman, like that tin-bum professor."

The men all raised their glasses in a toast of sorts before George excused himself, sitting down at one of the tables to open the letter. Elizabeth watched him reading it, noticing the furrow of his brow slowly deepening.

Peggy already had the attention of every other man in the room, expounding out loud. "So, fine gentlemen, no one is more deserving of a drink than all of you. Each and every one, coming through the interior like you have. So, what can I get you for a second round?"

Elizabeth sauntered around tidying up the kitchen, keeping one eye firmly on George as he finished the letter. As far as she knew that was the first communication George had had with Rodgers since she had arrived. Whatever was in that letter would surely affect her too. When she saw him fold it and look like he was about to get up, she moved quickly into the room. Acknowledging the men with a courteous bow of head as she passed, she started wiping down the long table where George was just getting up from. As he stood up to go, she moved quickly to position herself in front of him.

"Muttonbird tonight, I'm just cooking them now, out the back," she said matter of fact, smiling.

"You don't have to tell me; I can smell them. Tane must have come back, I never saw him. It always amazes me the way he can sneak into the hotel without me noticing. I hope you women are putting down all his drinks on his tab. Rodgers may tolerate him around, but I ain't got much time for him. Shouldn't have a ledger that's for sure."

Elizabeth moved slightly to block his way out, lowering her voice. "So, how is Mr Rodgers? I heard his name as that man handed you a letter."

George looked decidedly uncomfortable.

"He's coming back, week after next. Got his license. We'll be heading back to Invercargill Saturday week by the look of it."

Without so much as excusing himself, and avoiding her stare, George slid past her and left the room.

"Miss, what time is dinner?" One of the men with McKay piped up. Elizabeth didn't answer him, turning away to march back to the kitchen. She couldn't have spoken if she wanted to say something. She was dumbfounded, and damn angry too.

Chapter 13

Since coming back to Dunedin from Port Pegasus, Professor Black had found much adulation coming his way. Barely a day went past without some mention of him in the newspaper, and people were flocking in droves to hear his open public lectures. The man had proved himself a natural showman, and the admiring audience that now sat before him this evening proved it beyond any doubt. The university had not only forgiven him for his hurried departure and prolonged absence, but they had exonerated their esteemed professor of chemistry with the appointment of his own personal assistant, 'Wully' Gumbit, a scientifically inclined boffin described as calm and organised as the professor was impetuous and erratic.

The two worked perfectly together, quickly coming to a unique understanding of each other's purpose. To the amazement of them both, they found a special gift of communication, an intuitive one that barely required them to speak, anticipate each other's thoughts and movements. In the lab, they worked seamlessly together, like a well-oiled machine. Wully, well versed in laboratory work, quickly progressed to being an integral part of the professor's public lectures, where he assumed the subordinate role in what began to incorporate near slapstick routines. The two men became a natural comedy duo, and everybody loved their spontaneous acts. Every lecture was different, and entirely unrehearsed.

"Bring me a thousand gallons of sulphuric acid," the professor bellowed this evening to start his packed-out lecture. Wully immediately appeared from the wings to fetch him the small bottle of the stuff lying right under the professor's nose. Holding it aloft, like some magician in a circus, the professor would make an exaggerated show of pouring it in into his steaming cauldron to produce an explosion of billowing red smoke which enveloped not only his table, but Wully as well. As the smoke subsided to a haze, Wully was gone, disappeared completely. The professor would bellow for him again, facing where his assistant was last seen. But Wully would appear from the opposite side, carrying the very ingredient the professor now needed to complete his experiment. The crowd was not only reduced to laughter, but sheer wonder, for everything was explained in a revelatory way. This was not a chemistry show, but rather a divinely delivered lesson. The professor even delighted the audience with his ravings on the blackboard, filling every available blank space in a matter of minutes with his equations and symbols, shouting out his explanations as he went.

"Bring me forty thousand tons of chalk immediately!" he roared as soon as he'd filled the board. Wully promptly appeared carrying the smallest box of chalk and a duster. There was everything to like about the duo, but the professor shone as the lead actor. And so popular he had become in such a short time. His sheer passion for chemistry and geology were infectious, and he made sure that he imparted his wisdom in a way that made everyone appreciate not only himself, but how important his beloved science was to economic advancement in the colony. Anywhere he went, the faithful congregated, and he proved a top performer. Midway through the year 1890, the *Otago Daily Times* published its first list of influential go-getters of South Otago, undeniably the most go-ahead province in all the country. The extensive list included top business people, pastoralists, rising scholars, women's suffragette campaigners, journalists and politicians alike, everyone whose contribution was without reproach. But at the very top of the list was Professor John Gow Black of Otago University, second on the list being William Smith Fish, the controversial member of parliament for Dunedin South, a staunch opponent of women's suffrage and temperance advocate. Influential maybe, but few liked the staunch conservative, not like the professor who was adored by all. Above all, he had discovered the lodes of tin on Stewart Island that would soon make the province rich beyond measure.

His successful evening lecture over, the professor retired to the privacy of his office and bid his assistant goodbye. They were both exhausted, the showy lectures took it out of them both. They would tidy up tomorrow, but now the professor had something to examine, his third lot of samples, which had earlier that day arrived in the post from his two Cornish miners at Pegasus. As with the previous samples, their note with the latest samples succinctly advised of their progress, how far into the granite mountain they had tunnelled. "Seventeen-and-a-half fathoms in." Black was vaguely mused that the men still used the Cornish mine unit of measure, he quickly converting it on his pad—thirty-five yards. From his cursory inspection without a glass, he could tell they were still in the wolfram. A few hints of cassiterite for sure, mica and quartz too, but certainly not enough to get excited about. He took off his spectacles and rubbed his eyes. It was still early days. The next samples in two weeks' time would be more telling. He leaned back in his chair and let the glory of it all flood through him, remembering back to his six weeks camped atop the mountain, and what an eternity of ordeals that had proved to be. Twice his tent was blown away in the gales, ripped through by branches of leatherwoods. The first time it happened was at night, leaving him sleeping out with the wind raging all around him. Both times, it had taken him a full day to put back up again, get it tied down stronger than before. He imagined the great unexplored ice continent of Antarctica throwing all its wicked weather at him. At Pegasus, it was quite normal to experience all four seasons in one day. It could be fine and warm in the morning, then sleet and hail by afternoon, and snow on his tent by midnight. A warmish night could end with snow flurries and freezing by breakfast. When the sun came out or the wind died down, it could be delightful, but much of the time he spent near freezing to death. The professor reflected on his survival perched atop the lode. What had spurred him on to stay? Divine guidance and inspiration maybe? It didn't escape him that some great force was somehow conspiring to help him. But the knowledge he was sleeping on top of millions of pounds of ore surely helped also. He was going to be rich beyond all his dreams. No wonder he hadn't wanted to abandon that lode in a hurry. He closed his eyes, and as he snoozed off, he imagined looking down into the hold of a ship. It wasn't full of refrigerated sheep carcasses, the new export hope that everyone was suddenly hearing so much about. It was a far richer prize, pallets of meticulously stacked tin ingots, destined for all the Dominions of the British Empire. Slumped back in his chair, an immense feeling of satisfaction accompanied him as he fell into a deep sleep, pleased that his two miners were there, guarding the great treasure trove for him. Not only that, they were burrowing into it.

On that same day, those two miners on top of the mountain had also given thanks, not for the privilege of guarding the lode, which didn't occur to them, but because they weren't streamers, working out in the weather which had packed in again. Nineteen fathoms in, they were immune from its effect now. Cold yes, but they worked to keep warm, so what did temperature matter? Arthur pulled out his mining compass and inclinometer from its leather case and rechecked his bearing, 220 degrees exactly from the drop cut of the opening drift, exactly what he expected. He regarded himself as a good miner, and good miners didn't veer off course. But there was still something that concerned him. With the back of his hand, he smeared his sweat mixed with gritty black wolfram across his brow, and called out to his mate busy bogging out at the face. "When you finish loading that barrow, come take a look at this, will you?"

While he was waiting, Arthur felt along the ceiling fracture with one hand, holding up his candle with the other. Thank God, they weren't coal miners, having to worry about poisonous, explosive gases. Arthur had heard lots of coalminers were killed by explosive gas. Why they took canaries in cages down with them, 'cos the birds would do first.

Arthur's mate was alongside him now. "See this crack, I reckon it opened up since yesterday. We'll have to pitprop it here, otherwise we'll have a rockfall for sure. Still worries me we going in the wrong way as well, something just ain't right. Look here at these veins through here." Arthur ran his candle along a couple of yards before stopping at two glittering crevices forking across the ceiling. "I bet these are connected to the lode. It's running this way for sure, but we're going that way." He indicated along the drift before lowering the candle. "Second lot of samples I send out, I reckon we should ask the professor."

"I say don't bother," said Branock. "He thinks he's smarter than us, and maybe he is. Maybe he knows something we don't. We just miners after all." The man turned away chuckling to himself, then changed the subject. "Know what we should do? Boil the billy, that's what. Let me just spall up dump this barrow. Oh, for a pit pony, eh?"

"We got one," quipped Arthur, "it's you!"

"Aye, that's true!" laughed Branock. "Wouldn't mind couple more legs then. And some decent iron shoes, this granite sure slices through India rubber soles." The wind swirled around the portal and the daylight near blinded him as he pushed out yet another barrowload. The mullock was already 15 fathoms long, and Branock put in the effort to dump his barrow at the far end. The men had worked out that if they went in a hundred fathoms, they'd have two mullocks each the size of a good house on either side of the portal. The last thing they needed was to box themselves in. If everything went according to plan, a tramway would eventually be built to take out the tin ore, but until then they needed to be mindful of future access, not to mention dewatering. Every heavy rainfall left the ceiling dripping with water, so much so that they had to take their tea breaks crouched under their oilskins, which was marginally better than retreating outside where even getting a fire going under a billy in the extreme conditions was well-nigh impossible. That mine dug with their hard labour was their haven, as much as it was their hell.

It was on their fifty-third day of work into the mine that Arthur heard the voice echo along the drift.

"Yo! Wasson by bal, then?"

He stopped hammering his rock drill into the granite and put his hand up to Branock who was still shovelling. "Cheu chaunter! Another Cornish miner we have on the field, go and bring him by bal then."

Syd introduced himself to Branock at the portal, a hearty handshake establishing their Cornish connection. "Come by bal then, out of this wretched weather, wouldn't be saying to any incomer, we've had a few geeks come nosing, but we deal to 'em out 'er. So, where your family bal then?" Branock had already turned and was leading Syd down the drift.

"My father, he be bal dresser at Gwennap, where I grew up. Later, he became despatch captain at South Caraden, Great Consol too."

"Ah, Grand Consol, that's where my mate here worked." Branock raised him voice. "Arthur! this man's father despatched at Grand Consol."

Syd side-stepped the big wheelbarrow on his way to the man now waiting for him at the face. "'Tis pleasure indeed to meet you down bal," said Arthur, extending his hand to give Syd a hearty shake. Two candles in spiked holders driven into the wall at face height provided enough glow for Syd to make out Arthur's face covered in sweat and greasy grit. "Don't ya tell me now, your father wasn't Alwyn Braithwaite, surely not?"

"Aye, that's him."

"Well, here's to a great tin miner. Never favoured the lode master, always stuck up for the miners. Branock! Put that billy on will ya, now? It's time for a break. Wouldn't stop for everyone, ya know."

Little tongues of flame were soon caressing the underneath of the billy positioned on the floor, hard against the wall, a plume of smoke creeping up and spreading back out along the ceiling. The three crouched down to get out of the smoke as it became lower.

"So, what brought you here?" Syd asked the two men.

"You probably heard the writing on wall for Grand Consol. They weren't even renewing their lode contracts. No future, we could've got work at bal near Devon either. But then we heard about the gold at Bendigo, so we both quit and took off to Australia." Branock stopped talking as he attended to the billy, slipping a few dry twigs under it to hasten the boiling. "Only got two mugs, you'll have to share mine."

Arthur took over the story. "We ended up in Bendigo. But we were too late, all the best ground was taken. Never forget one night there though, soon after we got there, a huge storm came through, raged all night." Branock tapped the side of the billy with his pipe to let the tea leaves mash. Arthur let him finish before he continued.

"Morning once at Bendigo, we woke up to all these trees blown over, and there be gold nuggets all caught up in the roots. No one could believe it. It was a sight to see, hundreds of men, women and children, all dry panning the ground and hefting over cradles as quick as they could. I still got a few of the shiners in my skite tin."

The men laughed as Branock handed out the two cups of billy tea. "You go first, I'll have mine when you finish," he said to Syd, still reflecting on the story.

"Ha, if only it were that easy, eh," Syd commented. The conversation stopped as they sipped their tea. Syd reflected on how silent a mine can be, all the noises of the outside world silenced. It was Arthur who finally spoke again. "Aye, then, so what you know about another mine starting up, down by Diprose, is that right we heard?"

"Yes, Pegasus Mining Company, they call themselves. I haven't been to see it, but Tucker says he's been there. Told me they only just started, barely in past the drop cut, maybe four fathoms, that was last week. Hear they're expecting tough going, the granite is much harder down there than up here I hear."

The men talked for another quarter of an hour, their subjects flitting from one mining thing to the next, until Syd felt he had interrupted them enough.

"Only come up to say yo. I know you're both on contract, so I shall leave you to your work. You always welcome to come see my claim anytime. Goodbye and good luck with the digging." Branock followed Syd out, pushing his full barrow.

"Bring a pit pony next time, will ya?" Branock yelled his last words of farewell into the wind as Syd headed back around the mullock to begin his sidle down the mountain. Half turning to give a last wave, he carried on for only another two hundred yards before something caught his eye, causing him to come to an abrupt halt. Turning around, he just stared at it, the vein of gritty quartz running back up to the trig. He crouched down to touch it, fingering the gritty crystalline vein weaving up the slope. Then he walked up and down it, scratching his head as he established its direction. Looking over to where he had come out of the mine portal, he visualised the bearing of the adit and stretched out one arm parallel to that. Then he held out his other arm to indicate the direction of the vein. Syd stood like that for a good few minutes, just holding the position. Something was seriously not right. Those men were digging in the wrong way! These thoughts made Syd stay in the vicinity for more than half an hour, walking around in circles, examining all the other exposed veins in the rock that he could find amongst the windblown scrub. But there could be no mistaking the direction of the lode. He wondered about going back, telling the two miners that they could be making a huge mistake. But he thought better of the idea, they were both far more older and experienced than he, for a start. Knowing what direction to mine into a lode was one of the first things his father taught him. Every miner in Cornwall grew up appreciating that the drift went in against the lode, not with it. You had to cross it, hit it head on, otherwise there was a complete chance of missing it. Only then could you mine out to each side.

The wind had come up while Syd loitered, and it was howling by the time he made his way again. Even some of the lowest lying plants were flung about so much, he could imagine them all breaking off or even pulled out by their roots to be scattered down the mountain. Surely, nothing was meant to live up here, he thought to himself as he got more down out of the blasting wind. By the time he hit the relative shelter of the bush line, all thoughts of the mine were gone, and he was now completely taken up with Elizabeth again. The mail boat was coming in on Tuesday and he had written two more shareholder letters which needed to be posted. There could even be a letter from his father; it was a while since he'd received one. Who knows; one of the prospective shareholders may have changed their minds with rumours of the big consignment. He had sent out nine shareholder invitations, and only three had replied. He needed to get a few stores—a small sack of rolled oats, some flour, wax matches, he was nearly out. Some tins of bully beef would be welcome as well. He was sick of kiwi, having made two last three meals in the past week alone. A man cannot live on kiwi alone, and if he ever left this field, he had promised himself he would never eat another kiwi again as long as he lived. As he came onto his claim, Syd felt a joy fill his heart. And that joy came from the real reason that he was going down to the hotel in two days' time. He was going to present the brooch he'd made to Elizabeth. And tonight, in his tent, he was going to work out exactly what to say to her when he did. But first, he had some serious work to do, and that was shifting his riffle box down the tailrace. He was opening a new patch of ground, his latest prospect pit had been encouraging, not to mention catching him another kiwi. Maybe all his luck would come together all at once he thought. He had never felt happier to be a miner.

Chapter 14

Peggy hadn't had time to read the ballad penned by George Swain which he'd pinned to the wall the previous night. The great veteran of the Pegasus field had come down the mountain later in the evening after McKay and his colleagues had turned up at the hotel, joining them for drinks after their dinner of muttonbird and lamb. As the evening wore on, the men got rowdier, four other miners and two other guests joining the festivities as well, which lasted until well after midnight. Peggy had never served so much whisky, rum, and ale, at least a dozen bottles of hard liquor along with four crocks of ale she'd thrown over the bank that next morning. She'd noticed how the men separated into various groups as the evening progressed. wore on. The men who came with McKay had the most riotous time—not surprising after several days of deprivation along the tops. But the Pegasus streamers ended up in a huddle with McKay. He seemed to be asking them lots of questions, ones that made them pause and scratch their heads. More than once she'd noticed McKay pulling out a notebook from his waistcoat pocket to jot down what they were saying. Everything about the man showed serious investigative intent. Peggy knew she was nosey, but she recognised she was nothing compared to this man when it came to poking around for information. At the end of the previous evening, he'd even enquired of her if the hotel kept a 'gold book,' recording what miners brought in, to trade for supplies, drink, food or accommodation. Every store in every goldfield in the country was required to record such transactions, but since the field had converted to tin, there hadn't been any gold transactions. Rummaging around under the bar, she had finally located the dusty book which he opened to reveal only 15 transactions, all before June 1889. McKay had been interested enough in all those early one to write them all down. There was nothing this man was going to miss, thought Peggy as she packed everything away for the night. In bed, she lay awake, and that's when she remembered she'd forgotten to read the ballad penned by George Swain late in the evening. Quite a commotion had ensued when he got up on a chair to read it out aloud, then everyone in the room had fallen silent. She had tried to listen from behind the bar but was distracted by the urgent need to restock the bar. Considering there was only about 15 people in the room, she had been amazed at the applause when Swain finished reading it out.

The men had left earlier that morning, George farewelling McKay as he led his party away, all hefting heavy packs. His intention was to visit every resident claimholder. It was the measure of the man that his geology reports were regarded as gospel, such was the thoroughness of his field investigations. Swain had left also, leaving behind his ballad pinned to the wall. Now squinting, she was able to read it. Her eyes didn't seem as sharp as they used to be. Working under dim lamps and living above 47 degrees latitude meant it was getting dark by four thirty in the winter, which meant she worked under the steady flicker of dim whale oil lamps for a good part of the day.

Finally, focusing on the words, Peggy began humming the ballad as she thought it might go to music.

My clothes they are torn, my boots they are gone.
No gold we shall get anymore.
When I sit down and think what I've spent on drink,
Then I feel I deserve to be poor.

Let us throw away grief, we have faith in the reef,
And thoughts of it make us smile.
For no one can tell, a short time from this,
We'll be knocking about with a pile.

How true, thought Peggy, pinning it back up on the wall. Just the other day she'd commented to George that she was still waiting for a miner to come in saying he'd struck it rich. Fools and their dreams.

She glimpsed Elizabeth through the open door, passing through the cookhouse, on her way to the washroom. Peggy positioned herself by the stacked wooden crates near the door, making out she was sorting through more empties, a lioness positioning herself before pouncing on its unsuspecting prey. Peggy had found very early on in her life that the direct approach worked wonders in nearly every situation, the element of surprise even more advantageous when it came to soliciting confessions and disclosures. It didn't give them time to think, and her tried and true tactic was about to work perfectly this time around too.

Elizabeth nearly jumped out of her skin as Peggy leant out the door just as she passed, dispensing with any small talk.

"So, what happened last night? After you talked to George, you didn't hang around, couldn't help noticing. You left me with four stinkin' greasy muttonbirds to finish off and serve up. Not very pleasant, Lizzie, serving grog; I was smelling like fish-vomit." She flicked her hand out towards her, "Ah, don't worry, forgiven ya already." Peggy folded her arms as she stepped down to get closer to her prey. "Tell me though, what was in that letter from Rodgers? You asked George about it, didn't ya? I saw you purposely go out to wipe that table so you could ask him. So, what did you find out? Rodgers is my boss too. I wanna know, Lizzie!" Peggy kept her unblinking stare focused on her hapless victim.

Elizabeth felt the hot flush of alarm sudden ambush flood through her body. There was no avoiding Peggy on this one. "Rodgers is coming back, Saturday week…"

"And…so what did George reckon about that?"

"He said he and I are going back to Invercargill on the *Despatch* a couple days later."

"Well, it had to happen, I suppose that was the plan all along. Have you got any choice?"

Elizabeth stood tall, both hands on her hips now, and shouted, "I'm not going! Well, not with him anyway."

"Ah, Lizzie, watch yourself now. Might not bode well for a lassie like you, going off by yourself just yet. You could ask Rodgers to employ you awhile, help out for lodgings at least. I'll miss having another woman around if you go. I suggest you start by writing that letter to Rodgers tonight and make sure it goes on the first boat. But you'll have to tell George; you can't go behind his back on this one, you know Rodgers and him are like this." Peggy held up her two fingers, one of which was tightly twisted around the other.

Elizabeth spent the rest of her working day pondering her options. She could leave on the next boat for Invercargill and take her chances, but apart from availing herself of the good folk at the Presbyterian mission there, she knew she would be on her own in a town she barely knew. She could stay on at Pegasus, like Peggy suggested, but that would require the goodwill of Mr Rodgers, as the owner.

For the rest of her working day in the post office, she pondered her position. The more she thought about it, the more overwhelmed she became. In desperation, she drafted several letters, each time screwing them up to put on the fire in the bar later. In the end, she gave up and slipped the notepad away. The next boat wasn't coming for three days, so she had time to think more about it. "Never rush into big decisions," she remembered her father's wise advice.

Several miners came in to do their postings that day, all of them mentioning McKay's inspection of the field. The news of his arrival had ricocheted around the workings, not surprising, considering he was the most senior government official ever to visit, their chief geologist at that.

The first miner to arrive had been Thomas Cross, his claim being not far just up Pegasus Creek. Elizabeth had heard him talking to George in the hotel before he came into the post office clutching a handful of muttonbird-leaf postcards which he'd probably gone into the hotel to write at a table. He had probably spent all morning walking over to the hotel thinking about what he was going to write to everyone, picking the biggest leaves he could find along the way. A couple of them were twice the size of her hand, the largest she had ever seen. The man was full of McKay's visit, and wouldn't talk about anything else.

"I'm sure, he'll see all the riches that lie under the ground, the government will applaud us all for sticking it out here. You'll be the busiest postmistress in the province, mark my words." Elizabeth listened, stamping his leaf missives, managing half a smile as he left, wondering if her face betrayed the desperation she was feeling inside.

The second miner to come in, Robert McLeod from up McArthurs Creek, was one she had never met before. Even through his wispy beard, she could tell he was toothless, the gummy way he spoke. "May as well be a royal tour," he lisped lyrical about McKay's visit. "Least he'll be promoting the place. Mere fact that the government sent him here speaks volumes. We'll be shipping out tin ore next, you watch, lassie." As the man spoke, it dawned on Elizabeth how gaunt the man was, his trousers were held up with a frayed length of twine because he didn't have any hips to hang trousers on. She managed a distracted smile to him also as he bade goodbye and was about to lock up early for the day when Tucker arrived.

"Good afternoon, Miss. Just checking to see if there's any mail for me?"

"Yes, there is, two here for you," she said pulling them out of her rack. She could tell straight away he was going to be hard to get rid of, loitering intent oozed from him like sweat from a labourer on a hot day.

"McKay and his government cronies will be finished along Pegasus Creek tomorrow, then he'll be taking them down the south branch of McArthurs to check out the claims there. First Syd's, then mine."

Elizabeth's ears picked up now, and she visibly relaxed back in her chair.

"I'm sure he will be impressed with all the work you gentlemen have done in pursuit of the stream tin. So, Syd, is he all prepared for the visit?"

"Nope. Doesn't even know it's coming yet. I just learnt from Bill Cutten on my way down here. He wants me to tell Syd tonight after I head back up. I better make sure he knows too, because he told me he had something to do down here tomorrow. Can't let him miss McKay, can I now?"

Elizabeth's heart skipped a beat. Syd had been planning to come down to the hotel again. And if he couldn't come down tomorrow, he likely would the following day. Her desperation suddenly gave way to a glimmer of hope. Her smile was genuine this time.

"Why, thank you, Mr Tucker. It's been a real pleasure seeing you in Port Pegasus Post Office today. I hope to see you again soon."

As soon as Tucker left, she tidied her desk and locked up the post office. Her letter to Rodgers could wait a day or so; she had one of her fancy dresses to choose first.

Chapter 15

Alexander McKay could see that trudging through three claims in a row had taken it out of his three colleagues. Just about to turn 50, he was still waiting to find field companions who could keep up with him. Waiting for them to catch up, he climbed on top of a protruding slab of granite to survey the catchment they had just come walked up. Wisps of snowy white mist shrouded the hills, contrasting with the blackened patches of recent burn offs, one of which was still smouldering. A sudden rainstorm an hour earlier had come as a surprise, it was so localised, as if the clouds had diligently assembled over them, concentrating all their heavenly fullness to dump every drop they possibly could over them. It was like walking through a continuous waterfall and it left them completely drenched. The quiet roar of the river far below was testament to how much water had just fallen from the skies. McKay couldn't help thinking, even drenched how at home he felt here, the valley surrounding Pegasus Creek looked surprisingly like Carsphairn in Kirkcudbrightshire, Scotland, where he had been born and bred.

The product of good Calvinist shepherd stock, his father, William Sloane McKay, was his home-born town's wheelwright. He'd married Agnes MacClennan from just down the lane, the couple bringing up their eldest son to be an essential help in the family business. From the age of 11, they only let him attend school in winter, when their business was at its slowest, and in summer, they got him a job as a cowherd, sending him into the rocky hills to earn extra pennies for the family by helping local farmers. In a land without fences, it was his job to follow the cows around, pushing them back every so often to where they belonged. At first, this job proved exceedingly boring for the lad, but then something extraordinary happened. Without any prompting, young McKay began to notice the differences which existed between the outcrops of rocks. And in time, he began connecting them all together in his head, imagining how the sequences and strata made them flow in and out of the earth. Questioning passing miners, the lad found out the names of all the different rocks, then the minerals that they were comprised of, even their raw value when dug out of the earth. While the cows chewed their cud along the hillsides, he spent hours running his hands over the outcrops, feeling them, picking up rocks and examining them in detail, breaking them up to take home. His little sleeping loft became so littered with rocks; his mother feared it might collapse under the weight. Finally, his father ordered him to throw them all out, but the lad didn't care; there were plenty more rocks to find and bring home. Geology became his passion, and it was entirely self-taught.

McKay also found out exactly what a miner's life entailed, when aged 22, he emigrated out to New Zealand on the *Helenslee,* arriving in Bluff, then called Campbelltown, in 1863. He spent the next few years goldmining, first in the Otago Fields, then the Wakamarina diggings in Marlborough. After that, he headed over to New South Wales and Queensland where he went from diggings to diggings, following the overrated prospects. Returning to New Zealand, he spent four years wandering the remote south-west McKenzie Country, always alone and in all seasons. It was out in this lonesome land that McKay's path one day crossed with that of Julius Haast, the Canterbury provincial geologist. When they met again in the Ashley Gorge, while McKay was prospecting for coal, the esteemed geologist was so impressed with the young man's innate and entirely unacademic knowledge of geological matters that he hired him on the spot as his assistant. Together they had gone off to map Shag Point coalfield in North Otago, then went collecting reptilian fossils around the Waipara River. Under Haast's direction, he excavated and catalogued Moa-bone filled Point Cave at Sumner. Alexander McKay easily became Haast's uncontested second-in-command, until their very public falling out, that was.

Standing on his granite slab, McKay looked at his surveyor's map. By his reckoning, they should soon be able to soon drop down into the headwaters of the south branch of McArthurs Creek, hopefully into the claim of Syd Braithwaite. After lunch, they would start again there, then work their way back down in the afternoon, ending up at the old surveyor's camp where they would set up their tent for the night.

McKay was the first to make the saddle, where he stopped to admire the expansiveness of the field. And what a sight! To the south west were the naked granite domes and monoliths of the Fraser Peaks rising out of the bleak and barren moorland. Although partially cloud-draped, two peaks still stood out in all their magnificence: Gog and Magog. The men had first glimpsed them while walking in along the tops, and that initial sighting took their breath away.

Impressive country for sure, but was it a payable field? It was no wonder the government had sent him here, McKay thought. That professor in Dunedin was whipping up hysteria, and it was starting to cause the government some embarrassment that they weren't supporting the tin miners enough. Apart from a muddy surveyor's track up to a wooden trig, no capital works had been expended. No wonder, they wanted the report as soon as he got back. Ever since the public spat with his mentor, Julius von Haast, back in 1872, McKay had strived to free the country's earth sciences from the stuffy and staid strictures of European 'received wisdoms'. And it was here that McKay suspected he was about to debunk yet another academic, that man being Professor John Gow Black of Otago University. They would visit his mine in two days' time, and he was sure it would be revealing.

McKay waited for his charges to catch up again, then cleared his throat. There was little time to loiter, and he spoke briskly.

"So, gentlemen, taking in the limited number of claims we have inspected this morning, I would be interested in your first impressions."

The pompous representative from the Provincial Council answered first. "I would say exceedingly promising so far. All the miners we saw this morning reported good finds to date and appear to be most enthusiastically motivated."

"Aye, Aye," said the second. "They are all putting in the hard yards, surely it would be hard to fail with such determination and prospects."

"I agree," piped up the third. "Some capital works, maybe a dam and a tramway, certainly a wharf, and there would be no stopping them…"

"Look, over there!" his colleague suddenly interrupted, pointing upwards. Coming towards them was a flock of hundreds of bush parrots. The collective fluttering of their wings and raucous squawking became louder and louder until they were directly overhead, then receded again as the men turned to watch them disappear into the distance. A most splendid sight indeed, thought McKay, waiting until the spectacle was just a smudge on the far horizon before he spoke again.

"Once on D'urville Island, I witnessed a flock of maybe five thousand kaka flying over from the mainland to feast on kohekohe flowers, something I will never forget. Already they say the flocks are diminishing, no more food for them with all the burn offs and milling of the kohekohe I suspect. Such a shame. Our grandchildren, maybe even our children, will surely never know such a sight." He turned back around, summoning his charges back to attention.

"In all my experience you could never find a more decent, hardworking bunch of men than miners. I'm sure you will agree with me there." He waited for the men to utter their agreeance. "I would also like to assure you that supreme optimism is also another of their most prominent attributes, in sufficient proportions to distort the actual reality of their situation. Every claimholder on these workings has invested considerable money and toil, which makes them, each in varying degrees, blind to the truth. Now see down here…" McKay took one step forward to point down into the head of the Pegasus. "That last claimholder told us he was working up through far richer ground than when he started. But I saw a working face no deeper than one foot six inches at most, indicating little more than a smattering of stream tin. I would estimate less than half an ounce in every washing. I ignore everything a miner tells me about their prospects, it is usually nothing more than the product of their hopeful delusions. I look only for the truth, and I suggest you gentlemen do too from this point onwards."

"But surely, they impart information on their workings that has some bearing on the truth?"

"That is certainly true, but only in so far as finding out their effort to date, as it compares to their potential earnings. A well-worked claim does not immediately denote success, all it implies is a load of effort, nothing more. You must remember here that these are surficial placer deposits, formed by the mechanical concentration of mineral particles from weathered debris. This is nothing like the rich deep alluvial goldfields of Central Otago which extend down into the deeper gravels. Understanding the geology of the land lets us paint a far truer picture than what any diggers can tell us." McKay let his sobering words sink in. "Let us proceed now, gentlemen, we have at least three more claims to inspect this afternoon."

Syd had spent the morning rushing around, getting his claim half presentable, using his shovel to throw some gravel on a few of the softer parts of his access track. Tucker had certainly surprised him the previous evening when he'd come around to inform him of the impending 'inspection' by McKay and his party the following day. Syd had intended to walk down to the hotel at first light, to arrive when Elizabeth opened the post office around nine o'clock, and he'd felt disappointed that now he'd be lucky to get down before she shut up at the end of the day. Reminding himself that a visit from the government's top geologist and his cronies was not an everyday affair, he set about to work early. On his way up to his headrace, he noticed the cat was back, padded paw prints criss-crossing over an open section of half-dried mud. Almost a pet, he mused to himself, even if he only hadn't actually sighted the feral animal yet.

His first job was to roll back the big rock blocking the intake to his headrace before hefting the big log obliquely across the stream to divert the water. He watched with immense satisfaction as the water surged down the concisely cut channel to spread out over his freshly dug scarp. For the next three solid hours, Syd worked the face, picking consistently away at it, working one way, then the other, effectively double digging up into a wide face. As the grit and gravel dislodged, Syd picked up the larger rocks and stacked them into his new tailing which ran herring-bone to his last, the Cornish way. Syd still called them leats, Cornish miner's talk.

He had hoped his wash-up would be over by the time McKay turned up, but they came down earlier than he expected, just after he had closed off the water to retrieve his riffle plates.

Syd heard them coming down the track before he saw them. Carefully, he finished pouring the fine mix from his riffle box into his pan before standing up.

"Ahoy, there!" the man in front hailed from the other side of the creek. The sight of the chaotic looking man with a wild mop of hair and bushy beard took Syd slightly aback, not what he expected of someone from the government.

The introductions were minimal, McKay getting straight into it.

"So, gentlemen, we have come at exactly the right time. Now, Mr Braithwaite, would you please take us through your wash-up from emptying the riffle into the pan?"

The men gathered as Syd crouched down in the side flow of the creek, transferring the contents his riffles into his big pan and immersing it into the water before lifting it back out again. Rocking it forward and back in a continuous motion, a few of the coarser stones began falling out over the lip.

McKay kept up his running commentary. "That pan is not light, maybe 40 pounds to start with, a man needs a good back to keep this type of motion up in front of him like that. This man is young, so he has a few more years of streaming out in front of him before backache forces him to give it up."

Like hell, thought Syd, he felt more on the edge of riches. Surely, soon he would fall off into them.

McKay continued, "The stones and gravel and grit with lowest specific gravity quickly work to the top, it being the panner's job to coax them over the edge. In New South Wales where I prospected, they had a saying, 'mothers and miners must both learn to rock the cradle.' Let us be thankful, gentlemen, we have water in this bounteous country, which enables men like Mr Braithwaite here to become expert at panning and not cradling. There is no more dustier pursuit."

After five minutes of non-stop panning, the contents of Syds pan had reduced more than half.

"Now, we are coming closer to the moment of reckoning. If you could just stop now, Mr Braithwaite. May I ask you, roughly speaking, how much stream tin would you estimate is in that pan right now?"

Syd stopped to look up at McKay. "I'd say maybe a good pound, more or less. Still got some more panning to do of course, spill the dross."

"If we were in Cornwall; I'd say your estimate would be fairly bang on. But here where the tin is sparser, I am cautious of your estimate. If you would be so kind as to let me take a thimbleful of the wash, please." McKay stooped down to dip two fingers into the sludge, same time slipping his other hand into his pocket for his magnifying eyeglass. "Hold out a hand, gentlemen, I'll smear a bit on each and pass round this glass. Tell me what you see."

Syd resumed washing while the men took it in turns to peer at the sample of sand smeared onto their hands.

"I clearly see tin crystals," said one of the men.

"I see them too, but there's another mineral in here too," exclaimed the second.

The third man took his time before giving his verdict. "I see stream tin, and wolfram, they're both in there."

"Bang on! You are correct, exactly!" McKay slapped the man on the shoulder and began talking excitedly. "To the unaided eye, the two ores are near identical in appearance. The problem for a miner is that these two minerals have near identical specific gravity. This makes them impossible to separately pan out. Not one is favoured to rise to the surface. Panning only serves to better mix them up. Not a desirable situation."

McKay turned his attention back to Syd. "Please, carry on panning, young man, we are interested to see your final result."

The men watched as Syd rocked his pan back and forth at the side of the stream, the discoloured water spilling over gradually becoming clearer. Syd finally stood up with his bounty, a few handfuls of dark sand in the pan.

McKay was his usual blunt self. “A whole morning on the sluice paddock, and here is this man’s reward, maybe two pounds of placer deposit in his pan. My estimate would be around half is stream tin, cassiterite, the rest wolfram. I suspect one day this wolfram may be worth well in excess of what tin is now, but that won’t be until the twentieth century, at least ten years away, probably fifteen. Currently, smelting this tin off is problematical, and far too expensive.”

Syd couldn’t quite believe his ears, he felt like he had just participated in a school science experiment, he the unwitting subject who was fast failing. What about the professor in Dunedin? He said the place was rich with tin. All the stories in the paper even said so.

‘I would like to thank you, Mr Braithwaite,” McKay rounded off. “You have been most helpful, and I am sure that I speak for all here to wish you the very best.”

The men expressed their agreeance, shaking Syd’s hand in turn. He watched them go in single file behind McKay until they were out of sight. On any other day, he would have surely ruminated on what the great geologist had uttered in the creek. He felt the tinge of embarrassment, the type that comes from being caught out. It was a lesson for him, and not a very flattering one at that.

But today, he didn’t care; it could wait. Putting down his pan, he stripped off and walked naked up the side of his head race to the small sun dappled pool where he always bathed. On his way, he diverted to pick three or four *kumerahou* leaves as he went. He felt the cold stinging his body as he lay down and let the bitingly cold water submerge him, gasping for some fine gravel to rub over himself, abrasively scraping the worst of his sweat off before sitting up to palm the waxy leaves into a lather which he rubbed under his armpits. There was no time to waste if he was going to get down to the hotel before the post office closed. Picking up his pan under one arm and his muddy clothes in the other, he hurried back to his tent, not bothering to empty his pan into his tin, just throwing it into the corner. Quickly he dressed in his good clothes, feeling them soak up the excess moisture still on his body. ‘Best way to dry wet clothes, wear ’em,’ had always been Tucker’s advice. The last thing he did was get the tin brooch wrapped up in a bit of bandage he cut off, making sure it was safely stashed in his shirt pocket. He had an urgent delivery, and he set off without delay.

Chapter 16

In quiet and hopeful anticipation, Elizabeth had waited all afternoon for Syd to turn up. Peggy had commented about her dress, and she was bound to connect the dress with Syd's arrival, but for now, the barmaid didn't suspect he was going to turn up. Half of her was happy pretending nothing was happening; the other half was stricken with a slurry of excitement and anxiety. She still hadn't spoken to George or penned her letter to Mr Rodgers. She wanted to see Syd first, exactly why she didn't even want to ask herself. It just felt important to her.

If it hadn't been a visit from Tane, the morning would have surely dragged on. Peggy had brought him to the post office, the dark-skinned Maori man Elizabeth had only ever spied from across the other side of the hotel. He seemed to turn up irregularly, at the strangest times, and now he was standing outside.

"This is Tane," said Peggy, poking her head through the door. She smiled back at the man she was introducing. "Sorry, I still don't know your surname. Tane, meet Miss MacDonald, I call her Lizzie, I'm sure she wouldn't mind you calling her that either. Tane has a leaf postcard for you to stamp. Needs to go to his half folks back on Ruapuke Island."

"Why, come in, Tane," said Elizabeth, standing up to usher him in. Before he had even sat down in the chair, Peggy turned to go back to the hotel, muttering something about having a pot on the boil. The little man stepped lithely into post office with a broad smile, taking off his ragged hat to reveal grey hair that matched his short-cropped beard. Elizabeth surmised he was about 40, maybe a little older. Despite his worn clothes, which were in great need of darning, he struck her as exuding a most venerable air. Tane sat down in the spare chair and leaned forward to slide his leaf postcard across the desk with a half penny coin. He watched her as she wet the stamp over her roller and affixed it to the outside of the leaf. Only then did she notice that the postcard was addressed only to 'Ruapuke Island.'

"Is there a person who you are sending this to?" She enquired. "It may be best for you to put his or her name at the top, here." She used her pencil to indicate where.

At first the man looked blankly at her as though he did not understand; it suddenly occurring to her that this man was the first native she had spoken to since arriving in New Zealand. Is this what they were all like, she wondered to herself.

Suddenly, the man spoke, clearly and with a fluently that surprised her.

"The letter is not to one person. It is to my whole *whanau.*"

"Your *whanau*?" Elizabeth tilted her head in puzzlement, frowning over the unfamiliar word.

The man looked at her briefly before replying. "My family. No one else but my *whanau* live on Ruapuke, apart from Reverend Wohler and his wife Eliza. They won't be interested in reading it. It will be delivered to the person who needs to read it."

Elizabeth was perplexed. She imagined the postcard being delivered to Ruapuke Island, the postman not knowing who to give the card to. She wondered about turning the leaf over to read what the message was, to give her some steer on the matter, but the rule in the Rule Book came back to her. 'Article 5 Section D: On no account should a trusted employee of the New Zealand Post Office purposely read any mail addressed to a person other than themselves, nor should they indicate that they know the contents of any mail item, without first getting the permission of the sender to do so.'

"So, is Ruapuke your home?" It was all Elizabeth could think of asking.

"Yes, one of the ancestral homes of my ancestors. I spend half the year gathering *kai.*" The man sensed the postmistress did not understand. "Lucky, I am more fluent in English than you are in Maori," the man added with a grin. "*Kai*, food, we can only survive by harvesting kai from around the island. If it wasn't for the *titi* we would starve."

"Who is this Reverend Wohler? Why does he live amongst you, surely, he also stays in Bluff or Invercargill, at least the Neck at the top of the island where most of the European settlers live?"

Tane shook his head. "He has been on our island for 40 years now. Chief Te Tuhawaiki invited him there, to teach my people the ways of the bible."

"Oh, my goodness, a true missionary. Where did Reverend Wohler come from then?"

"He came from Germany. We have the bell from his town in our church on Ruapuke. It rings out to call us to service. Reverend Wohler told us all about it, the North German Missionary Society sent it to us. Our church has a steeple." Tane brought the tips of his upright fingers together. "When it rings, we all come together for prayer."

"Then, you indeed are a true Christian," pronounced Elizabeth, a warmth rising in her heart for the man. She thought back to all the comments the men made about Maori folk, about Tane in particular, and how wrong they all were. Here was a true believer, who impressed with his simple honesty and piety of purpose. Not once did he mention striking it rich or sluicing or minerals. The most important thing to him seemed only to provide food for his extended family. Up until a few minutes ago, she had only ever spied him in the distance. But after the exchange of words with him just now, she knew in her heart he was a good man.

She had one last question for him. "Pray tell me, sir, your English, it is so good. Who taught you?"

Tane smiled as he spoke, obviously pleased that she had noticed. "Reverend Wohler opened a native school on Ruapuke. My ancestors on my mother's side go back to the Waitaha tribe. They were peaceful, wanderers, foragers, but they were taken over. Some were wiped out, some taken prisoner, some even marrying into the new tribe, like my mother's ancestor did. Now, I am a mixture of tribes, and I carry the knowledge of many tribes. Every day on Ruapuke, we learnt English words. When Eliza arrived after marrying Reverend Wohler, we were surprised she could speak our language fluently. She always said we needed to share our words. It was her that made it easy for us."

Tane stood up to go, his goodbye most gracious. Only when she saw that he was going up the path back to the hotel, she turned over the leaf card to read his printed message.

I te huaraki ki a koe whitu poha titi.

Tane.

Elizabeth peered for several minutes at the words. Titi, the word he mentioned before, she had heard Peggy say that word, referring to the muttonbirds, and the islands where they came from. But beyond that the message was gobbledygook to her, and she stamped the card before slipping the card into her mail bag ready for the boat tomorrow. It made her remember the dreaded letter to Mr Rodgers which she was putting off. And talking to George too, she knew that time would have to come.

No one came in for the next three hours, and she busied herself tidying up her little post office, wiping down all the surfaces, finding herself drifting in and out of thinking about Syd. Perhaps, he wasn't coming down after all. Maybe McKay had waylaid him. A visit from the government geologist most important after all. If not today, tomorrow morning then, Syd would surely arrive. Every possibility went through her head.

At around four o'clock, Peggy poked her head back in the door.

"Isn't he here yet?" Peggy smile was mischievous.

"Who do you mean now?" Elizabeth replied. Damn, how did she know Syd was coming? That miner in yesterday must have mentioned it to her. Elizabeth had seen him go into the hotel after visiting the post office, he probably mentioned it, or more likely, she had gotten it out of him.

"Aah c'mon, Lizzie, Syd is was planning to come down to the post office, or should I say, to see you. The man is soft on you, you're his little bird." Peggy gave her a little wink. "And I know you feel the same, your misty eyes give it away." She straightened up, pausing as she turned to go. "So, have you written that letter to Rodgers?"

"Yes, it's in my room," Elizabeth lied. "It'll be in the mail bag on the boat tomorrow." That last part she fully intended to be true anyway. She was sure Peggy raised her eyebrows in disbelief before she finally turned and made back to the hotel. A terrible churning filled her stomach as she collapsed back in her chair. For a full half hour, she stayed in that position, nothing but desperate thoughts flooding through her head. She thought of the sea leopard. Maybe it was waiting down in her inlet, ready to grab her if she ventured down. Would that be so bad, trading her torment for a few moments of excruciating pain? She considered other ways of ending it, drowning herself in the sea. She had seen a rope in the storeroom…momentarily, considered it even, then dismissed it. She knew she was far too cowardly to carry out anything like that.

Footsteps! She could hear footsteps. Sitting bolt upright, she pulled her hands through her hair just in time to see Syd at the door.

"Why, Syd, what a surprise to see you today, I was just about to shut up here." She cleared her throat.

Syd stepped up into the doorway, hesitating slightly with one hand holding the doorframe. The situation had suddenly overwhelmed him, all the words he had practised suddenly slipping his mind.

"Hello, Elizabeth. It is my pleasure to see you again. How have you been?" Syd could hear his heart fair thumping.

Elizabeth was bursting to tell him about Rodgers coming back but decided against it. "To tell you the truth, Syd, I am unhappy here. I do my job, but that's it." She could tell Syd hadn't expected that answer and so soon after arriving, the way he looked taken aback. "Now, there is no mail for you, I'm afraid, maybe on the boat tomorrow."

"Yes, it'll be dark soon. I shall stay here tonight and wait for it to come in then, oh, now I have…I have something for you." Syd fumbled around in his shirt pocket to extract it, the brooch, wrapped in a piece of bandage cotton. He held it out for her. "I made this for you, out of tin which I panned myself. I hope you like it."

Every feeling of desperation that Elizabeth had felt that day flowed out of her as Syd lightly pressed his gift into her hand. Blood was rushing to her head, even as she did her best not to show it as she unwrapped the cloth.

"Oh, Syd, it's beautiful, I adore it," she said, admiring it in detail, turning this this way and that. "The thistle and the ferns, how thoughtful of you. However, did you do this?"

"The evenings can be long in a tent camped in the hills; it gives one time to be artistic, I suppose." He relieved his nervousness by shuffling from foot to foot, watching as she carefully undid the pin and fixed the brooch to the bodice of her lilac dress.

"It's not gold or silver I'm afraid, just tin."

"Shhhh now," she said quietly, putting a finger up to her lip and standing to come around her desk. Syd felt the press of her gracious hug against his body, the feel of her soft face against his stubble. She drew back a fraction to look him directly in the eyes, then slowly gave him a quick sweet kiss upon his lips. Syd was stunned, but as she drew away, he found himself muttering; "Oh, Elizabeth, this is the most wonderful moment of my whole life."

"Mine too," she said, looking him directly in the eye.

"Let me shut up this post office and get changed into something more comfortable. Tane was in before, a fine Christian he is too. Peggy invited him to eat supper with us tonight, and I would like to invite you to dine with us as well.

Peggy is threatening to cook a few of his muttonbirds again, you've tried them, I expect?"

"Why yes, I certainly have. I wouldn't say it's my top favourite now," replied Syd with a cheeky smile. "But then anything but a kiwi will be most welcome fare. I've had a few too many of those lately." Syd suspected anything that he ate tonight would be delicious.

Chapter 17

To fill in time before dinner, and while Elizabeth helped Peggy get ready for the evening, Syd went for a walk. The last thing he needed was Peggy coming out to plug him for information, so he headed up into the bush behind the hotel, sidling around until he came to the little creek which ran down into the narrow inlet on the far side of the hotel. Following the watercourse, he soon found himself working his way up the spur until he got to a bushy knoll and sat down. The last light of the day seemed different from normal, more diffused, tinged with a reddish colour, an entirely different perspective from what he was used to seeing high up in his encampment. Through the trees, he could see glimpses of North Arm, still as a millpond, Pearl Island rising in the near distance. Not only had the wind died down completely, but the sky had miraculously cleared, highly unusual thought Syd. How long ago had it ever been this calm, or clear? He couldn't recall. Laying back on the leaf litter, he let his mind drift. He thought of his mother and father back in Cornwall, at the other end of the day, still asleep in their beds most probably. There was nowhere further away on the globe that he could have emigrated to, his antipodean dream. And now Elizabeth was in his dream as well. Oh, that kiss, and upon his lips, so sweet and divine.

His indulgence did not last long, a heavy rustling noise nearby soon had him sitting upright, it was a seal waddling down the hill towards him. Syd picked up a stick as the animal advanced closer. Only at the last moment did they neatly sidestep each other and Syd watched it disappear down the spur. The animal had surprised him, so far up into the bush. He had no idea they came inland so far, or so high up. Syd guessed it would have been a good two hundred feet above the water. 'Never get bit by a seal,' an old sealer had warned him once. 'Seal finger' they called it, an infection that would never heal, just get more infected and poisoned by the day. You didn't even need to be bitten by one, just handling the pelts could get a man infected. Sealers died from it which could take six slow and painful months. You had to be careful around seals.

Darkness was falling now, and he was sure the redness of the sky had intensified as he made his way back down the spur. Maybe it was just his position, down low by the water, the fading light reflecting on the mirror calm surface.

Doubling back through the bush to the back of the hotel, he heard Peggy talking to George along with the clinking of bottles. Probably getting them out of cold storage in the tunnel he surmised. Coming back out above the boat landing, he saw Tane sitting on a rock by the water. The man with whom he had hardly ever spoken gave him a flick of his head in recognition, then turned back to stare back out over the water. Syd ambled up next to him.

Tane waved his hand across the sky. "Tahu-nui-a rangi," he said quietly.

It was a beautiful language that he spoke, reflected Syd. "I'm sorry, I don't speak Maori."

"Tahu-nui-a-rangi." Tane repeated gently again. "Tonight, it is coming, the big fire in the sky. When it starts to glow like this at nightfall in winter, it can happen."

Syd had no idea what the man was talking about. What was coming? Something to do with the sunset maybe. He sat down beside the man and stared out onto the still water. A fish jumped, then another and another. As darkness descended, the place was coming alive, and the sky only seemed to be getting brighter.

It was obvious Tane did not want much of a conversation, so Syd retreated into his thoughts. How eloquent Tane's few words were, almost poetical. Nothing like the rough talk and slang of the miners. Surely, he didn't learn it in a school? Not down here at the bottom of the world. The man baffled him. Syd's thoughts soon once again turned to Elizabeth, she would probably be helping Peggy now in the kitchen. All sorts of wonderings went through his mind. What would happen to Elizabeth when Rodgers came back? Would she dutifully disappear back to Invercargill with George? Surely not, it perplexed him greatly. He repositioned himself on the rock to get more comfortable. How still the man next to him was, just looking out over the water. He could have been a statue sitting there. Was he a man so primitive in nature that complicated thoughts did not affect him? Syd recalled back to the most learned gentleman on the boat out from England, who had given a talk one evening after supper about making a new life in the colony, and Syd could remember every detail, such an impression it had made on him.

The man had quoted a Genevan-born philosopher named Jean-Jacques Rousseau, who had put forward the argument that civilised people should incorporate primitive qualities into their disordered lives. The word 'disordered' had particularly stuck for Syd, made him reflect on his life in England which had been chaotic, a mad dash just to keep up in the world. Syd thought of his father, still a tin miner at 61 and well past his prime, a worn-out man. He had surprised the family not long before Syd emigrated when he started bringing books home to read. Where he got them, no one was quite sure, he'd just turn up with them saying a man had lent them to him. Suddenly, the words from the likes of William Wordsworth and Samuel Taylor Coleridge were being read out loud in the family home. No one could believe it. The passages they heard were selective, all advocating notions of returning to natural environments as an antidote to the sprawling depravities of the industrial revolution. Syd reflected that maybe he was sitting next to a wise man.

They said absolutely nothing for ten minutes. Tane broke the silence. "You like muttonbird?"

"Sometimes. I enjoy the saltiness, good for a man who works and sweats all day."

"They must be ready by now. Let us go." Tane got up and started for the hotel which was marked by a single whale oil lamp through the gathering dark. Syd followed him, noticing how agile he was, walking barefoot in the dark and barely making a sound, not like his own clobby old boots. You could hear an Englishman coming for miles.

The table was set and Peggy greeted them "Elizabeth and I are joining you two gentlemen tonight. We're just preparing your birds, Tane. Not too busy tonight. Syd, I bet you'd like an ale now?"

"Yes, please, that will do me nicely."

She didn't need to ask Tane, he always went for a tipple of rum. George may have gone on about how much he drunk, but in reality, it wasn't more than a few drams. She brought over their drinks just as Elizabeth stepped up from the cookhouse carrying the steaming muttonbirds piled together on a plate with sweet potato, puha and cress. Syd saw straight away that Elizabeth was still wearing his brooch, now on a light blue dress with a frilly neckline.

"Your brooch, Syd, it's beautiful, thanks again, I love it," she said quietly across the table to him with a smile. Peggy raised her eyebrows to give a knowing smile, making Elizabeth blush. Syd took the opportunity to say a rudimentary grace for the occasion, Tane adding several words at the end which no one understood. Soon, they were all ripping the muttonbirds apart with their fingers.

"Mmmm, these are delicious, far better than the ones I boiled for McKay the other night." Elizabeth licked her lips as she spoke, fishy bird grease dripping down her chin as she ate which made Syd laugh.

"Tane taught me, it's not how you cook 'em so much as what you cook 'em with," said Peggy, tearing off another thigh. Tane wasn't wasting any time talking, he was just quietly munching away. Syd looked for an opening to talk to Elizabeth, but Peggy was taking all the attention. "So, Syd, have you been up to those buttocks again. Climbed those titties maybe?" She roared with laughter, slobbering in the process.

Oh, my God, thought Syd, what will the woman say next.

'It's kind of strange though, ain't it?" said Peggy. "The names these mountains get called, like Gog, and Magog, can't say I seen those ones though."

"Named from the bible. Tucker told me. Book of Ezekiel," replied Syd, catching Elizabeth's eye. "They are incredible, you'll have to come up one day to spy them. They rise up like cathedrals, dominate the land all around…"

Tane butted in. "You English fellas give all your own names to our *maunga*." He paused. "Do you know what we call your Gog and Magog?"

"Tell us, Tane." said Peggy. "I think we need some water, this muttonbird makes me thirsty." She got up to fetch a flask of water. Tane waited for her to return.

"Gog is *Kaka-kura*. The red parrot. Look at the red streak across it at sunset, up high near the peak. It reminds us of the red neck and face feathers of the kaka, lifting its head to the sky."

"And Magog?" Syd was curious now.

"*Tu-pouri.* Dark and gloomy," said Tane. "The shape of it…" He used his hands to indicate its angular appearance. "You must see them at sunset or first light."

"Oh, I would love to see them one day, I miss all the peaks of Scotland," said Elizabeth.

Tane stood up, tipping his head at Peggy. "I need to look outside."

Elizabeth waited till he was outside before she leaned forward to say quietly. "What an interesting man, I like him, but why do people say unkind and horrid things about him?"

"Probably 'cos he's a native," said Peggy, already piling up the plates. "Ain't fair I know, but that's how it is. I don't believe a word of it, mind you."

"Can't be as bad as being a Chinaman," commented Syd. "Nobody trusts them, especially on the gold fields. Pretty mean thinking, I reckon. I met a few, they just all hard workers like us…"

"Come out. Look! Come out.'" Tane interrupted, calling through the door, gesticulating with one arm that they should all follow him out.

"Tahu-nui-a-rangi!" he exclaimed as they piled out. They moved forward to the edge of the bank, leaving the trees behind for an unobstructed view. Rising out of the hills all around the great port, a fabulous green glow was beginning to light up the waters all around with an eerie glow. What's more, magnificent shifting shafts of whitish light appeared to emanate from behind the very hills themselves, all shining up into the heavens all aglow with pink light. The spectacle was dancing before their eyes.

"Oh, my goodness," said Elizabeth slowly as she took it all in. "The polar lights, I saw them once in Scotland, when my father took me to the mission in Thurso. They were exactly like this. The whole town came out to see them." There was real awe in her voice.

"The first time I've seen 'em here, what a sight indeed!" said Syd quietly, sidling over to Elizabeth. He was sure she took a step over to meet him as well.

"Aye, aye," added Peggy. "Never seen such a show of lights. I wonder if they make you do strange things. Like the full moon does? Go mad like."

Peggy pointed over to the west, above Pearl Island. "Look, over there, it's becoming brighter," she hesitated briefly. "Oh my, it goes in waves across. Look!"

"Like curtains fluttering in the wind from an open window," murmured Elizabeth. "You can see the ripples." They watched in silence as the show of lights only got brighter and brighter, the cold of the arm descending on them. Syd wasn't sure if it was he who moved forward or Elizabeth who moved back, but he soon found himself with his hands gently resting on Elizabeth's shoulders. Their bodies naturally came together, seeking warmth.

"Whatever makes them?" Peggy wondered aloud.

Syd paused before answering, slowly sliding his hands down the outside of Elizabeth's arms. "That seaman, the one who told me about the sea leopard, he also told me about seeing polar lights, in the Southern Ocean. Said the ships compass used to go haywire, ya couldn't trust it. Something to do with the magnetism of the Earth, he reckoned. 'Tis a strange thing, magnetism, changes all the time. It's as the Earth can't control it." Syd was sure he had heard Elizabeth utter an appreciative, almost imperceptible sound when he slipped his hands around hers. They felt so small and delicate, the skin so soft and cold. He made sure they were well enfolded within his.

Tane hadn't said a word yet, he had been standing motionless, looking up into the heavens. When he spoke, his words came out slowly, and guttural, without emotion, "Tahu-nui-a-rangi. When we die, we believe our ancestors sail south in their canoes to a great land of ice and snow. They are trying to stay warm there. These are their great campfires, reflected in the sky. They are also letting us know that one day they will return."

No one said anything as they took in his words.

It was Elizabeth who finally broke the silence. "Can you hear that sound?"

They all stood stock still, listening.

"Yes, I can," said Peggy. "Like the sound…the sound that a field of grass in the distance makes rustling in the wind."

"Surely not, how could these lights make a sound?" Syd asked in a puzzled voice.

"Listen, I can hear it too," offered Elizabeth. "Not so much like grass I think, more like…a soft clicking of fingers."

They all listened awhile before Peggy spoke again.

"I hear what you mean, Lizzie. Perhaps, they are the ancestors talking, who are we to say what they are anyway."

"But, Tane," Elizabeth paused to choose her words carefully. "You read the Bible; how can you believe such things? Surely…" her voice trailed off.

Tane took what seemed like an eternity to reply.

"The Bible teaches us new ways, but the old ways stay with us. We would be unwise to forget them. Even Reverend Wohler tells us that. That is why he has been welcome with us for so long."

Elizabeth felt shocked. A reverend who encourages primitive people to believe in their old ways. Surely not? Tane had already turned back to watch the sky. He had spoken his truth, and the conversation was over.

"I'm too cold to stay out here," said Peggy briskly, "these lights are fading too, the fire's bound to need a log or two." Elizabeth and Syd could both feel her eyes upon them both as she turned back for the hotel. Tane had already slipped off without anyone noticing.

"Where did Tane go?" Elizabeth asked softly.

"Probably to go talk to his ancestors, I suspect his mind does not think like ours," replied Syd, letting his face rub against Elizabeth's silken hair, such a contrast against the hardness of her tortoiseshell comb.

"Oh, Elizabeth…I have such feelings for you. The more I dwell on it, the more certain I am." She savoured his whispered words, drawing a deep breath before replying, "Same for me too, Syd…" Elizabeth turned around, put her hands on his shoulders, looking straight at him.

"Syd, you're so kind to make me this brooch. It touches me to my heart. But there's something I've got to tell you…" He could feel her body go limp in his arms. "George told me Rodgers is coming back to manage the hotel. Said I have to go back to Invercargill with him Saturday week. I'm just not going." Her head collapsed into his chest as tears welled in her eyes.

"Oh, Elizabeth, I had no idea." Syd stroked her hair one with hand, holding her tight against him with the other."

"These lights tonight, Syd, I almost think they are a sign, don't you think?"

"What do you mean, a sign?"

"A sign we are meant to be together. Maybe for Tane, they are his ancestors, maybe that's true. But for us, our truth is just as valid. Maybe we are meant for each other…"

Syd wondered if she could feel his heart fair racing in his chest, or the flush of warmth filling his body. Their lips softly came together, Elizabeth surprised how soft and moist they felt against her as she let him gently kiss her. She had seen him as a rough-skinned muscular miner, but his lips felt so tender at that moment. Slowly, she lifted her hand to place around the head, pulling him gently in towards her. There was no going back she thought to herself.

"Elizabeth. Elizabeth! Where are you?" The holler came from the hotel.

"Oh, my God, it's George!" Elizabeth pushed herself back out of Syd's arms. "I have to go!" Without hesitation, she rushed off through the last faint glow of the evening, hurriedly hitching up her dress as she pushed through the cutty grass back towards the lone light in the distance.

The scene that greeted her at the hotel was not welcoming. Peggy and George were having an altercation, she could tell that immediately.

"…the Maori, I told you to book up all is drinks. But I can't see any on his ledger. Who's going to pay for them? He certainly won't." George was standing stiffly upright as he gruffly spoke, one hand palm down upon the table, the other holding a sheath of papers. Elizabeth could not believe how angry and accusing he looked.

"Arhhh...for God sakes, George," Peggy roared back at him, lowering her voice to continue, "the man gave us two kelp sacks of muttonbirds. Where would he get money from to pay us anyway? Twice I've given him half-a-penny to send his postcards, but that's my money. He's no different to a broke miner coming in asking for credit or swapping some gold or stream tin for grog. Surely now! You're just saying this 'cos he's a Maori, admit it now, will ya. And if ya don't, you're a far lesser man than him I say." Peggy's hands were firmly on her hips, and she stepped forward to face George fair and square. She wasn't having a bar of it.

Elizabeth went edged in slowly towards the fire, hoping to sit down unnoticed. But it was not to be, George turned around to face her now, taking a few paces forward to half throw down the papers on the table that separated them.

"Fill these in, will you?" His voice rough and commanding. "They have to be on the boat tomorrow, reconciliation returns for the post office."

Elizabeth jumped up to pick the papers up. As she roughly leafed through them, an anger rose in her.

"What? Why weren't these given to me sooner?" She stared George directly in the eyes. "How long have you had them?" She barked at him.

"Who cares? It's none of your business anyway, just fill them in," George flicked his hand disparagingly, then turned his attention back to Peggy.

"I want you to tell that Maori we don't want none of his muttonbirds no more, their stink gives this hotel a bad name too."

Elizabeth felt like throwing the papers at him, but the postmistress in her made her behave. It was a job she had to do, and she could hardly send them off dirty. Putting them under her arm, she marched over to join Peggy. They were both facing George now, there being nothing Elizabeth could hold back, and an uncontrolled rage rose in her.

"I'll fill in your blasted forms for you," she raised her voice with each word, "but don't expect me to come to Invercargill with you." Tears filled her eyes, and a choking anxiety filled her throat, but she still managed to say it. "You're a miserable man, George. I would never marry you! Ever!"

Peggy moved close to Elizabeth, putting her arm around her shoulder. There was no mistaking their solidarity. They both watched as George's eyes narrowed.

He swung on his heels to leave but stopped at the last moment. His face was contorted.

"If that's how you feel, Elizabeth, you can leave on the boat tomorrow, you are not welcome here anymore. Get out of my sight, and good riddance to ya! It was all your stupid uncle's idea that you should come out. I couldn't have cared less."

"Well, that showed us the truth, didn't it?" Elizabeth retorted as Peggy stepped forward to confront her.

"She's right, George, you are a miserable toad. What love have you ever shown her? You couldn't even be bothered meeting her off the immigrant boat. Face it, you only got her down so you can laze around all day. She's been nothing but a slave to you, admit it now!"

"Stupid women, both of you." George was shouting at the top of his voice now. He turned and headed for the door. That was when Syd stepped up from the step to block the man's way. He had been listening to it all from the darkness.

"Get out of my way," George went to push his way out, but Syd stayed staunch, throwing one hand up to the man's shoulder to stop him in his tracks.

"That's no way to talk to your workers, George. Certainly, no way to talk to these two fine lasses either." Syd voice was resolute, every muscle in his body tensing for a fight now, one in which he was sure he couldn't be beaten. The two men stared at each other for a few seconds before Peggy stormed over to intervene.

"Oh, for goodness sakes, you two, we don't need a barroom brawl now do we? You're the manager, George, and managers don't fight with their flamin' customers." She threw an arm past him to push Syd out to one side, same time using the other to push George away from him.

"Get to bed now, both of yas, we'll talk about it in the morning." Peggy spoke like she meant business.

George had to have the last word, turning back to face Syd. "Just get out of my hotel, you are not welcome here either anymore!" Syd and Peggy watched him disappear into the darkness.

"Awh, thank goodness that's over," said Peggy returning to Elizabeth who was sobbing out at the table. "Don't you worry tonight, rest yourself, its mailboat day tomorrow and we have much to do." She was already busily piling all the muttonbird scraps onto a plate ready for the cat. "George will calm down and see sense tomorrow. He knows he'll have endless work to do if you go. Mark my words now."

Peggy could make out Syd through the door, his back to her, leaning against a manuka tree, head hanging low. She took one step out the door towards him. "You shouldn't have confronted him, Syd, you made him feel cornered. It'll be right, give him a few days, let it all cool down."

Syd was too angry to reply. He stalked into the darkness. By the time Elizabeth realised he had gone, she knew it was too late to follow him. He could be anywhere. Her whole world was crashing down. Her head collapsed into her arms folded on the table, a terrible wailing coming from her mouth.

Chapter 18

In his office at Dunedin University, the professor was not only working late, but he was also perplexed. The fourth second sample sent to him by his two Cornish miners was showing even less cassiterite than the third. Fifty-six yards into the drift and still no hint of payable ore. He put down his magnifying glass and slumped back in his chair. Why? Going through all the possibilities, he could only come to one conclusion—that the lode was further in than he had initially calculated. After he reassured himself that the next sample would be definitely be more promising, his attention then focused on the note which had accompanied the samples. The message read…

"27 May-28 fathoms in, good progress. Is it possible 220 degrees drift is parallel to lode, not into it? Please reconfirm bearing. Arthur."

The professor grunted in disgust, throwing the note down on his desk. Without hesitation, he pulled out a sheet of watermarked paper impressed with his letterhead and scrawled upon it just three words, 'Stay the course!' Folding it roughly, he slipped it into an envelope which he addressed to Pegasus Mining Company, c/-Port Pegasus PO, Stewart Island.

As he sealed it and flicked it into his outward tray for his secretary to post first thing in the morning, he found himself asking aloud, "What would they know, anyway?"

At the same time, some 160 miles away, atop the Tin Range, the great government geologist Alexander McKay was waiting for the last of his party to come back into the tent from urinating outside. He expected his audience to be attentive, not to cause any interruptions, so he patiently waited until the man had come back in and repositioned himself under his blanket before taking out the book which always accompanied him wherever he went, Charles Lyell's *Principles of Geology.* Lighting the candle, he had set up on a rock of suitable height beside him, McKay waited for the man to finally settle and began reading in a soft and monotonous voice, starting from where he had finished the previous night. This was no picnic excursion, and the great geologist did not want to waste a moment instructing his charges in the words of the great masters. To his mind, the worst thing would be them going home knowing as little as they came with, and it was his job to ensure that did not happen.

All evening they had been treated, looking out over the great port of Pegasus, watching the polar lights intensify and wane, then intensify again into a brilliant display. What a great surprise it had been, McKay was visibly excited, likening its effect on him as experiencing the huge rocking power of an earthquake, feeling the immense energy thoroughly engulf and absorb him. What could be more impressive than great forces over which you had no control, the sheer unleashing of latent energy? The men did not need to ask any questions as to what caused the phenomena, McKay may as well have been a university lecturer beside them, expounding his bounteous knowledge.

"In Tasmania, the aborigines may be looking up, seeing this very sight at this very moment, the Indians of Patagonia too. So, why does this happen? Imagine if you can, the sun emitting a wind of sorts, not a wind that blows in the trees or makes waves upon the ocean, but invisible particles which get flung out into the heavens. It is still far from proven, but some scientists believe the magnetism around the poles has the effect of attracting these particles which flare up in our high skies." He paused to fling his arms aloft. "Gentlemen, this is indeed a show of God's infinite power, a power we do not yet quite understand." Not taking his eyes off the display, McKay was excitedly pacing now, his hand behind his back.

"Can it hurt our eyes, watching it?" One of the men asked. "Maybe we will go blind, like looking at the sun."

"No, no, certainly not. People have watched this sort of thing for eons." McKay hesitated for a few seconds, then added. "Twenty years ago, we had the Carrington Event, surely one of the most amazing things the Sun has affected upon our Earth in modern history. Scientists believe it was not so much a solar wind, but more a solar storm of sorts. It was so powerful, it set telegraph wires and telegraph machines alight." He paused now for effect before concluding. "Gentlemen, you are witnessing the power of nature, a nature that encompasses the entire universe, far beyond and greater than our Earth where we reside. As a life, we are no greater than ants upon its surface."

"I swear I can hear it, like a faint crackle. Can anyone hear it too?" One of the men asked suddenly. They all went quiet.

"Yes, I can too," replied another.

"Your ears are better than mine, gentlemen," said McKay. "But now you have pointed it out, I expect it's the static in the air. Well done, gentlemen, for picking that up. It is definitely the first time I have heard it like this."

They had all watched, and listened, to the show of lights until it all faded. The very last thing McKay told them was that some people had recently started calling the phenomena Aurorae, after the Roman goddess of the dawn. One by one, they retreated to the relative warmth of the tent. There was no doubt in any of the men's minds that they were in the presence of greatness, there seemed nothing the man did not know. McKay was widely read, even his great geology colleague, James Park, had publicly called him a man of high culture.

For a full hour, the men listened as McKay droned on and on, reading from his book. And as they were one by one lulled into sleep, he stopped to chide them for not listening to the great master. Finally, when he knew he was fighting a losing battle, he quietly put the book down and picked up his notebook and pencil and began writing.

McKay's most notable literary accomplishment to date by far had been *The Canterbury Gilpin,* which he had published anonymously ten years earlier. The poem had satirised the debate over Julius von Haast's long favoured view about the antiquity of the moa, and in particular moa hunters, which he had long theorised were a separate race that predated the Maori. McKay's poem had hilariously described the capture of the last sole surviving moa specimen, which after much fanfare, was paraded through the streets of Christchurch, riding on its back no other than Professor Haast himself. But as the crowds gathered close to cheer, the frightened animal bolts, the dismayed and terrified Haast having no option but to hang on for dear life as the bird disappears into the countryside, the two never to be seen again.

Haast had been greatly offended by the anonymous publication of the poem poking fun directly at him. He took it as an affront to both his personal and professional integrity, and he was under no illusion as to who had perpetrated it. Six years earlier, in 1874, in a paper read by James Hector and delivered to the Wellington Philosophical Society, McKay had expounded his interpretation of his excavation of Sumner Cave, his dynamic conclusion being that the moa hunters were in fact ancestral Maori, not a separate race of earlier palaeolithic people. Not only did it challenge Haast's long cherished view about a pre-Maori moa hunter culture, but it strategically pre-empted the publication of Haast's paper on the subject. Even more offensive to the eminent Austrian geologist, was when McKay's paper was published simultaneously with his, a year later. Haast was furious, that the younger geologist whom he had mentored had dared to challenge him in such a public way. Questions were even raised in the New Zealand Parliament about it, resulting in an appeal to the Royal Society of London for a ruling on the ethics of McKay's action. Many commentators of the day had suggested the highly public spat had more to do with the rivalry between Hector and Haast, than between McKay and Haast. Humourist Walter Mantell had had a field day, pointing out succinctly that the argument symbolised the clash between the new breed of explorer scientist such as McKay, and the established authorities of the time.

Under the soft glow of the candle in his tent that night, his colleagues all fast asleep, McKay meticulously recorded his observations from the day. They had seen seven more claims. Rolling out the surveyor's map, he recorded both the claim numbers and claim holders, then alongside each his exact observations. Whenever a miner had waxed lyrical about the result of his sluicing, he had quietly asked the man if he could see his chamois sack of stream tin, to inspect its quality. Two had fumbled, saying they had already sent it off, three had produced half bags, and another a mere cup with some covering the bottom. None could come up with more than £10 worth. He had not begrudged any of them for being untruthful, because he had been a miner himself, and he understood exactly what dreams of riches meant in a society where there was no hope of earning them. Those kinds of riches were the prerogative of the gentry, unless you could find them under the ground.

He also noted that six miners that week walked off their claims, their neighbours all giving vague excuses. One man had gone to get married; another had injured his leg and been unable to work, two had heard of rushes elsewhere and thought their prospects were better away. Only the sixth was reported to have left because of frustration that his riffles had produced little or no stream tin. McKay had diverted to inspect two of the vacated claims and had seen the tell-tale signs of abandonment, the discarded tools, the rain-soaked ash in the campfires, the square of bare earth where a tent once stood, a hut door swinging open, its interior clearly vacated. He had seen it all before. This was not a payable field, because even a vacated site would be occupied immediately by a new hopeful if it was payable. Intuitively, he already knew it, but his professional judgement would not allow him to declare that until he had the complete picture, and he would not have that until he inspected the lode claims. That would start in the morning, when they would head up the mountain to inspect Professor Black's audit. McKay had been informed two Cornish miners were working there, and he was keen to talk to them. Men on contract he knew were more honest that claimholders and shareholders. And being Cornish miners, they could be counted on to speak bluntly, their knowledge was generational, they weren't new chums to the game like most of the other miners in New Zealand.

McKay was exhausted. He drew a line under his day's observations, and started a new page, writing up his heading for the next day…

Cornish Mining Co. (Black's adit)

Underlining the words twice, he closed his notebook and tucked it away in its canvas cover, slipping it into the side pocket of his pack where he knew no rising damp could affect it. Blowing out the candle, he lay his head down on his sack pillow which he' had earlier filled with soft fern leaf, and pulled his blanket up around him. He tried to empty his head, free himself from the endless distractions of the day, but his mind full of them. At the top lurked Professor Black, for he knew the man was finally in his sights. The man reminded him of Haast, infinitely showier, but still just as opinionated with his 'received wisdoms.' What's worse, McKay suspected he had inflicted a whole field of gullible miners with his mistaken enthusiasms. Effectively, they had sweated blood and toil in his name, and now it was time to bring the man down, just like he had done with Haast.

McKay finally drifted off to sleep, satisfied that tomorrow his suspicions would be proven one way or the other.

Chapter 19

Elizabeth was distraught. Her world had fallen in around her. George had told her to leave, and Syd had disappeared into the night. Peggy tried her best to console her, reassuring her that the morrow would see things right. But inside herself, Elizabeth knew what she had to do. Using every bit of Scottish strength she could muster, she pulled herself together, wiped her tears away, and went about helping Peggy do the dishes and tidy up the kitchen. Peggy had much to say about the evening, and what she should do, but Elizabeth let it all waft past her.

"I'll see you in the morning, Peggy. Thank you for sticking by me tonight," said Elizabeth, giving Peggy an appreciative hug. Peggy didn't want to let her go, but Elizabeth pulled away. "I have to leave tomorrow, there's no other option," she said, going over the table to snap up the sheath of post office papers that George had insisted she fill in. "I'll do these tonight, they won't take long, and I'll get the mailbags ready, but that's it. I'm over it all."

"Oh, Lizzie! Honestly, tomorrow won't be so bad," Peggy extended out her thumb to smudge away a leftover tear on Elizabeth's face before placing both her arms on her shoulders again. "You know, I've seen George like this once before, just after he arrived. Ranted and raved his head off to me. I just shrugged off it all off. He was fine the next day. Just a bad tempered ol' selfish bastard, that's all he is."

"Yes, but it wasn't arranged for you to marry him, Peggy. I can't stand the man, and I don't want to be here another full day. Good night now, I'll see you in the morning."

Without even waiting for a reply, Elizabeth marched off to her room, pausing only to pick up her whale oil lamp. It was only then, trying to light it, that she realised her hands were trembling terribly. Her mind was racing, full of confusion. Why had Syd abandoned her? Where could he possibly be now? It was freezing outside. Surely, he wouldn't be walking back up to his claim, not without saying goodbye to her. Surely, after all the tender things he had whispered to her, he wouldn't just run off? Maybe he was just hiding out somewhere close by. Surely, she would see him in the morning. She ran her fingers over her tin brooch, still pinned upon her dress.

Making her way to her little post office, she unlocked it and set the lamp upon her desk where she spread out the reconciliation forms which George had thrust at her. Although she felt like just walking away from the hotel, she still felt an obligation to tie up all the loose ends. Her father's advice came back to her, 'Even if you feel jilted, remember it does not exclude you from your obligations. Do not leave loose ends, be it marriage, work or religion.' Getting out her transactions book, she wasted no time transcribing them over, double checking all the tallies added up correctly. On the final declaration page, she signed her full name, Elizabeth Jane MacDonald, dating and impressing the official Port Pegasus Post Office stamp carefully on one side. There was still one line to fill in, where it asked for the 'Position of person making Declaration.' She stared awhile at the page before picking up her pen again to write decisively 'Postmistress (resigned subsequent).' After checking the pages were all in order, she folded and placed them in an envelope and slipped it into the outward mail sack, padlocking the leather strap around its neck and throwing it over her desk to land by the door. Picking up the lamp, she cast her eye all around, making sure everything was in order. The little Rule Book was sticking out from the last time she pulled it, so she pushed it back to sit properly into the shelf. She placed her two stamp pads on top of each other, made sure the roller was tucked away properly. Sadness about the evening was flooding through her. She knew that she would never see her little post office again. Leaving her key on the table, she walked out with her lamp, quietly shutting the door behind her.

Back in her room, she opened her trunk. She would not need most of what was in it until she settled somewhere, so she would send for it later. She pulled out the clothes she thought she might need—two dresses, two woollen singlets, socks, woollen leggings, her bonnet, a scented candle. At any other time, the sight of her prayerbook would have fortified her, but now it seemed utterly ridiculous. Everyone had deserted her, even the good Lord.

After relocking the trunk, she refolded her selected items and stuffed them into her pillowcase that would have to suffice as her travelling bag. Then she collapsed on the bed, utterly exhausted. Too distraught to sleep, she tossed and turned, she couldn't help but go back over her life, her carefree childhood up to the death of her mother, her teenage years when the possibilities of the world began opening up for her. For the first time, she felt a deep resentment towards her father, the way he went about organising her to marry George. That was when it had all started going horribly wrong. She may have drifted off to sleep but kept waking up in fitful starts as the reality of her situation hit again and again. She remembered the dream she'd had soon after she arrived in Port Pegasus, imprisoned in some sort of enclosure. A man had appeared to pull her out. Oh, my goodness, that man was Syd, and the fiery sky had been the polar lights she realised, it had foretold what was going to happen. The realisation made her sit bolt upright, eventually collapsing back on the bed, utterly spent. On and on her torment raged, until she began to hear birds heralding in the dawn.

She got up and opened the door, listening for any stirrings. Hearing none, she tip-toed out of the building into the early dawn. She was looking for Syd, imagining where he might possibly have taken refuge close by in the night. She knew it was a new moon, that was the reason the polar lights had been so bright, so there was no way he would have walked up the hill. Surely, he still had to be about somewhere.

It wasn't until she climbed down the ladder to the landing beach that she saw it, Tucker's boat, not lying on the bank as it normally did, but propped up on one side a foot or so. As she drew closer, she could see it was a piece of driftwood that had been used, like a stick propping open the lid of a box. Then she spied his form, curled up under the boat, his back to her. It was Syd! She was sure of it, who else could it possibly be? It certainly wasn't Tane, she could tell by his clothes.

"Syd, Syd, is that you?" She whispered aloud, kneeling alongside the boat.

Before she had even finished asking, Syd had recoiled, banging his head on the thwart in the process.

"Ouch!" Elizabeth couldn't help chuckling, but it was more out of the relief of finding him.

"I was about to come find you," he said, turning over to face her. Already he was twisting his body to get out, only to dislodge the stick and have the wooden boat collapse on top of him. Elizabeth was laughing out loud now, helping lift the side of the boat as he used his legs to push it back up enough to slide out.

"Worst sleep I ever had," he said, finally picking himself up. He pulled her down to sit beside him on the rock cobbles. "Didn't think I slept at all, but I must have dozed off before the dawn. You surprised me." He drew up his knees, leaning forward with his arms around them. She did the same, they were both looking out over the arm.

"I had to find you, Syd, after all that commotion last night."

"Yes, I had to go, George made me so angry, If I'd stayed, I might have killed the man. I never liked him much." He paused, thinking whether to tell her. "When I heard he had an arranged bride coming out, I felt sorry for her, and it was you!"

"Syd, I can't stay here any longer, And I don't want to go off to Invercargill yet. I've packed a swag. Can you help me? Take me up to your claim."

"What! Elizabeth! Have you lost your mind?"

Elizabeth's voice spoke with surprising determination. "I was surely mad before, coming out here to marry a man I didn't know. I know what I want now, Syd, and it's got nothing to do with that man and that hotel any longer."

Syd butted in, "The boat…the boat is coming in this afternoon. You could be back in Invercargill tomorrow…we could meet later."

"No, Syd, you don't understand, this is about us, us here at Port Pegasus. Why should I leave? Break us apart…" The emotion made her throat thicken, and she turned her face to Syd who met her eye to eye.

"Right o, if we love each other, give me a good reason why I shouldn't go up with you then?" Elizabeth felt forceful, determined to settle something before the others got up and made it all complicated. Syd didn't know how to answer the question he had not expected. He turned to look back over the water while he thought about it.

"You'd be the only woman, Elizabeth, in the whole diggings. It just ain't done."

"I'm only one of two women down here. What about Little Biddy, up by Lyell? She was all the newspapers. Bog Irish, she couldn't even remember what village she came from in Ireland. Stood exactly four feet tall, not an ounce over seven stone. She found gold alright, working with two men whom she also lived with in a one room hut."

"What? You mean she lived with them both, married like?"

"Yep, the story said, '*in the nature of marriage.*' Sounded like a few people got offended, stuck up their churchy noses, but everyone else adored her, they said she got spirit. That's what I feel like I'm getting back now, Syd, my spirit!"

Syd was amazed, he hadn't heard anything about the woman gold miner. "Maybe the worst thing for people will be that you were betrothed to George, all the miners here know that. Just imagine what they'd say when they saw you up there with me?"

Elizabeth let her arms fall back behind for support as she leaned back. "If you don't want me, Syd, I'll should be on the boat out this afternoon." They were both silent until she spoke again. "I may as well be helping you up there, Syd. No one pays me down here, I'm only down here on George's account."

"Do you know how I live up there? In a cold tent, eating a kiwi here and there. The weather can be so foul, not like down here where it's sheltered most of the time."

"Nothing you say is going to put me off, Syd. Anything would be better than going back to that hotel today." The sound of empty bottles chinking and a metal bucket hitting the ground came from the hotel.

"Peggy's up. I better go tell her I'll be on that boat today then…" She got up to leave.

"No wait, Elizabeth!" He reached up to grab her arm, stop her going. He was thinking hard.

"Let's go then, up to my claim. Have you got your things? Warm clothes, you'll need them." Syd tried to pull her close, but she pulled back.

"I have to tell Peggy. I don't give a damn about George, but Peggy has to know what I'm doing. Wait for me at the start by the surveyors track, I'll meet you there, give me fifteen minutes."

Elizabeth ran back to her room to collect her pillow case swag, throwing her shawl around her as she went back to find Peggy sprottling away in the cookhouse.

Elizabeth wasted no time blurting out what she had to say, "I'm leaving today, Peggy. I've come to say goodbye."

"But the boat won't be in for hours…"

"I'm not going on the boat, Peggy, I'm going up with Syd to stay on his claim awhile."

Peggy's mouth dropped open as she dropped the dishrag she was holding onto the floor. "You're what!"

Elizabeth threw her swag on the bench, moving forward to grab Peggy around the middle. They were face to face.

"Absolutely nothing you say is going to stop me, Peggy, I've made up my mind. I might need a favour though; can you send my trunk on sometime? I'll advise you by letter when I know what's happening."

"Does George know any of this?"

"No, I haven't seen him since last night. Can you tell him…"

"That you've run off?" Peggy thought for a few seconds. "Aye, if you like, I can do that. But maybe it would be better if you should write him a letter, leave it here with me."

Elizabeth pulled back. "He doesn't deserve one, Peggy. It was him that told me to go. So, I'm going. Tell him the post bag is ready to go on the boat and the reconciliation is in it."

Peggy turned to the bench again, grabbing a small bag of rolled oats that lay open, along with an unopened tin of bully beef and some leftover biscuits from a tin. She moved around the kitchen adding whatever else she could see: a packet of wax matches, two candles, a little tin of curry powder, two onions, even the small salt shaker. "Here, take these, you will need them up there, Syd eats a few too many kiwi…" She stuffed them all into the little sack of rolled oats, wrapping its tie around the top to make sure nothing could fall out. "Take this too," Peggy said, grabbing the bottle of rum that was half full and stashing it into the swag.

"Remember, Elizabeth, I'm down here if you need me. Things will be different when Mr Rodgers comes back."

"Not for me, Peggy, it won't. Rodgers will always take George's side. He won't want anything to do with me. I got my eyes open now."

"Oh, Lizzie, I shall miss you so."

"Me too, Peggy, I couldn't have survived here a day without you." They fell into each other's arms, a farewell hug that seemed to go on forever. It was Elizabeth who finally drew away.

"I have to go; Syd is waiting on the track." Peggy followed her to the door to wave her on her way, but Elizabeth didn't turn back as the tears began streaming down her face. By the time Peggy made it back to the cookhouse, she was wiping her tears away too.

Chapter 20

Standing between the two head-high mullocks outside Professor Black's adit, McKay wondered if his eyes were deceiving him. The entrance to the mine half a chain ahead of him indicated to him that the bearing of the drift was clearly north east. Even before he had made it around the trig, he had figured that the lode almost certainly ran in the same direction. Several times, he had stopped as they neared the mine, pausing to kneel and examine the crevices in the granite. Each time the men had gathered around him, and each time, he had imparted a little more about the geology. If there was one thing McKay knew about informing bureaucratic laymen, it was to deliver it in small, measured doses.

"Gentlemen, you could be forgiven for thinking you are standing on a mountain stretching down in all directions. But imagine yourself, rather, on a huge dome of granite, more correctly a pluton, which eons ago was extruded into the softer shist. Let us move on."

It was only a chain on before he stopped again to inspect another gritty vein running up towards the trig, using the opportunity to carry on his lesson. Two of the men had been chatting, but he curtly brought them to attention by the gruff clearing of his throat. "Now, gentlemen, the surface of the shist that overlaid this landscape may have been several miles thick. As the massive forces pushed it up, it was eroded almost as fast by the inclement weather, leaving these much harder granite plutons sticking out like giant pimples, excuse the analogy there. These are what you admire today, Gog and Magog being the finest examples. Let us move on again now."

A short diversion took them to the trig, where they once again admired the splendid vista over Port Pegasus which was all covered in whitecaps, whipped up by the same wind that was buffeting them as well. They were pleased to move back into the shelter of the mountain where McKay stopped once again to appreciate another lode line, this one, a good six inches thick. Once again, he knelt alongside, and it spoke to him, as though he could see into the earth itself.

Finally, he arose. "We only think in terms of a few years, everything is defined by the few pitiful years we inhabit this Earth. But imagine the molten pluton I have spoken about taking thousands of years to cool down, insulated as it is by the miles of shist. The last act of this slow cooling process is the creation of a rock called pegmatite which contains the cassiterite, the ore of tin. And here we are, standing in the middle of a tin rush. Let us go onto Professor Black's mine. I believe the entrance should be just around this hillock."

McKay waited at the mine entrance for the two miners to come out.

"It's an honour to have you visit," said Arthur, shaking McKay's hand. "We heard you were coming. Have you met with the professor in Dunedin?"

"No. I prefer to let the mines speak for themselves," said McKay with a grin. "The ground always speaks the truth, wouldn't you not agree, being a Cornish miner?"

"Aye, aye, I agree, I like a man that can read what lies beneath. Would you like to inspect the bal? We're only in 23 fathoms, about halfway as far as the money goes."

Branock moved aside to usher the men in behind Arthur, then followed them in. The steady stream of water which flowed along the floor of the passage seemed to dry up soon after they entered. "Interesting watering," commented McKay, "I'd say the traverse pegmatite cuts through a spring just up ahead. You must have a prop up here."

"Aye, we put double in here, bloody heavy they were to drag up here too. We have another two further up."

Branock lit two extra candles, passing one to McKay and the other to the man in the middle. Arthur stopped at the crack in the ceiling, holding up his candle to run along its length. "What do you reckon here? A stress fracture? This one had me worried for a while."

McKay lifted his candle to inspect it. "I wouldn't worry. As the pluton here solidified, the thermal volume change created fractures. It looks typical to me." McKay turned to his three charges. "See here, gentlemen, we have the convenience of seeing exactly how the pluton is invaded. Through thoroughfares like this, the residual pegmatite migrated, slowly solidifying to form crystals which eventually seal off the cavity." He lowered his candle, causing it to illuminate his hairy face. Branock felt like telling him to watch out for his busy beard, so near the flame did it get, but settled for smiling to himself instead. McKay continued. "The crystals up here might be an inch at most, but I have heard of them reaching a yard, would you believe? The Eskimo people in the Arctic once used large sheets of muscovite mica from pegmatites as window panes for their igloos. The first European explorers to the Arctic thought they were glass, could not understand how they came by them."

"Well, ya learn something every day," piped up Arthur. A murmur of agreement came from the others. McKay ignored them. "Most of the crystals are just variations of the minerals found in the granite, but sometimes we get strange brews that just bubble away. That is when casserite and wolframite are made, and they are made together, that's why they are so similar."

"I can see why they made you government geologist," quipped Arthur, wiping some hot wax off his hand.

"Show me your working face then," asked McKay, pushing forward. "I can see your wedge fracturing is going well, you've taken off some good slabs."

"Yes, we've been lucky, consistent hardness, or should I say softness, comes away easy," replied Arthur.

McKay waited until he was at the working face before he popped the question. "So why are you digging in the wrong way?"

Arthur knew exactly what the government man meant, but he still replied with, "Pardon?"

"You're digging in parallel to the lode, not into it. Whose idea was that?"

"Professor Black's."

"Bloody amazing!"

"Why is that amazing?"

"Because somehow the most intelligent people can come up with the stupidest ideas," said McKay bluntly. "Surely, you've queried the man."

"Yes, we have, I sent him a note with the fourth lot of samples. To tell you the truth, I don't think he'll change his mind. He's set on us going it at 220 degrees."

McKay lifted his candle up to look around. "Well, apart from missing the lode completely, splendid work, gentlemen, a tidy mine. I think we have seen enough today."

Arthur and Branock watched them go from the mine entrance.

"Tell me, Arthur, what did you think of the man?" Branock asked.

"A bloody sight more intelligent than our employer, that's what I say."

"So, we are going the wrong way, then." Branock looked almost alarmed.

“Put it this way. Until the professor tells us otherwise, we’re still at 220. Whoever pays our wages dictates the drift, simple as that.” Arthur turned and walked back into the mine.

Chapter 21

Elizabeth looked at her mud-covered dress. The walk up the hill had not only exhausted her but left her splattered in mud. She had always imagined the Surveyors Track would be, well, a track, not a near-continuous ribbon of mud that entailed side stepping long bogs of thick mud, jumping over deep holes full of ink black water, or when neither was possible, wading through. Twice she had sunk up to her waste. Syd had laughed as he came to her rescue, grabbing onto her hand to pull her out. He was relieved that they met no one along the way, even Tucker had not spotted them, he knew that for sure, because if he had, he would have been out as quick as a flash. Funny how the diggings worked, everything was fair game when it came to gossip. Syd was now imagining what everyone would be saying: *'George's missus-to-be run off with Syd, would you believe it?'*

They had stopped three times, the first for Syd to re-adjust Elizabeth's swag and small sack which he now insisted on carrying. The second stop was to let Elizabeth catch her breath, which she did by collapsing backwards onto a steep incline of rock slab that bordered the track. Her arm was resting over her eyes, and Syd quietly crept up to lay beside her. Sure, she hadn't noticed him, he moved closer and closer with the intention of giving her a surprise kiss, but just as his lips were about to touch hers, she threw her arm around his neck and pulled his mouth in tight against hers. They kissed passionately before finally she playfully pushed him away.

"You'd better show me your camp first, Mr Braithwaite," she joked. "I expect some fine lodgings now."

"Oh yes, only the finest luxury digs awaits you," he replied in an exaggerated tone.

Their third stop was for water, sipping handfuls of the stuff from a mossy chute gushing onto the track. "How sweet it tastes when one is thirsty," commented Elizabeth wiping the drips off her chin.

"Nearly there," Syd said reassuring. Both their lips were still moist when they embraced and kissed again.

Finally, when they arrived, Syd flourished his arm to issue her ahead on the footworn track. "Welcome to 12A dash 54 Mayfair Lane," he said, using his claim number like an exclusive London address. She giggled as she passed him.

As they approached his tent, Syd remembered what a mess he'd left it in, such a hurry he'd been to get down to the hotel to give Elizabeth the brooch which she was still wearing. She could sense what was coming and pre-empted him. "Syd, don't apologise for your lodgings, I'm just happy to be here, away from that hotel, and with you." She poked her head into the tent, it seemed bare apart from a few personal items and a flattish mound of fern strewn with a red tartan blanket.

"So where do you cook?" She finally asked.

"Just around the place. Depends which way the winds blowing, I guess. Open the flap and cook on the fire if it's a south westerly or don't bother cooking if it's a northerly."

Elizabeth was fast getting the picture. "Aye, a right bachelor boy then, aren't you?" She said laughing.

She took his hand and pulled him out of the tent. "Take me around, show me what you get up to then, finding your tin. I want to see it all, Syd."

Taking the lead, he took her up to the head race, telling her in detail how he diverted the water to work his paddock below. Before they headed down, he grabbed her hand again to take her up to his bathing pool.

"This is my country bathing retreat, a private bubbling mountain spa, privacy guaranteed, and this is my soap," he said, diverting to pull off a kumarahou leaf. "The best lather your soft milky skin could ever desire."

She bent down to feel the water flowing past. "Oh, my goodness, Syd, it's freezing…"

"Only when you're under," he replied, already pulling her away to inspect his paddock and tailrace. She stopped him halfway, pulling him back by the arm so they could embrace.

"Syd, I feel so free. You rescued me. I had a dream this was going to happen."

"Aye, Elizabeth, you rescued me too. You've made me realise…" He paused.

"Realise what, Syd?"

He took a few seconds to compose his words. "Up here, just living with miners, you just keep going, but with you here…it shows me…" He stopped.

“Shows you what, Syd?”

“That maybe this ain’t the right place for me to be.”

“What do you mean? What about the tin? You came for the tin, Syd.”

“Exactly, I came for it, but to tell ya the truth, I don’t know how much there is.”

“What? How do you mean?

“It means there might not be enough of it. I could tell straightaway McKay wasn’t impressed. If anyone should know it’s him, he is the government geologist.”

“But what about that professor in Dunedin? Surely, he knows a thing or two, when I got here, all the miners were saying he was full of it…tin everywhere!”

“Forget him, I don’t think he knows half of what he claims…” Syd paused looking up at the sky. “Elizabeth, you know what I think, we have about two minutes to get back to the tent before we get saturated.” So engrossed in their exchange, they had been oblivious to the near black rainclouds sweeping in from the south east. They ran holding hands, he half dragging her along, as the big fat drops of rain began to fall on them, slowly at first but soon they were pelting down. Elizabeth shrieked with exhilaration as she ran, fleetingly reflecting how changeable, like the weather, her life was now. It was Syd pulling her along that brought it home, being pulled this way and that. The way her uncle too has pushed her into coming out to New Zealand, George too getting her down to Pegasus, then pushing her around at the hotel. Where were her decisions in it all, she wondered?

By the time they made it back under cover, the rain was pelting down in a near continuous roar.

“Weather! Never experienced anything like how it gets here,” grumbled Syd as he laced up the flap and went about breaking sticks of dry kindling and dry fern fronds he had stashed in the tent. “We’ll get a fire going out this side, it’ll be cosy in no time. You can only do it here when the breeze is to leeward, otherwise the tent would go up. Still got to watch for sparks though. Holding the smouldering kindling in one hand, he gently blew it until flames appeared, then, using his body to protect the flames, he carefully placed the smallest sticks until he was sure it had taken. Elizabeth watched him, amazed at both his dexterity in the fire lighting process as much as the primitiveness of the procedure. She tried to imagine herself doing it in such conditions. Glancing around, she saw there wasn’t even a chair, so she placed her swag on some dried fern and sat on it.

"Oh, Syd, that's nice, a fire to warm the cockles of my heart." The rain roared down unabated, streams of water running off the corners of the tent like waterfalls. She watched as the trickles inside the tent snaked across the ground towards her.

"Thank God for Peggy," said Syd, crouching down to retrieve the biscuits and a square-shaped tin from the side of the swag she sat on. He used his knife to open the tin of bully beef and smeared a blade-full of it across two biscuits and handed her one. Elizabeth hadn't realised how hungry she was. She bolted it down before he even had a chance to take a bite of his own. "My word, Syd, you live like a true wild man up here," she said reflectively. "Where do you even sit at night, before you go to bed like?"

He went over to place some larger sticks on the fire, bending down to blow it back to life. He waited until he was back beside her before replying. "Truth is, Elizabeth, I don't bother sitting down, I work until dark, grab something to eat then collapse on my bed. That's it until the next morning when I wake up and it all starts again."

"Don't tell me, a miner's life?" They both laughed as their heads came together. But the reality of her runaway situation was slowly beginning to dawn on her. Syd reached over and pulled out the half full bottle of rum. "Here, have a capful of this, it'll warm you up."

"Syd, I never had much alcohol, sneaked some once when my friends back in Glasgow offered me a swig, but it just made me dizzy. My father was a temperance campaigner all his life did you know."

Syd laughed as he slowly passed over the level capful. "Don't worry, I'm not out to get you rolling drunk. Just eases things up a bit. Life up here ain't that easy, you know."

"I can see that now, Syd, my eyes are wide open." She paused for a second before putting the capful to her lips and sipping.

"Oh my, it's so strong, I used to watch miners in the bar, slugging back half glasses, how do they do it?"

"Practise, plenty of practise," said Syd with a laugh, pouring a nip into his tin cup. The fire had taken as the rain eased, and suddenly, everything seemed a little easier. Elizabeth gave Syd a cheeky smile, nudging up to him.

"Oh my, these last few months have been absolutely momentous for me. Coming out from Glasgow to Dunedin, then Pegasus, meeting up with George, realising so quickly I was hanging on to a sad dream, now you, capturing my heart. Got to say, this all hasn't been easy, Syd." She sipped on the rum, noticing how the sipped dribble of drops was starting to slide down her throat more easily now. It made her think of Peggy. As abrasive and nosey she had been, she had been a great support. Syd interrupted her thoughts. "Let me show you something now, Elizabeth. I bet you ain't seen the way tin can cry?" Before she could even wonder what ever he was talking about, he pulled the finger-length ingot of tin out of his leather bag. "I made this on the same day I made your brooch," he said, holding it up to her brooch to compare the colour. "See, how grey and dull they have both become already, even more so as time goes on. White tin, it comes straight out of the smelter all shiny like, then it slowly turns grey in these cold latitudes. Can't stop it, white tin turns into grey tin. No other base metal does that, they all stay one colour. Guess you never played with tin soldiers, all shiny when you get them, then after a while they all turn dull and grey." He reached for the rum and refilled her cap before holding out the little bar again.

"This is what I want to show you now," he said, grasping the ends in the fingers of each hand. Waiting briefly for the rain to stop, he whispered to her gently, "Now, listen."

Slowly and deliberately, he began bending the bar at its middle. At first, she wasn't sure if she heard it, so she turned her ear to it, the sound of gentle rustling. Then with each bend, it became a discernible crunching sound until soon it was an audible crackle.

"That's the tin cry!" said Syd in a quiet voice. "Listen to it as it cries on and on," he lowered his voice to a whisper. It was like magic, she thought, the metal was crying out, as if quietly screaming in protest 'don't bend me, don't bend me.'

On and on, Syd bent it back and forth, each time as he did it the little bar cred out. "Oh, Syd," she murmured, "it's more a crackle really than a cry. Why does it do that?"

"'Tis the tin crystals shearing and breaking against one another. Watch how long it takes."

"Oh, Syd! It's like you are torturing the poor metal to death," she giggled, taking another sip of rum. She watched as he bent it a score more times, the cry getting more and more strained until finally it snapped apart into two. He held a piece in each hand, the broken ends were jagged, looking as though half chewed through.

"There you have it, the tin cry. How may lasses can say they have witnessed that?" He said it triumphantly. "Touch it," he said holding out his hand, "not at the broken ends, they will be far too hot." She noticed the broken end hung out over his palm. She extended her finger to feel it. The metal was cool at the unbroken end, but became warmer as she ran her finger along it. As she neared the broken end, she had to quickly lift her finer, so hot it still was.

In an instant, Elizabeth felt her life was revealed in that little metallic spectacle. Perhaps, the rum helped, but she could see it clearly now, the way all the external forces of her life bent her this way and that, made her cry out until she thought she might break.

"Oh, my goodness, Syd," she finally said, "that bar of tin is just like me, getting bent and twisted all about, writhing and screaming inside. When it gets too much, it suddenly stops and you feel like it's coming right, then bent over you go again, forced all against your will. There is no end to it all, except when you break in half."

Syd laughed. "So true, my dear, so true. But this is where the tin can teach us."

"Explain," said Elizabeth suddenly impatient.

"You see, the tin can take immense stress, it cries on and on. But how many times did I bend it?"

She could only guess. "Maybe fifty times."

"Yes, exactly, it's impossible to break at first. It is far too strong for that, like the human spirit, it has to be chipped away. But eventually, it can stand it no longer and then it gives…"

"So?"

"The thing I'm getting to, Elizabeth, is that it doesn't matter if its breaks, because in the end, we have two pieces that can be reformed by throwing them both in the crucible. All I have to do is heat it up to 450 degrees and it all melts together so it can be recast again, no damage at all done."

Syd poured himself another nip, offering to refill Elizabeth's cap at the same time, but she didn't notice, so absorbed she was, seeing herself as the tin, bending and bending and finally breaking, not realising how malleable her spirit could be.

"I'll have some more of that rum, thanks," she said, holding out her cap.

They talked on as darkness fell, becoming more and more playful with each other as the light faded into the dusk. The skies became clear and they ventured out to look at the starry heavens. “I’ve never seen such bright stars, Syd,” she whispered. “Do you know the names of them all?”

“Not all of them, of course, but a few.” He pointed over the horizon of mountains to a small cluster of stars.

“That’s the Southern Cross, you don’t see them in the old country. They move around the sky, but you can easily find them. Look for the two bright stars around them, they’re the Pointers, about brightest stars in the whole sky. They point to the cross. See there.” He put his head against hers as he pointed, same time holding her around the shoulders with his other arm. “The Cross changes during the year, in April its upright, but by October it’ll be upside down.” They stared upwards awhile, their thoughts all lost in the stars, but slowly they found their faces come to gently touch.

“It’s time for bed, don’t you think?” He whispered in her ear. “Aye, it surely is,” she replied.

Chapter 22

They spent three days alone, enjoying each other's company and exploring their love for one another. She had never felt her entire being so taken over by such a wonderful swirl of emotions. Nothing else seemed to matter except the warmth they were feeling. Even nature seemed to conspire with them, the weather treating them kindly as they did the chores that made life a little more comfortable. Gathering soft ferns, they enlarged their bed, she made two soft pillows, one for her out of her old swag pillowcase, and another for Syd from an old sack. Using Syd's one and only needle, she carefully unravelled some short lengths of thread from the hem of her dress to crudely sew the pillows, patting them this way and that to make them half presentable. Syd used his axe to chop dry trunks of burnt leatherwood into manageable lengths of firewood. On the second day, he came back with a freshly drowned kiwi out of one his prospect pits and cooked it in his camp oven. She had grimaced, at first, at the thought of eating a drowned wild animal, but it hadn't tasted so bad in the end. When the sun came out in all its glory on the afternoon of their third day, Syd invited her to have a bath.

"I'll watch, but don't expect me to get under, that water is far too freezing!" she had jokingly objected, but once they arrived the water was so clear and sparkling that she had willingly discarded her clothes and joined him in the water. Shrieking and screaming, she put her head under the freezing water, grabbing the waxy kumerahou leaves off him to lather the grime off her body.

"Oh, Syd, I feel so alive," she cried out as she dashed back to her pile of clothes, hugging them to her breasts before sprinting back up the track. Not far behind her, Syd had hesitated briefly alongside his head race, reflecting on how unimportant the tin frenzy seemed now. He needed to make a decision, but it could wait another day or two. Life had suddenly become a joy to him, and he ran to follow Elizabeth up the track. She waited for him to come past, hiding behind a bush to surprise him, and jumped upon his back. He grabbed her legs to keep her on his back and took off galloping like a horse. Together they screamed and hooted, like children frolicking in the wilderness.

Later that evening, he was thoughtful.

"Anything wrong?" She asked him, cutting up the damper for their supper.

"I need to see Conliffe tomorrow, over the hill. It won't take too long, five hours at most." The sudden announcement brought her back to the reality of their situation.

"What about?" She said, wondering if she was prying.

"Prospects, whether it's worth staying here," Syd said matter-of-factly.

She didn't comment as she stirred the left-over kiwi stew, suspecting there was something that he wasn't telling her. It didn't bother her that much; men she knew had trouble sharing their woes and worries, and she wasn't that much better. She wished Peggy was around, she missed her jibes and questions which always seemed to come with some good advice. Women understood each other, not like men and women.

They finished the last of the rum that night, listening to the trill of a kiwi not far from their tent, and talked about what awaited them.

"I can't imagine going back to that hotel, ever!" Elizabeth confessed vehemently.

"Neither could I, well maybe after George has left, I could, but even then, he will be sore with me, running off with his missus like I did." They both laughed at that.

She wondered if George might write a letter to her uncle in Scotland, advising him of the turn of events. It didn't bear thinking about. One day, she knew, she would have to explain everything to her Scottish relatives herself.

Next morning, Syd left early to see Conliffe. "I'll be back early afternoon," he said, holding her in a tight embrace as he left.

"Oh, Syd, I'm so happy you came into my life, I can hardly imagine life without you now." He didn't reply with words, just an appreciative look in his eye and a brushing kiss on her lips. She watched him walk off along the track, waiting for him to turn around and wave, but he didn't look back.

Feeling suddenly very alone, she busied herself tying back the tent flaps to let their canvas shelter get a good airing. Then she tidied up a bit, using a bushy branch of manuka to sweep out the tent floor. She went to the creek and got a billy of water, positioning it beside the fire ready for later. She shook out Syd's tartan blanket and draped it over a bush to air. Ever since arriving at Pegasus, she had only heard the miners talk about the forest as if it were a monstrous annoyance, something to dominate and get rid of at all costs, the big burn-offs treated with near jubilation. But since coming up here to Syd's camp, she had developed an appreciation just how varied the glory of creation was with the variety of plants that now surrounded here. Some were like spikey grasses, others leafy plants which grew all in a tangle, amongst them some type of thick leaved daisy flourished. Everything growing cheek to jowl. She had never seen so many different types of plants growing together, sharing the hillside as if planted by some divine hand.

After she was satisfied, the washing would stay put if any gusts came up, she returned to the tent to arrange their remaining food into days. Rolled oats for breakfast, she estimated five days' worth left. Flour, thankfully there was another weeks' worth at most, seven fine potatoes, and some left over damper. Survivable, she knew, but hardly luxury living.

She was just about to go foraging for more kindling when she heard the unmistakeable sound of a cat. There was no mistaking the meow coming from the undergrowth nearby.

Elizabeth remained stock still, not sure where it was coming from. Slowly, she leaned left, then right, peering to get a glimpse of it, but it remained out of sight. Reaching over the camp oven, she slipped the lid off and grabbed two pieces of left-over kiwi meat with her fingers. In one quick action, she threw them as far as she could out through the door of the tent to where she thought the noise had come from. Staying stock still, she waited and waited, but nothing appeared. Just as she was about to give up, she heard another 'meow,' then more silence. Finally, the feline came into full view. It was a tabby, and much larger than what she had expected. Its dull fur was matted and spikey. This was no domestic cat, that went without saying, it was a wild animal through and through. Smelling the bits of kiwi, she had thrown out, it paused awhile, looking around. Elizabeth could now make out its whiskers backlit by the sun which had just come up over the hilltops. The animal brought back memories of her parent's cat. Wondering if the wild animal might attack her, she stayed still and silent as the animal nibbled the offering of kiwi meat. Suddenly, it stopped chewing to look directly at her, then got back in munching. When it finished, the cat stretched on its stomach for a brief time, then got up and advanced slowly towards her. To her utter amazement, the animal came straight towards the tent, hesitating only briefly as it entered silently through the tent flap, pausing with every few footsteps to look this way and that. Elizabeth nearly shooed it away in cautious fright, but stopped, suddenly deciding it was safe. With little more hesitation, the animal took a few final decisive steps to finally rub itself against Elizabeth's dress.

"Oh, what a fine tabby you are," Elizabeth said gently. The animal began purring, rubbing itself one way then the other, back and forth along the bottom of her dress. Elizabeth could tell from its bulging stomach; it was probably in kitten. Slowly, she put her hand down to give it a rub behind the ear. "Oh, my tabby, I wonder if I am the first human to make your acquaintance. Tis' a pleasure to meet you." The visit didn't last long, a few minutes only before the cat was gone, dashing back out into the scrub. Elizabeth felt a tinge of sadness as it left. That cat was company, and company gone, all too quickly.

Conliffe waved when he saw Syd come towards his tent. The veteran Tasmanian miner was sitting on a rock, leaning over his billy, waiting for it to boil on the smouldering fire.

"Ha, Syd, good to see you, young man, I thought you might have packed up and left, like some of the others."

"Who do you mean exactly?"

"Fleming, Hall, Livingstone, even Old Dad. If they haven't gone already, they may as well be by next week."

"Why's that?" Syd asked enquiringly as he crouched alongside the miner. He already knew the answer but wanted to coax it out of the veteran in his own words.

"Writings on the wall, Syd. We got to face it. Not enough tin. Who the hell is getting rich here? No one! It's time to move on.'

"What about McKay's report? Surely, that will get everything going again."

Conliffe took his billy off the bubble and threw a small handful of China tea leaves into it. "You'll have to share my tin cup again, I'm afraid." He paused to think, his elbows leaning on his knees.

"His report ain't going to be flash, I have to warn you, Syd. I spoke to Swain yesterday; he said goodbye to McKay as he was getting on the *Despatch* back to Bluff. He was blunt, laddie. No one will ever make money from tin here. Said we were all dreamers if we persisted."

"Whew, that's hard to swallow," muttered Syd. He paused before adding, "It's inevitable I know, just coming to terms with it is the hard part."

"Is it though? What say you hear about another place, gold just waiting to be panned from the beach. Quartz in the hills, rich with it too."

"Where? Tell me." Syd asked, suddenly unable to contain himself.

"Knew you'd get excited," Conliffe sniggered. "I'll tell you, Syd. Cromarty and Kisbee Beach in Preservation Inlet. Drop everything and go there now, that's my advice to you today. Catch a boat there from Riverton easy."

Syd could barely speak. He could feel his stomach in his chest, all excited like. The very same feeling he got when he heard about the tin on Stewart Island.

The miner poured the tea into his cup and handed it to Syd.

"You first," there was a big pause, Syd suspected what was coming.

"Swain told me that post mistress run off with you. Is that right?"

"Yeah, it's true, she's at my camp now."

"Listen, I'm not a religious man, so no judgements here, that's all your business with the Almighty which don't concern me. But I'd watch George; Rodgers used to keep a revolver did you know, in case there was a robbery. George is probably looking after it, at least knows where it is. He's not a murderous man by any means, but jilted men can do strange things. Just warning ya here, laddie."

"Good advice. Thanks," said Syd. It hadn't occurred to him that George might shoot him, and the thought of it made him quiet.

Conliffe wasn't finished either. "If I was you, laddie, I'd keep away from the hotel, at least till George has gone. It'll blow over, things happen like this all the time, more than anyone dares to admit." The old miner gave a laugh as he bent over to prod the fire. "Sounds like he's told a few people by the sound of it. Here, hand over my cup, it's my turn now."

As Syd returned down the track back to his camp, he felt pleased he'd made the effort to see the wily Tasmanian. Somehow, the man always managed to give him a fresh outlook on things. Syd knew now he had to make sure to avoid George, make sure Elizabeth was safe too. The more he thought about it though, the more he knew George was not a rash man. There was no point in alarming Elizabeth, but he would definitely have to make sure she didn't visit the hotel either.

He already felt differently about the diggings, especially since speaking to Conliffe. Cromarty and Kisbee Bay were suddenly filling his head. He had to get there, and quick. It was always the first wave that made the money, the claimholders themselves, and he wanted to be one of them.

Syd found coming down so much easier than going up, and he still had a decided spring in his step as he made his camp. Elizabeth was draping some washing out over the nearby bushes, and he crept up the last few yards to surprise her. He could feel her jump as he grabbed her.

"You mustn't give me such a fright," she admonished him. He instantly felt guilty, especially considering his new resolve to keep her safe. But before he could apologise, she blurted out her news.

"A cat visited our camp, it even came into the tent, it let me stoke its neck." She gave a pleased giggle. "I think it was pregnant. Maybe it might come back, we could tame it to become our camp cat, maybe a couple of its kittens too. What do you think?"

It was as if he never heard what she said.

"Elizabeth, listen to me." He held her slightly away so he could look into her eyes. "I have some news, from Conliffe."

She looked at him expectantly.

"Elizabeth. The Tin Rush is over. Cromarty and Kisbee Bay, we must go there."

"What! Where?" She was shocked and pushed him back.

"Cromarty and Kisbee Bay in Preservation Inlet."

He was talking excitedly now. "Preservation Inlet, just three days from here. We have to leave, Elizabeth. There is no future here anymore."

Elizabeth felt perturbed. Once again, she was being directed, as though she was the last person to be considered.

"So, what is this place like? Is it a village or is it like Pegasus, maybe one building to get drunk in and the rest all just tents occupied by itinerant miners?" She was standing back now, her hands on her hips. Syd could tell she wanted answers.

"Soon it will be a town, Conliffe said they were finding gold on the beach, and the quartz there is full of gold."

"Yes, just like Pegasus, full of tin! You are dreaming, Syd." She stormed away, heading back to the ten.

He spent the next hour trying to convince her, but each time he came near to tell her something else that may convince her to shift on, but each time she walked off in a sulk. Finally, he couldn't hold back anymore. He stormed up to her as she was bringing in the washing.

"If you weren't here, Elizabeth, I would be gone already, this very afternoon. You don't realise what being a miner entails, shifting at a moment's notice is all part of the game, you have to follow the riches and get there before anyone else." With the bundle of clean washing under her arm, she turned to face him.

"Syd, I'm just not going." She pursed her lips before speaking on. "You're going to have to tell me more about the place first, what I can expect."

"But, Elizabeth…"

"Oh, shut up, Syd, your silly dreams and false hopes are making me tired." She started to walk off but turned back again at the last second. "You can take me down to the boat if you like. The *Invercargill* should be in tomorrow."

"Oh, Elizabeth, no, no no!" he implored. 'I love you, and I truly want us to stay together. There's another reason we can't go down too, I should warn you…"

"What?" She snapped.

"Rodgers kept a revolver at the hotel. George no doubt has access to it. He's been telling miners how angry he is about us running off. We shouldn't go down there under any circumstances, at least until he leaves anyway."

Elizabeth was taken aback, once again faced with the reality of her situation. "So, we are trapped here then, up this mountain?"

"Not quite," replied Syd as he moved closer to her, lowering his voice to not much more than a whisper.

"There is another way out, along the backbone of the island to Big Glory Bay. We could do it in three days."

"Oh, for heaven sakes, Syd, don't tell me it's another one of your surveyor tracks? Or probably no track at all."

Syd didn't want to tell her it that it would be far worse. "Listen to me. We will be doing it together and I will help you. But we must go as light as we can, starting early tomorrow morning." He stared into her eyes, watching for any flicker of acquiescence, but he couldn't detect anything. Only when tears began spilling down her face, did she finally turn away. Syd went to hold her, but she pulled away, only to relent and collapse against his chest. He ran his fingers through her unruly hair, gently kissing her forehead. He waited until he felt she had calmed down before he spoke again. "Elizabeth, we have to leave, tomorrow morning early. This is going to be our last night here, so decide what you want to take. I will be walking out of here. Apart from a few things I'll be leaving it all behind."

Elizabeth shook her head. Leaving what behind? He had almost nothing—no table, chair, pots and pans, the barest of cutlery. A tin mug and plate for sure, a few possessions in a leather satchel, but that was it. But she saw no alternative now. He was right, they had to go, and there was only one way out, and they had to walk it.

She spent the rest of the afternoon making small piles—a pile of fresh washing, all the food to take, her spare dress and clothes neatly folded. Syd came back from his paddock with only his pan which he threw down alongside his satchel. He spent an hour sharpening his big knife before putting it back into its leather sheath. His three spare boxes of matches he carefully wrapped in a piece of oilskin and tucked away into his satchel, rewrapping his crucible pipes and tongs in their square of chamois leather. Elizabeth noted how meticulous he was with it all.

They had the last of the potatoes that night, a feast roasted in their jackets on the edge of the coals. They used sticks to turn them around to cook evenly, dragging them back to cool before peel away their burnt skins. Syd had his on a flat rock while Elizabeth used his tin plate and fork to eat hers.

"You know, Syd, when I first came to Port Pegasus…" She paused to think about the cookhouse down at the hotel. "I used to think how primitive it was, but when I saw your camp, I realised how basic you can get."

"What about Tane?" Syd ventured. "No one even knows where he camps. He keeps it a secret, I don't know why, but I bet his camp has even less amenities than mine."

She pondered the difference for a while, then said. "I love you, Syd, but I'm not sure this life is for me. I need a few comforts. A feather pillow…"

"What's wrong with soft fern, it's as good as down…"

"No, Syd, you don't understand! I'm a woman, and women like a soft bed with cotton sheets, pots and pans in the kitchen, a desk to write letters at…but do you know what gets to me the most up here?"

"What's that?"

"I hate wiping my bum with those damn leaves, you can stick 'em, Syd. For sure, I can put up with them for a few more days, but after that, I never want to see another rangiora leaf again in my whole life, unless it's a postcard, of course." They both burst out laughing, and she moved over to him until they had their heads touching.

"Arrh, Lassie, I can't blame ya one bit. But I know, one day I'll strike it rich, and I'll be able to buy you a house with a veranda all around and dormer windows in the roof. It'll have a staircase and a kitchen just for you. There'll be a flower garden and a place to grow some vegetables…"

"Oh, Syd, so sweet of you to want that for us. Now, let me ask you something, you been a miner all your working life, eh?"

"Yeah, I have."

"And your father was all his life?"

"That's right. And his father…"

"And his father and his father no doubt, and probably his one before that," said Elizabeth in a voice tinged with sarcasm. "What makes you think you ae going to be any different, Syd? You'll be toiling all your life for sure. That's not much company for a woman like me."

"Arh, c'mon now, Elizabeth. It's going to be different because we are in a new country. This is New Zealand, not Cornwall, or Scotland!"

Elizabeth knew the conversation was going nowhere fast. "What time are we setting off tomorrow?" She asked.

"I'll make some damper to take early, at first light. Then we'll head off. We should hit the tops sometime after mid-day, then we'll see how we go. Hopefully, we'll get to the first big granite knob before it gets dark." Poking the fire, he seemed unable to leave it alone.

"How heavy is this tent?" She asked him.

"We're not taking it. It takes up too much room and weighs too much. We can sleep under the ferns. I'll bring the blanket of course."

Elizabeth spent a minute contemplating sleeping out along the mountain top in winter. "What say it rains?" She finally asked.

"Not if, just course it will. Let's just hope it don't snow, that's all."

"And what happens when we get to Big Glory Bay?"

"We should be able to get on a boat from the sawmill there, at Maori Beach."

Elizabeth went quiet, resorting to biting her lip. She thought about her coming out from Scotland to end up at Pegasus, what an ordeal it had all been. But now the prospect of the next few days felt like it might surpass everything she had been through.

Chapter 23

Elizabeth awoke to the crackle of the fire outside. It was still dark, even the birds had not yet woken for their dawn chorus. She stretched out, running one hand across the bed of fern to check if Syd had come back to bed, but she was lying alone.

"Good morning, my darling," said Syd re-entering the tent. "I have the damper on, it should be ready soon." He was pushing his heavy pack ahead of him into the tent. As he lit a candle, she could see his big gold pan strapped to the back of it.

"I've put your dress in my pack, but take all your warm clothes, you will need them. Let me take your pillowcase and tie it up so you can sling it over your back. It won't be heavy." He bent over to kiss her, at the same time lifting her head to slide her pillow out from under it. "Here, you can still have the fern," he said, pulling it all out. "But don't sleep in, we have to be going soon."

"Why so early?" She yawned.

"Because the earlier we go, the earlier we can make camp tonight." She watched groggily as he re-tied her swag, threading two strips of leather onto the rope.

"Adjust these over your shoulders, the ropes won't cut in so much." She could tell he was focused, systematically going about one chore after another, readying for leaving. "What about the camp oven, are we taking that?"

"Course not, far too heavy. I did think about throwing it on top of my pack, but not where we're going."

Elizabeth sat upright as he pulled the blanket off her and began rolling it up into a tight bundle which he tied to the side of his pack.

"The damper will be ready if you want to get it out of the camp oven," he said to her matter-of-factly. "Get some food into you. Keep you going all day." He disappeared outside, leaving Elizabeth to her thoughts, the huge reality of the day suddenly dawning on her. She arose from her stripped bed and went outside where Syd was now nowhere to be seen. Taking a few steps away, she crouched down to urinate on the ground. As she got up, she could hear it again, the cat, gently meowing. Staying crouched down, she silently waited, the meowing become closer and closer until she could see its shape in the gathering light. Something was different about the shape of it this time. It wasn't until the cat was right up to her before she realised, it had a bird hanging out of its mouth. The cat put it down and looked at her, then sniffed the ground around. Then Syd returned, frightening it away. It streaked off, leaving the lifeless bird on the ground. Elizabeth picked it up.

"Oh, my goodness," she said in wonder, "look at these feathers, Syd, it's beautiful, look at these tail feathers."

"Fantail," pronounced Syd, looking over the bird in a cursory manner. "Cats have to eat something up here, I guess. Can you put any damper we don't eat in your pack to have for lunch?"

Elizabeth was still chewing hers as they headed off. She glanced back at the camp they were abandoning, amazed at the way they were just walking off, leaving everything behind.

"What a shame we can't take the tent," she said wistfully.

"Forty pounds at least that tent," Syd had replied nonchalantly, not even bothering to turn around. "Three trips it took to get everything up here. I'm only doing one out."

They trudged for two hours without a single stop, Elizabeth doing her best to keep up with Syd, who every so often would stop and turn around to make sure she was still there. His stamina amazed her, especially carrying all that weight in his big oversized pack. She had tried to lift it when it was on the ground, just before they departed, but she couldn't even get it off the ground an inch. From behind, he looked a sight. His big gold pan completely covered his pack, and his two strong legs stuck out the bottom, with his head sticking out the top. The sight made her chuckle.

"Oh, just look at all these amazing plants," she said when they finally stopped. "See how they all hide from the wind, even the trunks of the leatherwoods grow along the crevices out of the wind."

Syd had to admit he had never noticed that much before, the way the plants cowered. "Aye, we're lucky today, no screaming winds from the roaring forties up here. No wonder, nothing grows much. This ain't been burnt off like down below, didn't need to be mind you, nothing much higher than a foot grows up here."

"It's so beautiful, Syd, a right picture, just like the paintings of the Scottish moors," she bent down to pick a pale green sprig. "It looks like heather, don't you think now?" She said, slipping it in behind her brooch. So pretty it looked.

"Once we get into the bush, I'd take that brooch off," Syd said sternly, "Brushing past a branch will take it off quick as a flash for sure."

They trudged on, across the spongy moorland tops littered with granite rocks, on their left flank a vast and verdant valley ran alongside. Slowly, they advanced towards a conspicuous granite knob rising rounded and high out of scrubland. At its base, they finally stopped to rest; Syd showing his weariness for the first time as he let his pack drop off his shoulders on a slab of granite.

"Look at this dome of rock, Syd, a thousand times the bulk of any vaulted roof of a cathedral back home," said Elizabeth in wonder. "The big slabs, they look like they're peeling off. How can that be?"

"It's the freezing weather, Elizabeth, the water freezes in the crevices; when it expands, it exerts a tremendous power. It wedges off the slabs, would ya believe now." His tone was flat and disinterested as he fiddled with his pack to finally pull out two biscuits. "Here, the last of 'em. Should keep us going till supper."

"I want to explore a bit, Syd. Climb up the granite, you stay here if you like. I won't go far, promise."

"Be careful then, call out if you need me and I'll come running," he said by way of goodbye. She felt strangely unencumbered by both swag and man as she took off up the sloping granite, its textured grey surface offering secure footholds to every one of her steps. Growing out of the lines of crevices were plants she had bever seen before, as she negotiated upwards, the slope of the dome became gentler and the exfoliated slabs of granite became more numerous as they had less chance to slide off. In her imagination, the more angular ones took on the shapes of faces, monsters, even a huge lizard, and she began to feel exhilarated. To be so alone amongst such grandeur of nature, how joyful it was!

Then she spotted it, a clear crystal lying in a shallow crevice. She picked it up, impressed that it stretched across her whole palm. She admired its beauty before holding it up to the sky and was amazed that she could see straight through, it was entirely translucent, just like glass. She continued on, following the crevice upwards. Suddenly, there were crystals everywhere. She picked up a few more, discarding those as she went that looked inferior to her eye. Soon, she was at the flat summit, taking in the magnificent vista. The wind of the open tops buffeted her now, chilled her to her bones, but she didn't care. Looking back from where she had come from, she could see straight down to the great harbour of Pegasus, its lush islands rising out of the steely grey water. Southwards, two peaks rose majestically out of the landscape, one a near perfect pyramid, the other more asymmetrical, but still nevertheless impressive. It only took a few seconds for it to come to her; they must be Gog and Magog. They made her think of Tane, even if there was no red feathered tinge to Gog today. The other didn't look sullen or angry either, but then, it wasn't early morning or sunset. Turning around to the east, she was treated to the sight of the unrestrained Southern Ocean stretching to the far horizon, its huge swells advancing towards the island's eastern flank to become line after line of big galloping breakers as they neared land. Far out at sea, dark clouds dominated, and she imagined them gathering for a great assault upon the land, just as an army might amass before a great battle. She had never witnessed anything like this so magnificent before. Turning back, she cupped her hands around mouth, calling out as loudly as she could to the tiny figure of Syd still leaning against the rock where she had left him. She knew he would never hear, not in this wind. Before she headed down, she paused to look along the ridge where she thought they might be headed. A verdant green and straw-coloured carpet of low vegetation dominated, but she also noticed the patches of forest and rocks which rose out of the landscape dominated by one particularly large granite hillock. Below it, off to one side a little tarn beckoned. She wanted to go there she thought as she headed back down, exhilarated by her foray.

"Look, Syd! Look what I found," she said, showing him the four biggest crystals, she had brought down with her. He took the largest one in his hand and examined it. "See how clear they are, like glass," she said enthusiastically.

He held it up to the light. "A lode crystal. Must say one of the clearest I seen." He handed it back. "Just what we need, more weight in our packs."

"I'm taking them, Syd, and I'll carry them, no problem there." She sounded annoyed.

"Didn't mean it like that, my darling." He said getting up. "It's been a hard walk up to here with this pack on, forgive me, will ya?"

She didn't bother replying as she pushed the two best crystals into her swag, dropping the other two on the ground to leave behind. "I saw where we have to go from up there, we should end up at a little tarn if I'm not mistaken."

Syd glanced around, looking somewhat surprised. "Tucker told me the route once and I've never forgotten, even if I thought I'd never have to do it. From here, we head down to that tarn, you are right there. But he said be careful, it can be confusing country, don't go following the ridge line to end up on the slopes of Mount Allen, best to sidle down and re-join the ridge once you're past it. Let's go."

The ground became spongier and spongier as they went on; in some places, they seemed to spring from one footing to the next; in others, they sank through to the bog underneath, only managing to pull their feet out with the greatest of effort. Syd seemed to cop it worse than her, sometimes he had to lean forward with his hands on the ground just so he could wrestle his foot out of the mud.

"It's my pack," he said at one point. "A man is not supposed to be carrying this much on ground like this." She might not have had his stamina, but she was nimble which gave her the true advantage.

Finally, they made the tarn, its dark water giving it a menacing and brooding appearance.

"Look, over there," Syd pointed to a large, tilted slab of flat rock on the opposite side, "We may find shelter under there tonight."

Sure enough, they found a cavity underneath, just big enough to crawl out of the deteriorating weather. Syd gathered some dead twigs got a fire going at the lee end, just managing to light it before the rainstorm hit.

"I saw it coming out at sea," she said as she pulled out the last of the damper from her swag. It felt stale and hard. "What will we eat tomorrow, I wonder."

"Don't worry, I will find something, maybe a big fat pigeon. Tucker told me the forest is thick with them once we get into it."

The rain was bucketing down now, and they could see the water pouring down in little cascades out both sides of their rock bivouac. "How far are we along the way?" She asked, peering through the dripping veil of water coming off their shelter.

"About a third," he said. "We follow the ridge along tomorrow; it will get us into forest. After that, we work our way around down to Big Glory." He ran his hand through her hair, then stroked her face. She cuddled up to Syd to share the warmth of his big body. He wrapped the blanket around them, and she found herself almost immediately drifting off to sleep, her body spent from the excursion of the day.

They woke several times in the night, at one point having to turn around and sit up the slope of their little cave to let the water flow through. That trickle became a steady flow, necessitating them to also prop their legs up against the rock on the opposite side so the water could flow through unobstructed. She had been too tired to care, but it all proved a night of fitful sleep that left them both exhausted.

Although, the rain had largely stopped by the time they woke up at first light, a thick mist had descended as they trudged off around the eastern flank of Mount Allen. The going was confusing as they negotiated fields of peat bogs that seemed to go on forever. Twice they had to retrace their steps to find their lead through the tussocks to get them back onto the main ridge of the island.

"I'm cold through to my bones. It makes me feel numb," Elizabeth called out to Syd when the wind came up. He hurried over, leading her into the lee of a rocky outcrop where he pulled out the blanket to wrap around her. He sat behind her, cradling her body to help warm her up.

"We'll be in the forest soon," he said reassuringly. "Hold on, it'll be much warmer in there. I'll find a pigeon and cook it for you."

Thankfully, they did make the forest that day, it starting out as thick manuka scrub which necessitated a full body wrestle to get through in places.

"Stay directly behind me," he advised her. "Let me carve the path through, stay in my wake, but watch for the branches flinging back. Wrap your scarf around your face, it will help."

Walking so close behind him gave her an appreciation of his progress, she could almost anticipate the route by just listening to his groans, moans and grunts as he heaved his way through, twisting and turning as he went to free his pack which got continuously snagged. The forest cover changed as they pushed through, the trunks of the towering trees soon festooned with beautiful mosses and hanging plants. At the first lancewood, Syd stopped and dropped his pack, pulling out his bowie knife to slice through the base of its slender trunk. She watched as he stripped the branches, up to a length of three yards and sharpened it to a fine point.

"Keep an eye out for pigeons, and the sharp end of my spear," he said as he hefted his pack back onto his shoulders. They didn't have to wait long before he spotted a pair in the lower branches of a *miro* tree down a bank. Dropping his pack, he indicated for her to stay back, stealthily working his way up to the birds. She was amazed they seemed so nonchalant as he positioned himself under them. Slowly, he brought up the spear until it was directly under the chest of one, edging it closer and closer until suddenly driving it upwards with as much force as he could gather, impaling the hapless bird which fluttered madly as he pulled it down to the ground. Elizabeth watched the other frantically fly off, its wings beating the air in noisy retreat.

"Let's camp early today, we deserve it," he said, carrying his prize back by its legs. "Once we stop, I'll light a fire. Roast pigeon tonight!"

Elizabeth was starving, but it took another hour of walking until he was satisfied with a place he deemed dry enough to camp, at the base of towering *rata,* the lean of its powerful contorted trunk affording shelter from overhead rain at least.

"Oh, Syd, everything is so wet, however will we light a fire?"

"Watch!" he said, "and find some dry sticks if you can. I shall be back soon." She ferreted around the bush as he disappeared, gathering an armful of damp wood, surely it would not burn she wondered. He soon returned with a huge armful of feathery dark green branches.

"Turpentine scrub," he said, pulling out his wax matches to light the oily leaves. Soon the flames were licking up, nearly touching his fingers. With a flourish, he whipped the flaming armful under the sticks she had gathered. Immediately, she could feel its warmth.

"This is where we need the camp oven," she said, turning around to warm her back. Already he had gathered more wood to pile on.

"There must be a puddle around from that rain. Let me look," he finally said. She watched as he pulled out the sack from his pack and wrapped up the pigeon in it, feathers and all, taking it all with him into the bush. Elizabeth's spirits were fast lifting, what a day it had been. She had thought she might not make it along the tops, she had become so cold. It was worse when the wind came up, chilling her to the bone. It had surprised her, how numb she felt from the exposure, as though nothing mattered anymore. She could have drifted off to sleep and never woken up.

Syd returned with his sacking bundle, dripping wet and plastered thickly with mud. He placed it by the edge of the fire.

"Supper will be served in two hours," he said, smiling to her.

"Thanks, Syd, I appreciate it. Today, I thought I might die up there, you know, but now, it all doesn't seem so bad."

"Over halfway now I reckon, it'll be over soon."

She didn't say a word, just stared into the fire as he dragged over a short length of fallen log for them to sit on. It was nice to feel his body alongside hers. She reflected on the fact that no one else had the slightest idea where they were. She thought about her uncle and Meg, whatever would they think if they knew? No doubt, they still thought she was with George in Invercargill, setting up his drapery shop. How ridiculous it all was, she couldn't help but think, suddenly sharing her thoughts out loud with Syd.

"Funny eh, don't you think, the way things happen?"

"What you mean like?"

"The muddles one can get into. Today was a bad one for me up there. What if I had died in your arms, what would you have done? You wouldn't have even be able to bury me without a shovel."

"It don't bear thinking about, Elizabeth, put your mind to happy things."

Elizabeth fell quiet. No, she wasn't going to make her mind happy, just because he said so. The day had been brutal. What if it had snowed, which it surely was close too. She would definitely have passed away. And why? All because Syd had to get to blasted Cromarty in a hurry, a place she didn't know the slightest thing about. It made her angry, but she kept it to herself.

The pigeon was delicious. Served up in his gold pan, it looked like a lavish banquet when Syd used his trusty bowie knife to peel back the skin and burnt feathers to reveal the soft pale brown flesh.

"I recall Conliffe telling me once, the best most flavourful pigeons are those you take feeding on the miro berry. Let's hope, he is right now."

"Oh, the smell, Syd, it's delicious already. I have never looked forward to a table bird as much as this one." They ripped into the bird, using their fingers to pull off chunks which they stuffed into their hungry mouths. They ate every last morsel, until there was just a pile of bones, feathers, skin, a few shrivelled guts.

"Maybe tomorrow we might get an owl parrot," said Syd. "Keep an eye out for their scratching bowls as we go, although they're usually more higher up."

The next day dawned clear if not chilly. Syd was keen to get started early again, to cover as much ground as they could. He had already cut her dress short with his knife so it would not encumber her, and she felt thankful for the spare one she had brought along to wear when they came out at Big Glory Bay. There would be men there for sure, and she did not want to appear like a wild woman. She had her standards to maintain, even if it was at the ends of the earth.

Coming up to Table Hill, everything changed when they got their first sight of the narrow slice of water that Syd guessed was South West Arm of Paterson Inlet. They hugged and congratulated each other, knowing the end was literally in sight now, even if was by no means over. They changed direction, to the north east now, following the flat open tops which Syd knew would take them down to Big Glory Bay. All day they trudged on, noticing the vegetation change as they descended; everything seemed lusher and taller, calm in the forest too. Flocks of colourful little parrots followed them, chattering amongst themselves as they remained elusive, high in the trees.

When they realised, they would not make the coast by nightfall, Elizabeth burst into tears.

"I can't take another night out in the bush," she sobbed. "I just want to be out of here," she sat down against a tree.

"Listen, Elizabeth," Syd tried to reassure her. "We'll be out by noon tomorrow."

"Damn you, Syd, bringing me here," she yelled at him, storming off to hide behind the nearest large tree trunk she could find. Her tears there were futile and she knew it, once again she had to face the reality of her situation. She was dependent on Syd to get her out of here, and it was all her own fault. In her heart, she had no one to blame but herself. Her eyes had been open, she even recalled how she told Syd that when they had discussed running off with him up the hill with him to his camp. Peggy's advice came back to her at that moment too. 'You don't wanna run off with the first man ya meet now.' Oh, my God, what a damn fool she felt suddenly.

She wiped away her tears and emerged to see Syd sitting on his pack, hands on his knees, head down, just staring at the ground. Taking a deep breath, she walked up behind him and placed one hand on his shoulder. Syd showed no reaction, not even lifting his head.

"Dear man," she said quietly, "I think this is a fine place to camp. Tomorrow morning, I shall look forward to bathing in the seawater with you." It didn't surprise her in the least Syd was not reacting to her, the way she had stormed off like some spoilt child not getting her way. Staying stock still, she waited beside him, her hand not leaving his shoulder. It was her breath she was aware of now, the deep inhale which made her bosom expand, the exhale which turned to condensation in the damp forest environment. So few times if ever she had ever considered her drawing of breath, the inexorable in and out that kept her alive. For a few moments, it made time stand still for her.

Slowly, Syd looked up and smiled at her. He had been thinking of nothing but Cromarty, but she didn't know that.

Epilogue

It was said about the great Tin Rush of 1889-90 on Stewart Island that it went off with a bang but ended with a whimper. And so, it was with Syd and Elizabeth.

After they arrived back in Bluff from Big Glory Bay, Syd set off almost immediately for Preservation Inlet. Their goodbyes proved tearful, especially for Elizabeth. The walk along the range from Pegasus had taken it out of her, and she had little to give as they parted. She knew in her heart that, no matter how much she loved Syd, he was always going to be a miner, forever on the move to the next prospect. It was just in his blood. They promised to write letters, which they did for several years, some expressing great passion, but he never came back for her in Dunedin where she settled. After her arrival there, she became strongly involved in the Suffragette Movement which culminated in women finally being accorded the vote in 1893. On one occasion, she was called up by Kate Shepperd herself at a public meeting to recount her experiences at Port Pegasus, and how it made her so determined to chart her own destiny and not let her male colleagues dictate it. Her experience running the little post office at Port Pegasus also served her in good stead, for she quickly got a job on the counter of the Green Bay Post Office where she worked her way up the civil service ladder to be appointed the first postmistress of a New Zealand metropolitan Post Office, Dunedin Central in the Hexagon. Nor did she ever forget the Rule Book, surprising her male subordinates in particular with her comprehensive understanding and ability to recite procedures. Still, when no one was looking, she could never resist reading the Muttonbird scrub leaf postcards that came through her office until 1915, when the New Zealand Post Office finally stopped accepting them. Despite being courted by various suitors, Elizabeth never married. After she died in her sleep in 1956, aged 89, tributes flowed in from near and far. She was remembered not only for her post office work, but support for the Suffragette Movement in Dunedin during the early 1890s. She is buried in the cemetery at Green Bay.

Syd worked his claim at Cromarty for two years, living in primitive conditions under canvas until he got a job at the Alpha Mine and Battery where he worked his way up to the position of mine manager, in time becoming regarded as one of the most proficient and knowledgeable men on the field. When the mine finally shut down in 1906, he stayed on awhile in the area, but eventually drifted off to find work in a sawmill at Tuatapere. After initially being turned down because of his advancing age, he was finally accepted for WW1 overseas service with the New Zealand Expeditionary Division because of his superb physical condition. It is assumed he was one of 2,100 New Zealand troops mown down by machine gun fire or blown to bits in the First Battle of the Somme. Although his body was never recovered, his name is inscribed on the New Zealand Memorial to the missing in the Caterpillar Valley Cemetery near the village of Longueval in Belgium.

As the number of miners dwindled, and with many creditors to pay, Louis Rodgers had little option but to put his Pioneer Hotel into bankruptcy. The hotel, store and little post office, along with the cat, were all sold in early 1891 for a pittance to an Irishman, Arthur Ford, for use as a house. Along with Shetlander Robert Fraser, they remained in residence there until 1914, prospecting and fishing as conditions allowed.

After Rodger's store closed, Peggy moved to the settlement of Oban, where she got a job as a barmaid at the South Seas Hotel, becoming the most trusted and long-time employee of the establishment. Such was her presence, many customers assumed she owned the place. Going out to warmly meet new arrivals on the beach, and later the wharf, became her forte, getting to know all their business before she even served them a drink.

George settled back in Invercargill, eventually opening his drapery in Leven Street. He married a local woman who assisted him in his shop. Although efficient enough, she acquired a reputation of being somewhat sullen with customers. They parted after ten years, after which time he closed up for good.

Tane gave up his seasonal *titi* gathering expeditions in 1895 after the death of Reverend Johans Wohler, returning to Ruapuke Island in Foveaux Strait to support his *whanau.* It is said that the cohesiveness of the islanders which Wohler encouraged quickly fell apart after his death. Many of the residents drifted off as the years went by, and the island was quickly overtaken by scrub.

If McKay's pessimistic report on the Pegasus Tin Field dashed the hopes of many, miners and investors alike, it was the well-reported comments of Harold

A Gordon, the government's chief inspector of mines, in mid-1890 that spelt the final death knoll for the field. Guided around the diggings by Mr Rusha of the Pegasus Co., he found a field with less than 20 men working, compared with 240 at the height of the rush only six months earlier. Gordon particularly criticised Professor Black's tunnel, then at 93 yards, for running parallel to the lode. "And considering the lode was not payable to work at the surface, whatever money has been expended may be considered thrown away." The criticism was remarkable in that Black and he had been partners in the mine. Summarising the prospects on the field, Gordon wrote, "As far as large deposits of tin being found in the alluvial drifts are concerned, the general character of the country does not hold any inducement for these being discovered. In short, it would never give employment to a large population."

For McKay, the Tin Range visit represented his last major exploratory expedition. He retired a year later, when the government retrenched its geological survey, but continued as a mine inspector for many years. Written with a flowing Victorian verbosity, his geological reports from four decades of work in the field 'proved to be an astonishingly accurate and reliable guide to the succession, structure, fossil content and distribution of strata of widely differing regions and geological ages.' Up to the 1940s, they were still regarded as the best account in nearly every region of New Zealand. Perhaps, his most last contribution to the understanding of New Zealand came out of his careful measuring of two displaced fence lines along the Hope Fault after the 1888 Glenn-Wye Earthquake, giving rise to his theory of horizontal movement along the Alpine Fault. Until then, only vertical displacements were thought possible from block faulting, and his work established our modern understanding that adjacent sections of the Earth's crust can be horizontally displaced, sometimes by hundreds of kilometres. Almost certainly, he was the first geologist in the world to document a transcurrent fault, not bad for an untrained geologist.

Largely thanks to his report to the government which he submitted immediately upon his return from Pegasus, the dreams of riches beyond avarice from a mountain of tin were finally put to rest. By January 1891, only two miners were reported as working the field, although two years later, a second, far more minor rush was reported after the supposed discovery of three tons of stream tin and 80 ounces of gold from an area on the far eastern side of the Tin Range. Amazingly, the find was never verified. A score or so miners descended once again, and the little post office reopened for eight months until a lack of mail forced its final closure.

The two Cornish miners finally laid down their tools in August 1890, at 46 fathoms (280 feet) in, after getting word from Professor Black that the money had run out. Despite being sent samples every two weeks, he never altered the course, and no payable cassiterite was ever found. The pick they used, it's wooden handle long since rotted, and the billy they used to make their last tea, remain at the inn face where a small alcove exists off to one side. Just like the miners, they walked away when they knew their prospects were up.

The professor was publicly blamed by many of the failed miners for leading them on a wild goose chase after a non-existent resource, indeed a deep malice was born by many. Nevertheless, Black never stopped being an enthusiastic proponent of the field, optimistically comparing it to its namesake in Greek mythology, expounding that 'Pegasus would shortly mount exultant on triumphant wing.' For many years, he continued to refer to Port Pegasus as the New Zealand's equivalent to Cornwall's Lands End, always alluding to the riches which lay beneath the ground.

For another two decades, he continued to deliver his fabulous lectures with flair and flourish. In 1910, at the age of 74, the professor retired to his beloved Stewart Island with his wife, with Mason Bay becoming one of his favourite haunts. On one such expedition, the alarm was raised when he failed to return for several days after he said he would. A search party went out looking for him, they arrived at the homestead in the dark, and seeing no lamp light on, took it as an ominous sign. But they found him inside, snoring in bed. On top of his blankets, he had somehow placed a heavy door which had come off its hinges. "Whatever's wrong?" asked one of the searches waking him up. "Were you scared that you would walk in your sleep?" They had all laughed at that. But the professor remained serious, retorting back to the laughing men. "Not at all. It's a cold night, gentlemen, and didn't you know that weight is conducive to heat."

Professor Black and his wife are buried in the cemetery at Oban.

The world cry for tin did not end with arrival of the twentieth century either. The Cornwall deposits, which had supplied the world or two thousand years, were fast drying up, and prices escalated as the century rolled over. Wolframite ore too, completely valueless in the original rush, was now fetching £100 per ton as tungsten became a mainstream hardener in new steel making process.

In 1912, the new developments led a group of Dunedin Investors to float a company to again work the Tin Range. Their overstated prospectus claiming returns per acre of 100oz of gold, two tons of tin and 4cwt of wolframite, from every acre of ground. That amounted to a return of £1,200 per acre, a dizzying amount for the day. They raised over £7,000, all spent on installing modern machinery, buildings, and a jetty at Diprose Bay. Their associated sawmill was soon milling up sleepers for the 'four miles and 48 chains' of tramway they dug out and installed up the western side of the Tin Range, ending in the headwaters of McArthurs Creek where water pipes and hydraulic fluming were all laid out. A small dam from the original field was extended to supply the water needed, the idea being that the fabulous profits earned from the hydraulic sluicing would pay for the development of extracting the ore body.

No profits were ever forthcoming, and the lode deposits remained untouched. A mine inspectors annual report from 1917 reveals a pitiful return from six months of work, just two-and-a-half hundredweight of tin and wolframite concentrates, which worked out as a return of £12 per acre, one hundred times less than projected.

A fish processing factory and freezer became the main emphasis of industry at Port Pegasus in the early twentieth century, and its remains can be seen next to Belltopper Falls which was utilised for power via fluming and a water wheel water. But the 1920s did see a few prospectors turn up, one notable being a Dane named Carl Yunge, or 'Big Charlie,' and a giant of a man. He credited his father with inspiring him with stories of the original rushes in Otago. The last of the tin miners was Ted Carrington, a former city engineer from Napier. He first arrived in 1937 and made numerous trips to Port Pegasus, blazing a route that started at the southern end of the Tin Range that went via Scollay's Flat all the way to Maori Bay. He stayed for months at a time at Port Pegasus, constructing a storehouse with help of islander Peter McKellar. Together, they packed tinstone down off the range, where it was picked up by Bill Thomson in his 'pride of Pegasus,' the 21-metre-long ketch *Rahui* which he'd built and launched there in 1936.

Among the 'relics' Carrington left behind were two draughthorses, which he let loose after his stay there ended. Eventually, they made their way up to the open tops, where, according to islander Roy Traill, they could get a decent feed. Unable to return to the low country as the tracks became overgrown, one died, but the other hung on, using a cave as its stable when the weather turned foul. Almost certainly, it was the loneliest horse in the whole world.

The Pegasus tin field remains the most intact alluvial mining field in the country, thanks to its isolation. The discovery of kakapo in the area in 1977 brought hope for the survival of the species, along with the establishment of a 'cat catchers camp' not far up the hill from the little inlet alongside where the hotel once stood. The area was deemed feral cat free around 1982.

It is a great irony of Pegasus that goldminers ended getting more tin than they bargained for, and tin miners ended up selling more gold than tin. May they all be remembered for their tin dreams, a stupendous effort in the most inhospitable conditions.

Glossary of Nineteenth Century Mining Terms

Adit: An almost horizontal passage dug into a hillside from which a mine working is entered and dewatered.

Alluvial/Alluvium: Deposits of eroded sediments which have been sorted by water action, invariably streams and rivers. Usually unconsolidated and unlithified. Alluvial mining is the extraction of valuable minerals from these deposits, usually by washing with water.

Bal: Cornish word for a mine, often used in association with the mine's name.

Borrow Pit: An extraction, usually into a bank, where material, such as soil, clay, or gravel is taken to be used somewhere else, such as in construction of a dam or embankment.

Casserite: Tin ore, a heavy mineral known as stream tin when found in alluvial deposits, or tinstone if found in bedrock. Usually reddish brown to black, but also sometimes grey or whitish. Commonly found in *pegamatites* associated with *granites*.

Drift: The near horizontal passageway into a mine.

Drop Cut: The opening cut into a new mine, usually made into a hillside.

Eluvium: Deposits that have formed in situ by natural weathering of rock, or having been shifted by wind. In contrast with alluvial deposits which have been sorted only by water.

Ground sluicing: A mining technique that uses running water to wash away the ground. Water is supplied by a head race, and is directed across a face that is eroded by the running water.

Hydraulic sluicing: A mining technique that uses high pressure water cannons (monitors) to wash away the ore-bearing ground. Usually associated with a large reservoir of water.

Iron pan" A type of sub soil hardpan (a hard impervious layer usually cemented by insoluble materials) in which an excess of iron oxide is usually present.

Leat: Cornish name for tailings.

Lode: A tabular mineral deposit or vein in consolidated rock. A tin lode was a deposit of tin ore within its parent rock, as opposed to alluvial and eluvial deposits in which tin ore has been eroded out of the rock and deposited downstream.

Mullock: Waste rock from a mine, containing no payable ore.

Ore: A raw mineral or aggregate of minerals that contains a metal or other desirable substances.

Paddock: A mining pit, often square or rectangle shaped, which can be backfilled with waste rock or tailings.

Pegmatite: Coarse-grained igneous rock found usually as dikes associated with plutonic rock (usually granite). Forms from the molten residue left after most of the pluton solidifies. Often contains traces of valuable minerals such as cassiterite and wolframite.

Placer deposits: A surficial mineral deposit formed by mechanical concentration of mineral particles from weathered debris. The mechanical agent is usually alluvial, but can be marine, colian, lacustrine, or glacial.

Pluton: A body of igneous rock that has formed deep below the earth's surface by consolidation from magma. In the case of the Tin Range, the Knob Plutons formed beneath the older schists which subsequently eroded away.

Riffles: Bars set across a tailrace channel in a sluicing operation, designed to catch the heavy ore such as stream tin or gold.

Tailings: Waste rock from an alluvial mining operation, usually stacked back into worked areas. Also, the waste material discharged from a hard rock crushing battery.